SOLO

WILLIAM BOYD

Solo

VINTAGE BOOKS
London

Published by Vintage 2014

2 4 6 8 10 9 7 5 3 1

First published in Great Britain in 2013
by Jonathan Cape

Vintage
Random House, 20 Vauxhall Bridge Road,
London SW1V 2SA

www.vintage-books.co.uk

Addresses for companies within The Random House Group Limited
can be found at: www.randomhouse.co.uk/offices.htm

The Random House Group Limited Reg. No. 954009

A CIP catalogue record for this book
is available from the British Library

ISBN: 9780099578970

The Random House Group Limited supports the Forest Stewardship
Council® (FSC®), the leading international forest-certification
organisation. Our books carrying the FSC label are printed on FSC®-
certified paper. FSC is the only forest-certification scheme supported
by the leading environmental organisations, including Greenpeace.
Our paper procurement policy can be found at:
www.randomhouse.co.uk/environment

Printed and bound by CPI Group (UK) Ltd, Croydon, CR0 4YY

For Susan

Not for these I raise
The song of thanks and praise;
But for those obstinate questionings
Of sense and outward things,
Fallings from us, vanishings;
Blank misgivings of a Creature
Moving about in worlds not realised . . .

WILLIAM WORDSWORTH, *Intimations of Immortality*

AUTHOR'S NOTE

In the writing of this novel I have been governed by the details and chronology of James Bond's life that were published in the 'obituary' in *You Only Live Twice*. The novel was the last to be published in Ian Fleming's lifetime. It is reasonable to assume, therefore, that these were the key facts about Bond and his life that he wanted to be in the public domain – facts that would cancel out various anomalies and illogicalities that had appeared in the earlier novels. Consequently, as far as this novel is concerned, and in line with Ian Fleming's decision, James Bond was born in 1924.

PART ONE

BREAKING AND ENTERING

·1·

IN DREAMS BEGIN RESPONSIBILITIES

James Bond was dreaming. Curiously, he knew at once where and when the dream was taking place – it was in the war and he was very young and was walking along a sunken country lane in Normandy, a dirt track between dense blackthorn hedges. In his dream, Bond turned a corner and saw, in a shallow ditch at the side of the muddy roadway, the sodden bodies of three dead British paratroopers, clumped together. In some shock, he paused instinctively to look at them – they seemed in their huddled inert mass to be part of the earth, in a strange way, some vegetable growth germinating there rather than human beings – but an angry shout from the rear told him to keep moving. Beyond the ditch a farmer strode behind his team of two toiling shire horses, busy ploughing his field as if the war were not taking place and these dead men and this small patrol of commandos walking uneasily and watchfully down his farm lane had nothing at all to do with his life and work—

Bond woke and sat up in bed, troubled and disturbed by the dream and its intense vividness and eerie precision. His heart was beating palpably, as if he were still walking down that muddy track past the dead paratroopers, heading for his objective. He thought about the moment: he could identify it exactly – it had been the late morning of 7 June 1944, a day after the invasion of France – D-Day plus one. Why was he dreaming about the war? Bond rarely ventured into the haunted forest of memory that made up his recollections of that time. He ran his hands through his hair and swallowed, feeling his throat sore, sharp. Too much alcohol last night? He reached over for the glass of water on his bedside table and drank some mouthfuls. He lay back and further considered the events of 7 June 1944.

Bond smiled grimly to himself, slid out of bed and walked naked into the en suite bathroom. The Dorchester had the most powerful showers in London and as Bond stood under the needle jets, feeling his skin respond to the almost painful pressure, he sensed the traumatic memories of that day in 1944 begin to retreat slowly, washed away. He turned the tap to cold for the last twenty seconds of his shower and began to contemplate breakfast. Should he have it in his room or go downstairs? Downstairs, he thought, everything will be fresher.

Bond shaved and dressed in a dark blue worsted suit with a pale blue shirt and a black silk knitted tie. As he tightened the knot at his throat more details of his dream began to return to him, unbidden. He had been nineteen years old, a lieutenant in the Special Branch of the Royal Naval Volunteer Reserve, attached as an 'observer' to BRODFORCE, part of 30 Assault Unit, an elite commando charged specifically with the task of capturing enemy secrets: documents, files and encoding devices – all the legitimate plunder available in the aftermath of battle. Bond was in fact looking for a new variation of a *Wehrmacht* cipher machine, hoping that swift advance would create surprise and pre-empt destruction.

Various small units of 30 AU were landed on the Normandy beaches on D-Day and immediately thereafter. BRODFORCE was the smallest of them, just ten commandos, with an officer, Major Niven Brodie – and Lieutenant Bond. They had stepped ashore from their landing craft an hour after dawn at Jig Sector on 'Gold' beach and had been driven inland in an army lorry towards the country town of Sainte-Sabine, close to the Chateau Malflacon, the SS headquarters of that region of Normandy. They left their lorry with a forward unit of Canadian infantry and advanced on foot, down the deep narrow lanes of the Normandy *bocage*, into the fastness of the countryside. The push inland from 'Gold' had been so speedy that there was no front line, as such. BRODFORCE was leapfrogging the British and Canadian forces and racing with all speed for whatever booty might be waiting for them in the Chateau Malflacon. Then they had seen the dead paratroopers and it had been Major Brodie himself who had shouted to Bond to keep moving . . .

Bond combed his hair, smoothing back the forelock that kept falling forward out of position, as if it had a life of its own. Maybe he should change his hairstyle, he wondered, idly, like that television-presenter fellow – what was his name? – and comb his hair forward in a short fringe, not bother with a parting at all, in the contemporary fashion. No, he thought, *pas mon style*. He swallowed again – his throat *was* sore. He left his room, locking the door behind him, and wandered down the corridor, heading for the lift. He pressed the button to summon it, thinking, yes, scrambled eggs and bacon, many cups of coffee, a cigarette, that would set him on his feet again—

The lift doors opened.

'Good morning,' a woman's voice said from inside.

'Morning,' Bond replied automatically as he stepped into the lift. He recognised the unforgettable scent immediately – the vanilla and iris of Guerlain's 'Shalimar' – unforgettable because it was the perfume his mother used to wear. It was like opening a door to his childhood – so much of his past crowding in on him today, Bond thought, looking over to meet the eyes of the woman leaning in the corner. She smiled at him, quizzically, an eyebrow raised.

'Happy birthday?' she asked.

'How do you know it's my birthday?' Bond just managed to keep the surprise from his voice, he thought.

'Just a good guess,' she said. 'I could tell you were celebrating something last night. So was I – you sense these things. We celebrants, celebrating.'

Bond touched the knot of his tie and cleared his throat, recalling. The woman had been sitting in the dining room last night, a few tables away from him.

'Yes,' Bond said, somewhat ruefully. 'It is indeed my birthday . . .' He was buying a few seconds' time, his mind beginning to work. He was definitely off colour this morning. The lift hummed down to the lobby.

'So – what were *you* celebrating?' he asked. He remembered now – they had both been drinking champagne and had simultaneously raised their glasses across the room to each other.

'The fourth anniversary of my divorce,' she said, drily. 'It's a tradition I keep. I treat myself to cocktails, dinner, vintage champagne and a night in a suite in the Dorchester – and then I send him the bill.'

She was a tall rangy woman in her mid-thirties, Bond estimated, with a strong handsome face and thick honey-blonde hair brushed back from her forehead and falling in an outward curve to her shoulders. Blue eyes. Scandinavian? She was wearing a jersey all-in-one navy catsuit with an ostentatious gold zip that ran from just above her groin to her neck. The tightness of the close-fitting material revealed the full swell of her breasts. Bond allowed the nature of his carnal appraisal to register in his eyes for a split second and saw her own eyes flash back: message received.

The lift doors slid open with a muffled 'ping' at the ground floor.

'Enjoy the rest of your day,' she said with a quick smile and strode out into the wide lobby.

In the dining room, Bond ordered four eggs, scrambled, and half a dozen rashers of unsmoked back bacon, well done, on the side. He drank a long draught of strong black coffee and lit his first cigarette of the day as he waited for his breakfast to arrive.

He had been given the same table that he'd occupied at dinner the night before. The woman had been sitting to his left, three tables away, and at an angle of the room so that if Bond turned his head slightly they had a good view of each other. Earlier in the evening, Bond had drunk two dry martinis in Fielding's, the private casino where he'd managed to lose almost

£100 at chemin de fer in about twenty minutes, but he wasn't going to let that spoil his night. He had ordered a bottle of Taittinger Rosé 1960 to go with his first course of pan-fried Scottish scallops with a beurre blanc sauce and, as he had raised the glass to himself – silently wishing himself a happy forty-fifth birthday – he had spotted the woman lifting her glass of champagne in an identical self-reflecting gestural toast. Their eyes had met – Bond had shrugged, smiled and toasted her, amused. She toasted him back and he had not thought about it further. She had left as he was preoccupied with assessing the bottle of Chateau Batailley 1959 that he had ordered for his main course – fillet of beef, rare, with pommes dauphinoises – and consequently hadn't really taken her in as she swept briskly past his table, registering only that she was tall, blonde, wearing a cream dress and that her shoes had small chunky gold heels that flashed in the glow of the table lights as she walked out of the dining room.

He sprinkled some pepper on his scrambled eggs. A good breakfast was the first essential component to set any day off to a proper start. He had told his secretary he wouldn't be coming in – part of his present to himself. It would be as impossible to face his forty-fifth birthday with the routine prospect of work as it would without a decent breakfast. He ordered another pot of coffee – the hot liquid was easing his throat. Strange that the woman should be in the lift like that, he thought, and stranger still for her to guess it had been his birthday . . . Funny coincidence. He recalled one of the first rules of his profession: if it looks like a coincidence then it probably isn't. Still – life *was* full of genuine coincidences, he reasoned, you couldn't deny that. Very attractive woman, also. He liked the way she wore her hair. Groomed yet natural-looking—

The maître d' offered Bond a copy of *The Times* to read. Bond glanced at the headline – 'Viet Cong Offensive Checked With Many Casualties' – and waved it away. Not today, thank you. That zip on the front of her outfit – her catsuit – was like a provocation, a challenge, crying out to be pulled down. Bond smiled to himself as he imagined doing precisely that and drank more coffee – there was life in the old dog yet.

Bond returned to his room and packed up his dinner suit, shirt and underwear from the night before. He threw his toilet bag into his grip and checked that he'd left nothing behind. He needed a couple of aspirin for his throat, he thought: the coffee had soothed it momentarily but now it was feeling thick and lumpy, swallowing was uncomfortable. Flu? A cold, probably – he had no temperature, thank God. However, the day was his to do with as he pleased – he had a few necessary chores, but there were plenty of birthday treats that he had promised himself along the way.

At the checkout desk it seemed that a group of a dozen Japanese tourists were collectively querying their bill. Bond took out his cigarette case and, as he selected a cigarette and put it in his mouth, noted with mild concern that he must have smoked over thirty cigarettes the previous night. He'd filled the case before he'd gone to the casino. But this was not the day to entertain thoughts of discipline and cutting down, he told himself, no, no – today was a day for judicious self-indulgence – then, as he fished in his pocket for his lighter, he smelled Guerlain's 'Shalimar' once more and heard the woman's voice again.

'May I trouble you for a light?'

As Bond lit her cigarette she steadied his hand with two fingers on his knuckles. She had a small cream-leather travelling bag at her feet. She was checking out also – coincidence . . . ? Bond lit his cigarette and looked squarely at her. She plumed smoke sideways and returned his gaze, unperturbed.

'Are you following me, or am I following you?' she said.

'We are seeing rather a lot of each other, you're right,' Bond said. He offered his hand. 'My name's Bond, James Bond.'

'Bryce Fitzjohn,' she said. They shook hands. Bond noticed her fingernails were cut short, unvarnished – he liked that – and her grip was firm. 'Do you always celebrate your birthday alone?' she asked.

'Not always,' Bond said. 'I just didn't feel like company this year.'

She glanced up as the phalanx of tourists began to move away.

'At bloody last,' she said. There was the hint of an accent, Bond thought. Bryce Fitzjohn – Irish?

'After you,' Bond said.

She opened her handbag and took out a card, offering it to him.

'I end my divorce celebrations with a cocktail party. It's at my house, this evening. A few amusing and interesting people. You're most welcome to come. We start at six o'clock and see how it rolls along from there.'

Bond took the card – a small alarm bell ringing in his head, now. The invitation was overt; the blue eyes were candid. I'd like to see you again, was the message – and there might be some sexual fun to be had, was the subtext.

Bond smiled, apologetically, pocketing the card anyway. 'I'm afraid my day is spoken for,' he said. 'Alas.'

'Never mind,' she said, breezily. 'Maybe I'll see you here next year. Goodbye, Mr Bond.'

She sauntered to the checkout desk, Bond noting the lean perfection of her figure, rear view. It had been the correct thing to do, in terms of proper procedure, but all the same he wondered if perhaps he'd been a bit hasty saying no quite so unequivocally . . .

Bond took a taxi back to his flat in Chelsea. As it swung into Sloane Square he felt his spirits lift. Sloane Square and Albert Bridge were the two London landmarks that gladdened his heart whenever he saw them, day or night, all seasons – signals that he was coming home. He liked living in Chelsea – 'that leafy tranquil cultivated *spielraum* . . . where I worked and wandered'. Who had said that . . . ? Anyway, he thought, telling the taxi to stop just before tree-filled Wellington Square, whoever it was, he agreed with the sentiment. He strolled into the square and made for his front door. He was searching his pockets for his keys when the door opened and his housekeeper, Donalda, stood there.

'Ah, glad you're back, sir,' she said. 'There's a wee bit of a crisis – the painters have found some damp in the drawing room.'

Bond followed Donalda into his flat, dropping his grip in the hall. She had been with him for six months now – she was the niece of May, his trusted housekeeper of many years, who had finally, reluctantly, retired, creeping arthritis encouraging the decision. It had been May who suggested Donalda. 'Best to keep it in the family, Mr James,' she'd said. 'We're very close.' Donalda was a slim, severe-looking young woman in her late twenties with a rare and diffident smile. She never wore make-up and her hair was cut in a short bob with a fringe – a nun's hairstyle, Bond thought. He supposed with a little effort she might have made herself less plain and more attractive but the handover of May's housekeeping responsibilities had been achieved so seamlessly that he had no desire to see that quiet efficiency alter in any way. One morning it had been May, as ever, then the next day Donalda had been introduced. There was an apprentice period of two weeks when both May and Donalda had run his household life, then May had gone and Donalda took over. Absolutely nothing in his domestic routine had been altered: his coffee was brewed to the same strength, his scrambled eggs had the same consistency, his shirts were ironed identically, the shopping was done, the place kept unimprovably clean. Donalda slipped into his life as if she'd been in training for the job since childhood.

Bond stepped into his drawing room. The rugs were rolled up, the tall bookshelves empty of his books – all boxed and in store – the floorboards were bare and the furniture was grouped in the centre of the room under dust sheets. His nose tingled with the astringent smell of fresh paint. Tom Doig, the decorator, pointed out the patch of damp in the room's western corner, revealed when a bureau had been moved. Bond reluctantly authorised him to investigate further and wrote a cheque for £125 to cover the next period of work. He had been promising himself for years to redecorate his flat. He liked his home – its scale and situation – and had no intention of moving. Besides, his lease still had forty-four years left to run. Bond calculated – I'll be eighty-nine if I last that long, he thought. Which would be extremely unlikely, he reasoned, given his line of work – then he grew angry with himself. What was he doing thinking about the future? It was the here and now that intrigued and fulfilled him and, as if to prove the truth of this adage to himself, he spent an hour going over all the work in the flat that Doig had completed, deliberately finding fault everywhere.

When he'd thoroughly irritated and discomfited Doig and his team he told Donalda not to bother preparing a cold supper for him (she went home at six) and he left the decorators to swear and curse at him behind his back.

There was a hazy afternoon sun and the day was agreeably mild and balmy. He wandered pleasurably west along the King's Road towards the Café Picasso pondering a late lunch of some kind. The King's Road was busy but Bond found his mind wasn't concentrating on the passing parade – the throng of shoppers, the poseurs, the curious, the gilded, carefree young, dressed as if for a fabulous harlequinade somewhere; a noise, a random image, had triggered memories of his dream that morning and he was back in northern France in 1944 walking through an ancient oak wood towards an isolated chateau . . .

To Bond's eyes, it looked as if the Chateau Malflacon had been the victim of a rocket attack by a Hawker Typhoon on D-Day. The classic stone facade was cratered with the shallow impact-bursts of the Typhoon's RP-3 rockets and the left-hand wing of the building had been burnt out, the exposed, charred roof timbers still smouldering in the weak sunshine. Bizarrely, there was a dead Shetland pony lying on the oval patch of lawn surrounded by the gravelled sweep of the driveway. There were no vehicles in sight and everything seemed quiet and deserted. The men of BRODFORCE crouched down amongst the trees of the wooded parkland around the chateau waiting while Major Brodie scanned the building with his binoculars. Birds were singing loudly, Bond remembered. The faint breeze blowing was cool and fresh.

Then Major Brodie suggested that Corporal Dave Tozer and Mr Bond might circle round the back of the chateau and see if there was any sign of activity there. He would give them ten minutes before the rest of the men stormed through the front door, took occupancy and began their search.

It was the same kind of hazy, weak sunshine, Bond recalled, as he neared the Café Picasso – that was what had started him thinking, again – the same sort of day as that 7 June – soft, lemony, peaceful. He and Dave Tozer had cut through the woodland and darted past an empty stable block before finding themselves in a sizeable orchard, unkempt and brambly, with some sixty or seventy trees – apple, quince and pear in the main but with some cherries here and there, already showing clumps of heavy maroon fruit. 'Look at this, Mr Bond,' Tozer had said with a grin. 'Let's snaffle this lot before the others come.' Bond had raised his hand in caution – he had caught a scent of woodsmoke and thought he heard voices coming from the other side of the orchard. But Tozer had already stepped forward to seize the glossy cherries. His left foot sank into a rabbit hole and his ankle snapped with a crisp, distinctly audible sound, like dry kindling caught by a flame.

Tozer grunted with pain but managed not to cry out. He also heard the voices now. He waved Bond to him and whispered, 'Take my Sten.' Bond was armed: he had a Webley .38 revolver in a holster at his waist and he handed it to Tozer, with some reluctance, picking up Tozer's Sten gun and creeping cautiously forward through the orchard towards the sound of men's voices . . .

Bond sat down at a pavement table outside the Café Picasso, his mind active and distracted. He looked at the menu and forced himself to concentrate and ordered a portion of lasagne and a glass of Valpolicella from the waitress. Calm down, he said to himself, this all happened a quarter of a century ago – in another life. But the images he was summoning up were as fresh as if they had taken place last week. The fat glossy cherries, Dave Tozer's grimacing face, the drifting scent of woodsmoke and the sound of conversing German voices – all coming back to him with the clarity of total recall.

He forced himself to look around, glad of the diversion afforded by the Café Picasso's eccentric clientele – the dark-eyed girls in their tiny short dresses; the long-haired young men in their crushed velvet and their shaggy Afghan coats. He ate his impromptu late lunch and kept his gaze on the move, easily distracted by the comings and goings. He ordered another glass of wine and an espresso and admired the small-nippled breasts of the girl on the next table, clearly visible through the transparent gauze of her blouse. There was something to be said for modern fashion after all, Bond considered, cheered by the unselfconscious sexuality of the scene. The girl with the see-through blouse was now kissing her boyfriend with patent enthusiasm, his hand resting easily on her upper thigh.

Bond lit a cigarette and found his thoughts turning to the woman in the Dorchester – Bryce Fitzjohn – and their series of encounters over the last twelve hours or so. Was there anything to be suspicious about? He played with various explanations and found the improbabilities too compelling. How could she have known he was staying at the Dorchester? How could she have contrived to be in the lift when he decided to go to the dining room for breakfast? Impossible. Well, not impossible but highly unlikely. True, she could have waited in the lobby for him to check out, he supposed . . . But it didn't add up. He took her card out of his pocket. She lived in Richmond, he saw. A cocktail party at six o'clock with some 'amusing and interesting' friends . . .

Bond stubbed out his cigarette and called for his bill. He found he was thinking about her and her rangy, alluring body. He felt a little animalistic quiver of desire low in his gut and his loins. Lust, more like. The prehistoric instinct – *this is the one for me*. He hadn't felt this sensation in a long time, he had to acknowledge. She was a very attractive woman, he told himself, and, more to the point, she clearly found him attractive also. Perhaps he should check her out further – it would be correct procedure after all – and perhaps the gods of luck were conspiring to send him a birthday present. He threw down a pound note and some coins to cover his bill and a tip, stepped out into the King's Road and hailed a taxi.

·2·

THE JENSEN FF

'Back again, Mr Bond, nice to see you,' the salesman said with a wide sincere smile as Bond circled the chocolate-brown Jensen Interceptor I. It was parked on the forecourt of a showroom just off Park Lane, in Mayfair. Bond had visited it three times already, checking out the Interceptor, hence the salesman's welcoming smile. What was his name? Brian, that was it, Brian Richards. Bond's Bentley was out of action, having its gearbox replaced. The old car, much loved, and lovingly customised over the years, was showing signs of its age and its rambunctious history and was beginning to cost him serious money just to keep it road-worthy. It was like an old thoroughbred racehorse – its time had come to be put out to grass. But what to replace the Bentley with? He wasn't particularly enamoured of modern cars – he'd test-driven an E-type Jaguar and an MGB GT but they didn't trigger any pulse of pleasure in him, didn't make his heart beat. But the Interceptor was different – big and beautiful – and this was what kept bringing him back to Park Lane.

Brian, the salesman, sidled up and lowered his voice.

'I'll have the Interceptor II in a few weeks, Mr Bond, after the Motor Show. And I can do you a very fair price – so buying the One wouldn't be that clever, what with the Two coming out, know what I mean? But . . .' He looked around as if he was about to divulge a dark secret. 'In the meantime, come through the back and have a look at this.' Bond followed Brian across the showroom and through a door to a small mews courtyard at the rear. Here were the workshops and extra space for cars to be waxed and polished before they went to the forecourt on display. Brian gestured to what looked like another Interceptor, painted a dull gunmetal silver. Bond walked around it. An Interceptor but somehow longer, he thought, and with two air vents set behind the front wheels.

'The Jensen FF,' Brian said softly in veneration, almost with a catch in his voice. 'Four-wheel drive.' He opened the door. 'Step in, Mr Bond. Try her for size.'

Bond slipped into the driving seat and rested his hands on the wooden rim of the steering wheel, his eyes taking in the grouped dials on the fascia, his nostrils filled with the smell of new leather. It worked on him like an aphrodisiac.

'Take her out for a spin,' Brian suggested.

'I just might,' he said.

'Be my guest, Mr Bond. Take her out on the motorway, give her some gas. You'll be amazed. Take all the time you need, sir.'

Bond was thinking. 'Right. When do you close? I may be a couple of hours.'

'I'm working late tonight. I'll be here till ten. Just bring her round the back and ring the bell on the gate.'

'Perfect,' Bond said and switched on the engine.

* * *

Bond felt he was in a low-flying plane rather than an automobile as he accelerated the Jensen down the A316 towards Twickenham. The wide curved sweep of the windscreen filled the car with light and the powerful rumble of the engine sounded like the roar of jet propulsion. The four-wheel drive meant the tightest corner could be negotiated with hardly any diminution of speed. When he stopped at traffic lights pedestrians openly gaped at the car as it idled throatily, heads turning, fingers pointing. If you needed a car to boost your ego, Bond thought, then the Jensen FF would do the job admirably. Not that he needed an ego boost, Bond reminded himself as he accelerated away, the speed forcing him back in the seat, cutting up and leaving a Series V Sunbeam Alpine for dead, its driver gesticulating in frustration.

Bond turned left before Richmond Bridge. He went into a post office to ask directions to Chapel Close, where Bryce Fitzjohn lived. He motored down Petersham Road, along the river's edge, found the narrow lane, turned the corner and parked. It was just before six o'clock and he rather liked the idea of being the first to arrive at her little party. A few minutes alone would negate or confirm any lingering doubts he had about her.

Bryce Fitzjohn's home turned out to be a pretty Georgian 'cottage' with a walled garden, the grand houses of Richmond Hill rising behind and beyond. Bond surveyed the driveway and the house's facade from across the lane. Worn, patinated red stock-brick, a slate roof, a moulded half-shell pediment over the front door, three big sash windows on the ground floor and three above – a restrained and elegant design. They weren't cheap, these refined houses on the river – so she wasn't short of money. However bitter her divorce had been, perhaps it had proved lucrative, Bond wondered as he crossed the road, noting that there were no cars parked outside. He was the first to arrive – excellent. He rang the doorbell.

There was no response. Bond listened, then rang again. And again. Now new intimations of alarm began to cluster. What kind of invitation was this? Bond was unarmed and felt suddenly vulnerable, wondering if he was being watched from some vantage point. He looked around him and stepped back out on to the road. A mother pushing her pram. A boy walking his dog. Nothing out of the ordinary. He returned to the house and slipped through the ornate iron gate at the side that led to the walled garden. Bond saw well-tended herbaceous borders edging a neatly mown lawn with a large stone birdbath set on a carved plinth in the centre. At the bottom of the garden, under a gnarled and ancient fig tree, was a wrought-iron bench and table. All very ordered and civilised. Bond followed paving stones set in the turf round to a conservatory at the rear. Beside it was a door that led into the kitchen.

Bond peered through the window. Here, laid out on a scrubbed pine kitchen table were trays of canapés, ranked glasses of various sorts and bowls of nuts, cheese balls and olives. So, there *was* going to be a party . . . But where was the hostess? Bond thought about returning home to Chelsea, but his curiosity was piqued and he felt it was his professional duty to find out if there was anything more clandestine going on here. He just had to gain access to this house. Needs must, he thought to himself, and reached down and removed one of his loafers. He twisted off the heel, revealing the two-inch, dirk-like stabbing blade that projected from it, sheathed by the specially constructed sole. He slipped the blade into the gap by the Yale lock, probed, eased and then turned it, feeling the tongue of the lock spring back and the door yield. He pushed it open. It was all too easy, this breaking and entering.

Bond replaced the heel and slipped his shoe back on. He allowed himself a couple of seconds' reflection – he could close the door and return home, no one would be the wiser – but he felt that having achieved ingress, as it were, it would be wrong not to explore further. Who knew what he might discover? So he stepped in and wandered around the kitchen, listening intently, and, hearing no sound of anyone stirring, he helped himself to a chicken vol-au-vent and then a triangle of smoked salmon. Delicious. There was a drinks trolley with an impressive display of alcohol set upon it. Bond contemplated the array of bottles (some serious drinkers were expected, clearly) and was tempted to have a dram of the Scotch on offer as it was Dimple Haig, one of his favourites – but decided this wasn't the moment. Then he decided it was, so he poured three fingers into a tumbler and left the kitchen to investigate the house.

The rooms were high-ceilinged and generously sized on the ground floor: there was a dining room and a drawing room with fine cornicing and French windows that gave on to the lawn. To the other side of the entrance hall was a cloakroom-bathroom and a small study. He spent some time in the study, one wall of which was lined with bookshelves – mainly biographies and non-fiction, he saw, with a distinct showbiz slant. He opened the bottom drawer of the small partners' desk that sat in a corner (always start with the bottom drawer) and was surprised to find a cache of large glossy professional photographs of Bryce Fitzjohn nearly and provocatively naked. In some she was wearing a tiny leather bikini; in others she was topless, her arm held demurely across her breasts;

and there were others of her in full make-up, hair blown awry by a wind machine, her cleavage plungingly on display. There was one set of her sitting up in a rumpled bed, naked, her back to the camera, the cleft of her buttocks visible, her hair tousled, her eyes half closed and invitingly come-hither. The name at the foot of each photograph was 'Astrid Ostergard'. So, Bryce Fitzjohn was Astrid Ostergard in another life. The name seemed familiar to Bond – where had he seen it before? He leafed through the photos – an actress, a dancer, a model? A high-class prostitute? Bond was tempted to take a photo as a souvenir.

He quickly went through the other drawers of the desk and found nothing out of the ordinary. Her passport confirmed her name was indeed Bryce Connor Fitzjohn (aged thirty-seven) born in Kilkenny, Ireland. It was time to go upstairs. Bond drained his glass of Haig and left it on the desk.

On the first floor there were two bedrooms, one with a bathroom en suite and clearly Bryce's. Bond opened cupboards and drawers and the medicine cabinet in the bathroom – he noticed there seemed no trace of a male presence anywhere. In the guest bedroom the bottom drawer of the bedside table revealed an ancient, desiccated half-pack of Gauloises cigarettes and a well-thumbed copy of Frank Harris's *My Life and Loves*. Scant evidence of a man in her life. No, there was really nothing to go on apart from the pseudonymous photographs—

The sound of a motor – diesel – and a tyre-scatter of gravel made Bond freeze for a second before he strode to the window, peering out cautiously. A breakdown van towing a Triumph Herald 13/60 convertible pulled up outside. Bryce Fitzjohn stepped out of the cab of the van and, from the other door, an overalled mechanic emerged, who unhitched the Herald. Bond watched Bryce write a cheque for the driver and see him and his van off with a cursory wave, and then Bond drew back as she unlocked the front door to her house.

Bond moved quickly to the top of the stairs, the better to overhear the series of calls she proceeded to make from the telephone on the small table in the hallway. 'Yes,' he heard her say, 'me again. Nightmare . . . After the breakdown in Kingston . . . It got worse – completely dead . . .', 'Hello, darling, *so* sorry . . . No we'll do it another time . . .', 'I might have been in Siberia, nobody offered to help . . . Took me three hours after I called you to find a garage . . .', 'And then the man said the car was fixed but it still wouldn't fucking start . . . Exactly, so I had to find another garage . . . Day from hell . . . Yes, I'm going to have a hot bath and an enormous gin and tonic . . .', 'Bye, my dear . . . Yes, it is a shame . . . everything was ready . . . No, we'll do it again. Promise . . .' and so on for another few minutes as she rang around apologising to the friends who were meant to have come to her party, Bond assumed.

As he stood there listening he began to wonder what his best course of action would be. Reveal himself? Or try to slip out unnoticed? He heard her go into the kitchen and then a minute later head back across the hall for the stairs. He ducked into the spare bedroom. He heard her kick off her shoes on the landing and the chime of ice in a glass, then, moments after, the sound of water tumbling into a bath. Bond peered out, carefully. She had left the door to her bedroom open and he was able to watch her undress, partially, in a kind of jump-cut striptease, as she crossed and recrossed her room, shedding clothes. He moved cautiously out into the corridor and saw her reflected in the mirror of her dressing table. She was wearing a red brassiere and red panties, and her skin was very white. He noted the furrow of her spine deepen as she arched her arms back to unclip the fastener of her brassiere. And then she slipped out of vision.

Bond stepped back into the spare bedroom – he was both excited and, at the same time, made vaguely uneasy by this unsought-for act of voyeurism. Everything seemed unexceptionable and explicable: there had indeed been a party planned – that was then cancelled when her car broke down in Kingston on the way back from London. No honey trap after all; sheer coincidence being the explanation behind everything – yet again. Still, he thought, better to be secure in this knowledge than worry that some sort of elaborate scheme of entrapment had been set in motion.

He eased past the door of the spare room, pulling it closed behind him, and paused for a moment on the landing. It was quiet. She seemed to have gone into the bathroom, no doubt luxuriating in a deep bath. For a crazy second he contemplated walking in on her – no, madness, slip out unnoticed while you have the chance. He stepped over her discarded high-heeled shoes and swiftly went down the stairs and into her study. On a piece of her writing paper he wrote 'Thanks for the cocktail. James' and weighted it with his empty whisky glass in the centre of her desk. What would she make of that? he wondered, pleased with his mischief, not bothering to question the professional wisdom of the gesture. To hell with it – it was his day off. He let himself out of the front door, closed it silently behind him and strolled, hands in pockets, nonchalantly back to where he'd parked the Jensen.

*   *   *

Bond drove steadily back to Chelsea, not testing the powerful car at all, so caught up was he with the images crowding his brain. Images of Bryce undressing – the red of her brassiere offset by the alabaster whiteness of her skin; the way she'd used a finger to hook and tug the caught hem of her panties back over the swell of her buttock. What was it about this woman, this virtual stranger, that so nagged at him? Maybe it was the fact that he had broken into her home and had spied on her, that his illicit presence in her house made his glimpses of her more . . . what? More charged, more erotic, more perversely exciting? At the back of his mind was the thought that, come what may, he had to contrive a way of seeing her again. It wasn't over.

He wound down the window to allow some cool air into the car. His face was hot, he wiped his lips with the back of his hand, and as he crossed over Chiswick Bridge he drove through the drifting smoke of some early evening bonfire. Instantly, the trigger-effect of the association worked on him and he was back once again in the world of his wartime dream, back in the orchard of the Chateau Malflacon, flitting from tree to tree, Corporal Tozer's Sten gun heavy in his hand, listening to the sound of German voices – chatting, unconcerned – growing louder as he approached.

Bond pulled up at a traffic light. Somebody, seeing the Jensen, shouted, 'Nice motor, mate!' Bond didn't even look round – he was in another place, twenty-five years ago. The woodsmoke, he thought, recalling it as if he was actually there in that Normandy orchard, moving cautiously from tree to tree. As he had reached the edge of the orchard he had seen the actual bonfire, heaped high with concertina files and flung boxes of documents, smouldering weakly, wisps of smoke seeping from the mass of paper but no sign of flames catching. Three young German soldiers – his age, teenagers – were emptying the last boxes of documents on to the bonfire, laughing and bantering. One of them, his jacket off, exposing his woollen vest and his olive-green braces, was using a long-handled French gardening fork to spear and heave the tied bundles of paper on to the mound. Filing clerks, stenographers, radio operators, Bond supposed, the last to leave the chateau, instructed to burn everything, unaware that Major Brodie and the rest of BRODFORCE were about to thunder in the front door.

The boy threw down his fork and began to empty a jerrycan of petrol over the pile of papers, sloshing the fuel on the bonfire. He dumped his jerrycan on the grass and searched his pockets for some matches. One of the others tossed him a box.

Bond stepped out from the trees, the Sten gun levelled.

'*Weg vom Feuer,*' he said, ordering them to move away from the fire.

They froze – completely shocked to see a British soldier, and then to realise he was speaking fluent German. Two of the clerks turned immediately and raced away, panicked, for the woods beyond. Bond let them go. The boy in the braces fumbled with his matches, trying to be a hero. There was something wrong with them, they wouldn't light.

'*Lass das,*' Bond warned him, cocking the Sten. '*Sonst schiess ich.*'

The boy in the braces managed to light a match and immediately dropped it on the grass. He scrabbled for another. Was he insane, Bond thought?

'Don't be a fool,' he said, in German. He raised the Sten and fired it into the air.

Nothing. The redundant click of the trigger. The gun had

jammed. Jamming – the curse of the Sten gun. Carbon build-up in the breech, or a feed malfunction in the magazine. The operating instructions when this occurred were to remove the magazine, tap against knee and reinsert. Bond didn't think he was going to do this.

The boy in the braces looked at Bond and seemed to smile. With deliberate care he took out another match and struck it. It caught and flared.

'Now you are fool,' the boy said, in English. He dropped the match on the bonfire and small flames flickered.

Bond slapped the Sten's magazine and worked the cocking bolt.

Bond pulled the trigger again and again. Nothing. Click-click-click. The boy stooped and picked up the long-handled fork. It had three tines, Bond saw, curved, ten inches long.

Bond worked the bolt again. He aimed the Sten at the boy.

'*Forke weg,*' Bond said. '*Sonst bring ich dich um.*'

The boy quickly stepped towards him and thrust the fork upward. The sharp, curved gleaming tines were suddenly two inches from Bond's chest and throat. Bond imagined them entering his body, effortlessly, puncturing the material of his uniform and then his skin, plunging deep inside him. He couldn't turn and run – he'd be speared in the back. He still had the useless Sten in his hands; he thought in the mad scrambling seconds left to him he could fling himself sideways and smash the gun against the boy's head. Somewhere in the back of his mind rose up the absolute determination that he was not going to die here, in this Normandy orchard.

The boy smiled thinly and pressed the tines of the fork closer, so that they actually touched the serge of Bond's jacket, ready for the fatal thrust.

'*Dummkopf Englander,*' he said.

Tozer's first shot hit the boy full in the throat, the second in the chest and flung him backwards.

Bond glanced round. Tozer was leaning against an apple tree. He lowered Bond's Webley, smoke drifting from its barrel.

'Sorry about that, Mr Bond,' he said. 'Bloody useless Sten, always has been.' He limped forward, raising the revolver to cover the German lying on the ground. 'I think I got him fair and square,' Tozer said, with a satisfied smile.

Bond realised he was shuddering, as if suddenly very cold. He took a few steps towards the boy and looked down at him. His woollen vest was drenched in his blood. The round that had caught him in the throat had torn it wide open. Big thick pink bubbles formed and burst, popping quietly as his lungs emptied.

Bond sank to his knees. He laid the Sten carefully on the ground and vomited.

The traffic light changed to green. Bond put the Jensen in gear and accelerated cleanly away. Now he knew why the dream had so haunted him, summoned up from his unconscious mind like a minatory symbol. Why had he remembered it? What had provoked this recollection in every detail and texture? His birthday? The fact that he was aware he was growing older? Whatever it was, the memorable part of that particular day, he realised, 7 June 1944, was that he had been confronted with the possibility that his life was about to end, there and then – it marked the first time he had stared death full in the face. He could have had no idea that this was to be the pattern of the life ahead of him.

PART TWO

HOW TO
STOP
A WAR

· 1 ·

ELEMENTS OF RISK

'Happy birthday, James,' Miss Moneypenny said, as Bond stepped into her office. 'Rather, happy birthday in arrears. Did you have an enjoyable day off, last week?'

'I'd rather hoped you'd forgotten it was my birthday,' Bond said, his voice thick and raspy. He could hardly swallow.

'No, no. It's my business to know these things,' she said, standing and going to a filing cabinet. 'All the mundane little facts of your life.'

Sometimes, Bond thought, Moneypenny's banter could verge on the annoyingly self-satisfied. He was vaguely irritated that she must know how old he was.

'You don't happen to have a couple of aspirin, do you?' he asked.

'You've obviously been celebrating far too enthusiastically,' she said, returning to her desk and handing him a file. Bond took it, unreflectingly.

'I've got a sore throat,' he said. 'Touch of flu, I think. I've been in bed by eight the last two nights.'

'Your secret's safe with me,' she said in the same dry tone, somehow producing a glass of water and then two aspirins from

31

a drawer in her desk. Bond took them, thankfully, swallowing the pills down.

The light above M's office door changed from red to green.

'Off you go, James,' Moneypenny said and turned to her type-writer.

M was standing at one of the three windows of his office that looked out over Regent's Park. His head seemed hunched down on his shoulders as if his back were tense and knotted. He seemed deeply thoughtful, not registering Bond's entrance in any way. His pipe, Bond noticed, lay on his desk blotter, empty of tobacco, and Bond wondered if he'd have to sit through the usual interminable, tantalising, pipe-filling, pipe-lighting routine before he found out why he'd been summoned. Bond cleared his throat and winced.

'You wanted to see me, sir,' Bond said, going to stand in front of the wide desk, placing Moneypenny's file to one side.

M turned – his face looked tanned, weather-beaten. Working in his garden, Bond thought. He looked fit, full of vigour for an elderly man. What age would M be, Bond found himself wondering? He must be at least—

'What's wrong with your voice?' M asked, suspiciously.

'Bit of a sore throat. Shaking off a cold,' Bond said. 'Moneypenny's given me some medication.'

'Smoking too much, more like,' M said, sitting down and picking up and flourishing his pipe. 'You want to take up one of these. Haven't had a sore throat since I was at school.'

'Interesting idea, sir,' Bond said, diplomatically. He would rather give up smoking than smoke a pipe.

'Sit down, 007, and do light up if you want to.'

Bond sat down and took out a cigarette as M rummaged in a drawer of his desk and drew out an atlas. He opened it, turned it and pushed it across the desk towards Bond.

'Tell me what you know about this place,' M said.

Bond looked at the open page. An African country. A small West African country called Zanzarim.

'Zanzarim,' Bond said, thinking. 'There's a war going on there. A civil war. Civilians starving to death by the thousand.'

'By the tens of thousand, some would have it,' M said, leaning back in his chair. 'Anything else?'

'Used to be a British colony, didn't it?' Bond said. 'Before they changed the name.'

'League of Nations mandated territory to be precise. Upper Zanza State. Got independence five years ago. Old German colony established in 1906. We and the French liberated it in 1914 – split it in two. There was a plebiscite in 1953 and the Zanzaris voted for us.'

'Unusual.'

'You forget how dominant and impressive the British Empire was, even in those days, 007. It was the sensible, obvious thing to do.'

'Oh, yes. Moneypenny gave me this file.' Bond handed it over.

'No, no. It's for you. Open it.'

Bond did so and saw a mass of newspaper clippings and documents entitled 'Agence Presse Libre' – then something fell on the floor and Bond picked it up. It was a plastic identity card and his photograph was on it. 'James Bond. Journalist. Agence Presse Libre' it stated.

'Right . . .' Bond said slowly. 'So I'm to be a journalist for this French press agency.'

M smiled, knowingly. Bond knew he was enjoying himself, drip-feeding the information about his mission this way, toying with him.

'Small, left-of-centre press agency. Good reputation. International reach,' M said. 'Your old friend René Mathis from the Deuxième Bureau arranged it all, cleared everything.'

'And where am I going to be doing my journalism?' Bond asked dutifully, playing along, knowing the answer.

'Zanzarim.'

'And what am I meant to do once I get there?'

M smiled, again, more broadly. 'Stop the war, of course.'

Bond told his new secretary, Araminta Beauchamp (pronounced Beecham) that he was not to be disturbed and sat down at his desk to read through all the material on Zanzarim contained in the file that Moneypenny had handed him.

Bond leafed through the newspaper cuttings. The civil war in Zanzarim had become an international crisis because of the mass malnutrition of civilians. There were many shocking and heart-rending images of starving children – stick figures with macrocephalic heads, protruding bellies and glaucous, staring, uncomprehending eyes. Bond selected a Foreign Office briefing document entitled 'The Origins of the Zanzarim Civil War' and began to read.

* * *

Zanzarim had been a small stable West African country when it gained independence in 1964. The name of the country was changed and so was the name of the capital city – to Sinsikrou (it had been Gustavberg, Victoireville and Shackleton in its short colonial history). Zanzarim had a creditable balance of trade surplus, its main exports being cocoa beans, bananas, copper and timber. Then oil had been discovered in the Zanza River Delta – a vast, apparently limitless, subterranean ocean of oil. This benediction soon began to turn sour. The problem was that Zanzarim's capital and seat of government, Sinsikrou, was in the north. The government, moreover, was dominated by the Lowele tribe, the largest in a country of some two dozen tribes. In the south, in the river delta, the paramount tribe was the Fakassa. All the oil deposits had been discovered squarely in the middle of the Fakassa's tribal lands. Not surprisingly, the Fakassa viewed the prospect of an endless flow of petro-dollars as a blessing conferred primarily on them. The Zanzarim government, and the Lowele tribe, disagreed: the oil was for the benefit of the whole country and all Zanzaris regardless of their tribal affiliation. Internecine bickering ensued between Fakassa and Lowele representatives and became more aggressive as it seemed no compromise could be reached. There was a form of uneasy stalemate until 1967 when the first proper assessments of the potential reserves and the scale of their potential revenues were made known.

In Port Dunbar, the central town in the river delta, 200,000 Fakassa took to the streets in protest against this Lowele 'theft' of their patrimony. There were anti-Fakassa riots in Sinsikrou and over 300 Fakassa were massacred by a rampaging Lowele mob. In the south a revanchist anti-Lowele pogrom took place – shops were burnt, traders expelled and their assets seized. Eight Lowele policemen, attempting to flee, were caught and lynched. As the trouble increased and more indiscriminate slaughter ensued, attempts to broker a peace by British and UN diplomats failed and tensions rose inexorably on both sides as massacre and counter-massacre occurred in a deadly and inhuman tit-for-tat. A rush of Fakassa refugees from elsewhere in Zanzarim fled into the tribal heartlands around Port Dunbar. Towards the end of 1967 the south of the country – effectively the Fakassa tribal lands – formally seceded from Zanzarim and a new independent state was created: the Democratic Republic of Dahum. Two brigades of the Zanzarim army invaded Dahum and were repulsed. The Zanzarim civil war had begun.

Bond put the briefing document down. It was like that old Chinese curse: 'May you live in interesting times' – reconfigured as 'May vast reserves of oil be discovered in your country.' He shuffled through the newspaper clippings and selected one written by a defence expert whose name he recognised. In the two years since the war had begun the overwhelmingly superior Zanzarim forces had managed to drive the Dahumians back from their ostensible frontiers to a small hinterland in the river delta concentrated around the town of Port Dunbar. The Democratic Republic of Dahum now consisted of Port Dunbar, an airstrip near a place called Janjaville and a few hundred square miles of dense forest, river creeks and mangrove swamps. Dahum was surrounded and a blockade commenced. The desperate population of Fakassa began to starve and die.

Her Majesty's Government supported Zanzarim (as well as

providing military materiel for the Zanzarim army) and urged Dahum to sue for peace and return to the 'status quo ante'. To all observers it seemed that unless this occurred there would be a human catastrophe. It had seemed inconceivable that Dahum could hold out for more than a week or two.

Bond recalled what M had recounted.

'However, it simply hasn't happened,' he had said, shrugging his shoulders. 'It seems heroic – this small, makeshift Dahum army holding out against hugely superior and well-equipped forces. To be sure, there's a clandestine air-bridge flying in supplies at night to this airstrip at Janjaville. But somehow they've completely stopped the Zanzari advance. Every time there's a push from the Zanzarim army it ends in humiliating disaster. It seems the Dahumian army is being brilliantly led by some kind of tactical genius producing victory after victory. The war could drag on forever at this rate.'

Bond picked up a clipping from *Time* magazine that showed an African soldier, a brigadier, with a black beret and a scarlet cockade standing on top of a burnt-out Zanzari armoured car. The caption beneath read: 'Brigadier Solomon "The Scorpion" Adeka – the African Napoleon'. So, this was the soldier who was the architect of Dahum's astonishing resilience – a military prodigy who was somehow contriving to inflict defeat upon defeat on an army ten times the size of his.

'Brigadier Adeka is the key,' M had said, simply. 'He's the man who's single-handedly keeping this war going, by all accounts. He's the target – the object of your mission. I want you to go to Zanzarim, infiltrate yourself into Dahum and get close to this man.'

'And what am I meant to do then, sir?' Bond had asked, knowing the answer but keeping his face impassive, giving nothing away.

'I'd like you to find a way of making him a less efficient soldier,' M had said with a vague smile.

There was a knock on his door and Bond looked up, irritated, and Araminta Beauchamp stepped in. She was a pretty girl with a fringe of dark hair that almost covered her eyes. She kept flicking it away with a toss of her head.

Bond sighed. 'Minty, I said absolutely no interruptions. Don't you understand plain English?'

'Sorry, sir. Q Branch has just called to say that they can see you any time that's convenient to you.'

'I know that. I've just been speaking to M.'

'I thought it was important . . .' Her chin quivered and she dragged her fringe away with a finger to reveal eyes about to weep tears of penitence.

'Thank you,' Bond said, gently. 'You're right. It probably is. And please don't cry, Minty.'

Bond rode the lift down to Q Branch's domain in the basement and announced himself. He was met by a young bespectacled man who introduced himself as Quentin Dale. He looked about twenty-five years old and had the eager proselytising manner of a doorstep missionary.

'I don't think we've met before, Commander,' Dale said, cheerfully. 'I've only been here a couple of months.' He led Bond down a corridor to his small office, showed him to a seat and sat down opposite, removing a file from his desk and pushing his spectacles back on his nose.

'You'll need some inoculations if you're going to West Africa,' he said. 'Shall we arrange them or would you prefer your own doctor?'

'I'll deal with that,' Bond said.

'Yellow fever, smallpox, polio – and you'll need a supply of antimalarials. They say Daraprim is very good.'

'Fine,' Bond said, thinking that the only problem with Q Branch was that they treated everyone as a naive, innocent, not to say ignorant, fool.

'We don't think you should go to Zanzarim armed,' Dale said, consulting the notes in his file. 'Because of the war the airport searches at Sinsikrou can be very thorough. And you're working for a French press agency . . .' Dale smiled, sympathetically, as if he was about to break bad news. 'And the French aren't very popular with the Zanzaris.'

'Why's that?'

'They've given a kind of de facto recognition of the Dahum state. The French embassy here in London is where the Dahum diplomatic mission is based.' He screwed up his face.

'I suppose it was their colony for a while.'

'True,' Dale said.

'But I'll be pretty popular in Dahum itself.'

'Exactly – that's the logic.' Dale smiled again, this time approvingly, as if the most backward boy in the class had answered a difficult question. He reached into another drawer and took out a zipped pigskin toilet bag, opening it and showing Bond its contents. Bond saw that it was a luxury shaving kit: safety razor,

Old Spice shaving stick and badger-bristle brush, aftershave, talcum powder, a deodorant roll-on, all tucked in their respective pockets and slings.

'We can't give you a gun, but we can give you some potency,' Dale said. He held up the aftershave. 'A tablespoonful of this will knock a man out for twelve hours. Add a teaspoon of this' – he showed Bond the talcum powder – 'and he'll go into a coma for two to three days. It's completely tasteless, by the way. You can put it in any drink or food, no one will notice.'

'What if I add two teaspoons?' Bond asked.

'You'll probably kill him. Best to make it three teaspoons to be on the safe side, if you want to bring about death. Coma, then a massive heart attack,' he smiled and pushed his spectacles back on his nose again. 'Should give you plenty of time to make your escape.'

He took an envelope from his file and handed it over.

'This contains all the information you need. And your plane ticket to Zanzarim. BOAC on Friday evening. One way.'

'So I'm not coming back,' Bond said, drily.

'Our station head in Sinsikrou will arrange your journey home. It's not clear how long you'll be in the country, anyway – or even if you'll be leaving from it.'

'I suppose not. Who's our station head?'

'Ah . . .' he looked at his file. 'One E. B. Ogilvy-Grant. It's been very recently set up. A business card with the address and phone number is in the envelope and confirmation of your reservation at the Excelsior Gateway Hotel. It's near the airport. Ogilvy-Grant will make contact with you after you've landed.'

Bond took the business card from the envelope. It read:

'E. B. Ogilvy-Grant MA (Cantab). Palm Oil Export and Agricultural Services.' There was a telephone number in the corner.

'Anything else, Commander?'

Bond zipped up the toilet bag.

'What about communications? Connecting with base, here?'

'Ogilvy-Grant will take care of all that.'

Bond stood up, slowly. Something was bothering him. It all seemed a bit vague, a bit wing-and-a-prayer, a bit improvised. But maybe this was what a mission to a civil-war-torn West African country involved. Once he was actually in Zanzarim and had met Ogilvy-Grant the picture would be clearer, surely. He had a few days before his plane left, in any event, so it might be a good idea to do some extra homework himself.

'Good luck,' Dale said, flashing him his boyish smile. He didn't offer Bond his hand to shake.

·2·

HOMEWORK

Bond strolled down the street in Bayswater for the second time and joined the back of a long queue at a bus stop and took in his surroundings at leisure. Across the street was a small shabby parade of shops – an ironmonger, a newsagent, a grocery store and a seemingly empty premises with a hand-painted sign above the grimy plate glass window that said 'AfricaKIN'. Sellotaped to the glass was a poster of a starving child with rheumy eyes and a distended belly holding out a claw-like begging hand. The caption was: 'Genocide in Dahum. Please give generously.'

Bond crossed the road and rang the bell.

He heard a clatter of footsteps descending some stairs and sensed a presence behind the door scrutinising him through the peephole.

'Who are you? What do you want?' an educated English voice said.

'My name's James Bond. I'm a journalist,' Bond explained, adding, 'I'm going to Zanzarim on Friday.'

The door was opened after a key had turned in a lock and two bolts were drawn. A slim African man stood there, in his forties, smart in a pinstriped suit with his head completely shaven and a neat goatee beard. His gaze was watchful and unwelcoming.

Bond showed his Agence Presse Libre card. The man smiled and visibly relaxed.

'I'm looking for Gabriel Adeka,' Bond said.

'You've found him. Come on in.'

Bond knew from his further researches that Gabriel Adeka was Brigadier Solomon Adeka's older brother. A successful barrister, educated at Rugby School and Merton College, Oxford, he had given up his lucrative legal career to found AfricaKIN, a charity dedicated to alleviating the suffering in Dahum. Bond saw, as he entered, that the linoleum-covered ground floor contained a fifth-hand photocopier and, to one side on a decorator's trestle table, a light box and a typewriter. It must be quite a contrast to his chambers in Lincoln's Inn, Bond thought, as he followed Adeka up the creaking carpetless stairs to his small office on the floor above.

Adeka's office was papered with his various distressing posters and was occupied by a table and chair surrounded by yellowing piles of flyers, news-sheets and booklets about AfricaKIN and the plight of Dahum. He shifted some cardboard boxes and found a stool behind them, placing it in front of his desk for Bond to sit on.

'May I offer you a cup of tea?' Adeka said, gesturing towards an electric kettle and some mugs on a tray on the floor.

'No, thank you . . . I don't drink tea,' Bond added in explanation.

'And you call yourself an Englishman?' Adeka smiled.

'Actually, I'm not English,' Bond said, then changed the subject. 'You seem to be very much on your own here. One-man band.'

43

'I've a ready supply of volunteers when the need arises,' Adeka said, with a weary smile. 'But most of my funds have gone. I gave up my practice two years ago and as we all know, money – alas – doesn't grow on trees. Also, we find ourselves very harassed by the state. Inexplicable electricity failures, visits by aggressive bailiffs claiming we haven't paid our bills, break-ins, vandalism. All this costs me. AfricaKIN isn't welcome – Her Majesty's Government has made that very clear.'

'Maybe you should move to Paris,' Bond said.

'I've thought about it, believe me. Without our French friends . . .' He stopped. 'I wouldn't be talking to you, Mr Bond, if you didn't work for a French press agency.'

'I'm very grateful.'

'So, what takes you to our benighted country?'

'I'm flying in to Sinsikrou, yes – but then I plan to make my way south, to Dahum. I want to interview your brother – which is why I'm here.'

The kettle had boiled and Adeka made himself a cup of tea – no milk, no sugar. He sat behind his desk and looked at Bond, candidly, silently for a second or two, as if weighing him up, analysing him. Bond sat there, happy to be scrutinised – for some reason he liked Gabriel Adeka and admired his futile ambitions, his sacrifice, his crazy integrity.

'Why do you think I might be able to help you?'

'Well, you are his brother.'

'True. But I haven't spoken to my "little brother" since Dahum seceded in '67,' he said with heavy cynicism. 'Solomon can be very persuasive. He told me what he was planning to do – to secede, to establish a "new" country, keep the potential oil revenues for the Fakassa people. He had very, very big dreams. I begged him not to do it, told him it would be a disaster for the Fakassa, a kind of race-suicide.' His face tautened. 'I derive no satisfaction from being proved right.'

'So why didn't he listen to you?'

'You wouldn't understand, Mr Bond. You have to be a Fakassa to have that depth of feeling, that closeness . . .' The words seemed to fail him. 'We've lived in the Zanza River Delta for hundreds, perhaps thousands of years. It's our homeland – our heartland – in every passionate, instinctive sense of the words.' He smiled, emptily. 'I don't expect you to know what I'm talking about. You're not African.'

'No, I can understand,' Bond said. 'You make sense. There's no need to patronise me.'

'I apologise. Do you own a house?'

'I have a flat.'

'Do you like living there?'

'Very much.'

'What would you say if your neighbours came in one day and took away your carpets and your furniture, your treasured possessions?'

Bond shrugged. 'It doesn't relate. The Zanza River Delta is part of Zanzarim.'

Adeka looked a little contemptuous. 'Zanzarim, and before that, Upper Zanza State, and before that Neu Zanza Staat was a construct of European colonialists. They only arrived a few decades ago, at the end of the last century. They drew the country's boundaries on a whim one afternoon when they had nothing better to do.' He grew more serious. 'To the Fakassa people the

Zanza River Delta, our tribal homeland, is our birthright. It has no connection with twentieth-century neocolonial politics or the venal ambitions of European adventurers. Can you understand that?'

'Yes, I think so.'

Adeka yielded a little. 'All the same, my brother, Solomon, should never have tried to create an independent state. It was madness. I told him so. We fought, spoke very harsh words to each other and we haven't seen each other since.'

'Your arguments didn't impress.'

'He couldn't see sense. Wouldn't. Not surprisingly.'

'What do you mean?'

'Have you any idea how much oil lies beneath the Zanza River Delta, Mr Bond?'

'No.'

'Well, I suggest you try to find out – and then calculate roughly how many hundreds of millions of dollars will go to whoever owns it.'

He stood up. 'I can't help you, I'm afraid. You'll have to find someone else who can introduce you to my brother. All I ask is, if and when you reach Dahum, you tell the world exactly and honestly what you see there.'

Bond rose to his feet. 'You can count on that,' he said. 'We're not in the propaganda business.'

Adeka led him back downstairs and at the door handed him his business card.

'I'd be most grateful if you'd send me your articles.'

He extended his hand and Bond shook it, firmly, not thinking about the reality that lay behind his journey to Zanzarim.

'I'll give your salutations to your brother,' Bond said.

'Save your breath,' Adeka said evenly, with no bitterness. 'Solomon looks on me as the worst kind of traitor – he thinks I've betrayed my people.'

They made their farewells and Bond stepped out of the small shop on to the street and heard the bolts on the door slide shut behind him.

Bond wandered up the street, thinking, heading for the Bayswater Road. He glanced around him, remembering Adeka's words about continual harassment, wondering if the AfricaKIN office was under surveillance and, if it were, whether his visit would have been noted and logged. Something was making him uneasy, a prickling between his shoulder blades, an uncomfortableness. He always responded to these instinctive promptings – whenever he'd ignored them he had usually regretted it – so, looking for an opportunity to check his back, he turned into a convenient cinema and bought a ticket for the show but, instead of going into the auditorium, lingered in the foyer, to see who might be following him in. After five minutes he began to relax. No one else arriving at the kiosk to buy a ticket could have been any threat at all.

An usherette approached him asking if she could be of any help, reminding him that the film was due to start in 'four and a half minutes'. Bond reassured her he was aware of that fact and moved outside beneath the cinema's awning, glancing up and down the street. Nothing. Then his eye was caught by the poster. *The Curse of Dracula's Daughter* starring Astrid Ostergard. Bond smiled. There was Astrid/Bryce, naked in a bed, a tattered blood-boltered sheet just about covering her impossibly ripe body, a dark looming shadow of some vengeful monster cast over her. It wasn't a bad likeness, Bond reflected, remembering the glimpses he'd been afforded a few days ago. So this was where he'd seen her name before – B-movie horror-shockers. At least that much was clear now. Yet here was Bryce Fitzjohn/Astrid Ostergard again. Was there any significance in this curious recurrence? Anything he'd missed . . . ? Stepping into a random cinema foyer couldn't be construed as anything malign or manipulated – this was a harmless coincidence pure and simple. He had another look at the poster and smiled to himself, thinking he really had to make contact with her again once this whole Zanzarim business was over, and turned on to the street and strode confidently on towards the Bayswater Road, looking for a passing taxi he could hail.

·3·

WELCOME TO ZANZARIM

The BOAC VC10 levelled into its cruising altitude and the 'fasten seat belts' sign was extinguished. Bond ordered a double brandy and soda from the stewardess and as he sipped his drink thought about what lay ahead of him and what unforeseen perils he might have to face. It was always like this as he departed on a mission – and while the unknown generated a certain alarm and pre-emptive caution, Bond also recognised the frisson of excitement that ran through him. This was what he had been trained and honed to do, he re-emphasised to himself; sometimes he wondered if it was what he was born to do. He glanced over his shoulder, checking the cabin – the plane was only half full and Bond had two empty seats beside him. Not many people going to Zanzarim these days, he reflected, even though this flight was routed on to Banjul and Accra. Bond ordered another drink, running over the events of the last few days in his mind. He couldn't remember M sending him on such a vague assignment before: to find a way of infiltrating himself into Dahum and, one way or another, to 'immobilise' the brigadier . . . Perhaps, as far as M thought, his instructions were perfectly explicit, however concise. But, from Bond's point of view there was a lot of room being left for his initiative. Conceivably Ogilvy-Grant would be able to put some flesh on these bare bones.

The plane flew south into the darkening evening sky. Bond switched on his reading light and took out his book – Graham Greene's *The Heart of the Matter*. Bond had been to West Africa only once before, years ago – to shoot down a helicopter, as it happened – but he had not lingered; it had been an in-and-out visit. Greene had served in Sierra Leone during the war – as a spy, moreover – and Bond was hoping that his West African novel might furnish some shrewder insight to the place.

Eight hours later the VC10 touched down at Sinsikrou International Airport. As the plane taxied towards the terminal buildings Bond gazed out of the window at Africa, lit by the early morning sun. They passed gangs of crouching workers cutting the runway verges with long thin knives like sabres. Beyond the perimeter fence was undulating dry scrubland dotted with trees – orchard bush, as it was known – that sprawled away in the heat-haze. A row of olive-green MiG-15 'Fagot' fighters and a couple of sun-bleached, oil-stained Bell UH-1 helicopters were drawn up on a separate apron. The Zanzarim air force, Bond assumed. A few soldiers squatted listlessly in the shade cast by the planes' wings.

The VC10 came to a halt and the passengers bound for Sinsikrou headed for the door. All men, Bond noted, and none of them looking particularly salubrious. As he passed through the door on to the aircraft steps the humid warmth hit him with almost palpable force and, as he crossed the parched, piebald asphalt towards the airport buildings, he sensed his body breaking out in sweat beneath his clothes. Soldiers, wearing an assortment of camouflage uniforms and carrying various weapons, looked on lazily as the passengers filed into customs and immigration. Bond glanced around quickly. Parked by the fuel depot was a shiny new six-wheeled Saracen armoured car – recently imported from Britain, Bond supposed, the first patent indication of whose side we were on in this war.

As if to give credence to this analysis Bond's British passport was barely examined. It was stamped, the immigration officer said 'Welcome to Zanzarim,' and waved him through to the customs hall, which was surprisingly busy with a traffic of people who apparently had nothing to do with customs. As he waited for his suitcase to arrive, Bond declined to have his shoes polished, rejected the invitation to be driven in a 'luxury' Mercedes-Benz private car to his hotel and politely refused a small boy's whispered offer of sex with his 'very beautiful' big sister.

A surly customs officer asked him to open his case, rummaged through his clothes and even unzipped his pigskin toilet bag and – finding no contraband – scratched a hieroglyph on the suitcase's lid with a piece of blue chalk and moved on to the next piece of baggage in the queue.

Bond again refused the offer of help with his case as a young man physically tried to prise it from his grasp, and walked out of the building to find a taxi rank. He climbed into the back of a racing-green Morris Minor and happily agreed to pay extra in order not to share the car with others. He instructed the driver to take him to the Excelsior Gateway Hotel.

Even though the Excelsior was barely a mile from the airport the journey there was not straightforward. Almost as soon as they left the airport perimeter they were waved to a halt at an army roadblock and Bond was asked to step out of the car and show the customs mark on his suitcase. Despite the clear evidence of the chalk scribble he was asked to open the suitcase again. The soldiers at the roadblock were bored and this was a diversion to enliven their long and weary day, Bond realised. Other taxis were halted behind them and soon voices were being raised in angry protest. Bond wondered if he should give the soldier who was listlessly picking through his case some money – a 'dash', as he now knew it was called, thanks to his reading of *The Heart of the Matter* – but before he could do so an officer appeared, shouting in furious rage at his men and waved everyone on.

A further 500 yards down the road they were halted at another so-called roadblock consisting of two oil drums with a plank across them. This looked less official and the demeanour of the soldiers manning it was more lackadaisical, the men contenting themselves with peering curiously through the open windows into the back of the taxi.

'Good morning,' Bond said. 'How are you today?'

'American cigarette?' one soldier said, grinning. He was wearing a tin helmet, a red T-shirt and camouflage trousers.

'English,' Bond said and gave him the Morlands that remained in his cigarette case.

When they eventually reached the hotel entrance Bond paid his fare and pushed through the crowd of hawkers that surrounded him – offering thorn carvings, painted calabashes, beaded necklaces – and finally gained the cool lobby of the Excelsior Gateway, formerly the Prince Clarence Hotel, as an old painted sign on the wall informed him. Ceiling fans turned above his head and Bond gave his suitcase to a bellhop in a scarlet waist-coat with a scarlet fez on his head. He crossed the glossy teak floorboards towards the reception desk where he was checked in. There, an envelope was handed to him that contained a slip of paper with Ogilvy-Grant's address and new contact telephone number at an industrial park. Bond folded the note up and tucked it in his pocket, looking around him as the receptionist busied himself writing down Bond's details from his passport. Potted palms swayed in the breeze produced by the ceiling fans. Through glass doors Bond looked into a long dark bar where a barman in a white jacket was polishing glasses. On the other side of the lobby was the entrance to the dining room, where a sign requested 'Gentlemen, please no shorts'. Another receptionist wearing a crisp white tunic with gold buttons arrived on duty and wished him a smiling 'Good morning, Mr Bond.' For a moment Bond savoured the illusion of time travel, when the Excelsior Gateway had been the Prince Clarence Hotel and Zanzarim had been Upper Zanza State and civil war, mass starvation and illimitable oil revenues were all in an unimaginable future.

·4·

CHRISTMAS

The bellhop in the scarlet fez took Bond to his small chalet in the hotel grounds at the rear of the main building. There were a dozen of these mini-bungalows linked to the hotel buildings by weed-badged concrete pathways, a remnant of the Excelsior Gateway's colonial past. After independence an Olympic-sized swimming pool had been constructed, flanked by two five-storey modern annexes – 'executive rooms with pool-view balconies'. Bond was glad to be in his shabby bungalow. He tipped the bellhop.

'Water he close at noon, sar,' the boy said. 'But we have electric light twenty-four hours.' He smiled. 'We have gen'rator.'

Bond took his advice and had a cold shower while the water pressure was still there. He changed into a cotton khaki-drill suit, a white short-sleeved Aertex shirt and a navy-blue knitted tie. He slipped his feet into soft brown moccasins, thought about removing his socks but decided against it. He reloaded his cigarette case with some of the Morlands he'd brought with him in a 200-cigarette carton and, ready for action, headed out to the hotel entrance.

The doorman shooed away the hawkers and Bond gave him $10.

'I need a taxi with a good driver for several hours,' Bond said. 'Twenty US dollars for the day – and if he's good, I'll give you another ten.'

'Five seconds, sar,' the doorman said and raced off.

Two minutes later a mustard yellow Toyota Corona lurched to a halt opposite Bond. A skinny young man, smart in a white shirt and white shorts, stepped out and saluted.

'Hello, sar. I am your driver, Christmas.'

Bond shook Christmas's hand and eased himself into the back of the Corona.

'Where to, sar?'

'Do you know where the military headquarters are?'

'Zanza Force HQ. I know him. Ridgeway Barracks.'

'Good. Let's go.'

Ridgeway Barracks was a large four-storey pre-war building of faded cream stucco set in a park of mature casuarina pines. Christmas dropped him at the main entrance and Bond showed his press card to the soldier at the gate and was told to follow a sign that said 'Press Liaison'. In an office at the end of a corridor a young captain with an American accent looked over his documentation.

'Agence Presse Libre? This is French. Are you French?'

'No. I'm from the London office. I file all copy in English. It's an international press agency, founded in 1923. Global. Like Reuters.'

The captain thought about it for a moment then stamped and signed a new accredited press card. He smiled, insincerely – Bond suspected that he didn't like journalists or his job – and handed it over.

'The daily briefing is in twenty minutes,' he said. 'Let me take you to your colleagues.'

The captain led Bond out through the back of the building where, at the edge of a beaten earth parade ground, a large canvas tent had been pitched.

'Take a seat – we'll be there shortly.'

Bond slipped in the back and sat down, looking around him. The filtered sunlight coming through the canvas was aqueous and shadowless. It was hot. Sitting randomly on rows of folding chairs were about two dozen journalists – almost all white – facing an empty dais beneath a huge map of Zanzarim. On this map, at the foot, a small bashed circle that was now the diminishing heartland of the Democratic Republic of Dahum was outlined in red chalk. Clusters of sticky-backed arrows threatening the circle indicated offensives by the federal Zanzarim forces, Bond supposed. He wandered down an aisle between rows of empty chairs to get a closer look.

The scale of the map revealed in great detail the massive and complex network of creeks and watercourses that made up the Zanza River Delta. Port Dunbar was at the southern extremity, the notional capital of the secessionist state. Above it, written on a card and stuck on the map, was the name Janjaville, where the vital airstrip was to be found. It was immediately apparent to Bond that bringing an end to Dahum would be no easy task. One main highway crossing many bridges and causeways led south into Port Dunbar and it was here, judging from the clustered arrows, that the main federal thrust into the heartland was taking place. All other roadways were symbolised by dotted red lines, meandering around the obstacles posed by the creeks, swamps and lakes, crossing hundreds of makeshift bridges, Bond imagined. You didn't need to be a military genius to defend this small patch of territory, it seemed to him. Bond wandered back to his seat – his close look at the map had also allowed him to calculate the distance from Sinsikrou to Port Dunbar – some 300 miles, he reckoned. He began to wonder how Ogilvy-Grant planned to 'infiltrate' him – it didn't seem that straightforward . . .

Suddenly there was a jaded tremor of interest amongst the waiting journalists as a bemedalled colonel in crisp, brutally starched camouflage fatigues pushed through a flap at the rear of the tent and took up his position on the dais, followed by the captain with the American accent, who was carrying a thin six-foot rod, like a billiard cue.

'Good day to you, gentlemen,' the colonel said. 'Welcome to the briefing. We have interesting news for you today.' The colonel took the pointing-stick from the captain and, indicating with it on the map, began to enumerate various federal victories and advances into the rebel heartland. Under his instructions the captain rubbed out a portion of the Dahum circle and redrew it with the red chalk so that a pronounced salient appeared on the main highway south. Bond sensed the minimal credulity in the room diminish, suddenly, like a balloon deflating.

'With the capture yesterday of the village of Ikot-Dussa the Zanzari forces are now forty-two kilometres from Port Dunbar,' the colonel said, triumphantly, turned and left the tent.

A journalist raised his hand.

'Yes, Geoffrey,' the captain said.

'According to my notes,' Geoffrey said, his voice flat, 'the village of Ikot-Dussa was liberated ten days ago.'

'That was Ikot-Darema,' the captain said without a pause. 'Maybe our Zanzari names are confusing you.'

'Yes, that's probably it – my mistake. Apologies.' There was a subdued ripple of badly suppressed chuckles amongst the journalists and many knowing glances were exchanged.

Another journalist's hand was raised.

'You were predicting the unconditional surrender of rebel forces five weeks ago. What's happened?'

The captain leaned the stick against the wall.

'You may have noticed, John,' the captain said, not quite managing to disguise his weariness, 'now you've been in the country for so long, that it's been raining rather heavily these last couple of months. And now it's stopped raining and the dry season has begun – therefore military operations are resuming at full strength.'

And so the briefing continued for another listless twenty minutes as each loaded question was either batted away or rebuffed with confident fabrication. Bond found he rather admired the captain's tireless ability to lie so fluently and with manifest conviction. He was good at his job but no one was fooled. This war had ground to a semi-permanent halt, no doubt about it. Bond stood up and slipped out of the tent. He had learned a surprising amount on his first day as an accredited journalist for APL. It was time, he felt, to make contact with the British Secret Service's head of station in Zanzarim.

·5·

E. B. OGILVY-GRANT MA (CANTAB)

OG Palm Oil Export and Agricultural Services Ltd was to be found in a light-industrial estate halfway between Sinsikrou city and the airport. Bond had telephoned from Ridgeway Barracks, but there had been no reply, so he decided to pay a personal visit. Christmas drove Bond into the complex and stopped in the shade of a Bata Shoe warehouse. Opposite was a small row of premises with storage space below and offices above. OG Palm Oil Export and Agricultural Services was at the end.

'I won't be long,' Bond said, opening the door.

'I stay here, sar.'

Bond crossed the road to the OG section of the building. Sun-blistered metal blinds were padlocked down and the electric bell-push dangled from its flex by the door that accessed the stairwell. Bond rang the bell but it seemed dead to him. He pushed at the door and it swayed open. All very impressive, he thought: as 'cover' went, this might work – a tenth-rate palm-oil exporter on its uppers. He closed the door behind him and walked up the stairs to the offices. He knocked on the door but there was no reply, he tried the handle and the door opened – so, no locked doors at OG Palm Qil Export and Agricultural

Services Ltd. Bond stepped into the office and raised his voice – 'Hello? Anybody in?' Silence. Bond looked around: a metal desk with a typewriter and an empty in tray, a wooden filing cabinet, a fan on a tea chest, last year's calendar on the wall, a display table with various dusty sample tins of palm oil set out on it and – touchingly, Bond thought – hanging by the door, a faded reproduction of Annigoni's 1956 portrait of the Queen, a small symbol of the covert business being done here.

Someone's throat was cleared loudly behind him.

Bond turned round slowly. 'Hello,' he said.

A young African woman stood there – a pale-skinned Zanzari, Bond thought, slim, petite, pretty, her hair knotted in tight neat rows, flat against her skull, which had the curious effect of making her brown eyes seem wider and more alert. She was wearing a 'Ban the Bomb' T-shirt, pale denim jeans cut off raggedly at the knee and around her neck hung a string of heavy amber beads. Ogilvy-Grant's secretary, Bond assumed. Well, he could certainly pick them – she was a beautiful young woman.

'My name's Bond, James Bond,' he said. 'I want to buy some palm oil. I'd like to arrange a meeting with Ogilvy-Grant.'

'Your wish is granted,' she said. 'I'm Ogilvy-Grant.'

Bond managed to suppress his sudden smile of incredulity.

'Listen, I don't think you understand—'

'I'm Efua Blessing Ogilvy-Grant,' the young woman said, then added with overt cynicism, 'oh, yes, I'm E. B. Ogilvy-Grant, managing director.' She had a clipped English accent, rather posh, Bond thought, rather like Araminta Beauchamp's.

'Nice to meet you, Mr Bond,' she said and they shook hands. 'My friends all call me Blessing.'

60

'A Blessing in disguise,' Bond said without thinking.

'Funny – I've never heard that one before,' she said, clearly unamused.

'I apologise,' Bond said, feeling vaguely shamefaced that he'd uttered it.

'I was waiting for you at the airport this morning,' she said. 'Didn't London tell you I'd be there?'

'They didn't, actually . . .' Bond watched her take her seat behind the desk.

'We were meant to meet by the Independence Monument.'

'No one told me.'

'Standard London cock-up.'

She opened a drawer and took out a pack of cigarettes, offering it to Bond.

'They're our local brand,' she said. 'Tuskers – strong and oddly addictive.'

Bond took one, fished out his Ronson and lit her cigarette, then his.

'So – you're our head of station in Zanzarim.'

'Go to the top of the class. That's me.'

Her accent sat oddly with the radical-chic, love-in outfit, Bond thought.

'When were you appointed, if you don't mind my asking?' he went on.

'I don't mind at all. Just over two months ago. Weirdly, we had no one here. Everything was run through the embassy.' She smiled, relaxing a bit. 'My mother is a Lowele. All her family's here in Sinsikrou – my family. I speak Lowele. And my father was a Scottish engineer, Fraser Ogilvy-Grant, who helped build the big dam in the north at Mogasso just before the war. My mother worked as his interpreter – and they fell in love.'

'A Scottish engineer?' Bond said. 'So was my father, funnily enough. And my mother was Swiss,' he added, as if the fact that they were both of mixed nationalities would form an affinity between them.

In fact the information did seem to make her relax even more, Bond thought. That old Celtic blood tie established, the home-land noted – however fragile the connection, however meaning-less – worked its temporary magic.

'You don't sound Scottish,' he said.

'Neither do you.' She smiled. 'I was educated in England. Cheltenham Ladies' College, then Cambridge, then Harvard. I hardly know Scotland, to be honest.'

Bond stubbed out his Tusker in the ashtray on her desk, his throat raw.

'Did they recruit you at Cambridge?'

'Yes. Then they arranged for me to go to Harvard. I think they had plans for me in America. But, because of my family connec-tions, this was the perfect first assignment.'

Bond was trying to calculate her age – Cambridge then Harvard, born in the war, maybe twenty-six, or twenty-seven. She was remarkably assured for one so young; but he suspected this job was going to prove harder than he had ever imagined.

'I'm staying at the Excelsior,' he said.

'Yes, I do know that,' she said with elaborate patience. 'And Christmas is your driver.'

'Ah, so you must have arranged—'

'I'm here to help, Commander Bond.' She stood up. 'I must

say it's a great privilege to be working with you. Your reputation precedes you, even out here in the sticks.'

'Please call me James, Blessing.'

'I'm here to help, James,' she repeated. 'Shall we have dinner tonight? There's a good Lebanese restaurant in town. We can talk through everything then.' She walked him to the door. 'Make our plans. I'll pick you up at the Excelsior at seven.'

·6·

SYRIAN BURGUNDY-TYPE

Bond had ordered malfouf – stuffed cabbage rolls – followed by shish tawook – a simple chicken kebab with salty pickles. The food was good. Bond had spent three weeks on a tedious job in Beirut in 1960 and in his endless spare time had developed a taste for Lebanese cuisine. The wine list, however, was a joke, given that he had drunk excellent Lebanese wines in Beirut – all that was on offer here was Blue Nun Riesling and a red described as 'Syrian Burgundy-type' – so Bond played safe and ordered the local beer, Green Star. It was something of a first for him to drink beer with dinner, but the lager was light and very cold and complemented the strong flavours of the garlic and the pickles. Blessing had a cold lentil soup and a dried-mint omelette.

'You're not a vegetarian, are you?' Bond asked, suspiciously.

'No,' she said. 'Just not very hungry. Would it matter if I was?'

'It might,' Bond said, with a smile. 'I've never met a vegetarian I liked, curiously. You might have been the exception, of course.'

'Ha-ha,' she remarked, drily. 'By their food shall ye judge them.'

'You'd be surprised, it's not a bad touchstone,' Bond said, and called for another Green Star. 'Or so I've found in my experience.'

Since he had left her office she had had her hair redone. The plaited rows had gone and it was now oiled flat back against her head almost as if it was painted on. She had a shiny transparent gloss on her lips and was wearing a black silk Nehru jacket over wide flared white cotton trousers, and had some sort of crudely beaten pewter disc hanging round her neck on a leather thong. She looked very futuristic, Bond thought, with her perfect caramel skin, the colour of milky coffee, as if she were an extra from a science-fiction film.

The restaurant was in downtown Sinsikrou, near to the law courts and the barracks. It had a deliberately modest facade with a flickering neon sign that bluntly read 'El Kebab – Best Lebanon', but the first-floor dining room was air-conditioned and there were white linen cloths on the tables and waiters in velvet waist-coats and tasselled tarbooshes. Bond had spotted several high-ranking soldiers and also some of the journalists who'd been at the briefing earlier that day. El Kebab was obviously the only place in town.

They chatted idly as they ate, keeping off the subject of their business with each other – the tables were close and it would be easy to overhear or eavesdrop. Blessing told him more about the civil war and its origins from her perspective. Being half-Lowele, she explained, she thought that the Fakassa junta that had provoked and engineered secession were crazy. What did they think the rest of the country was going to do? Sit on their collective hands? Allow themselves to become impoverished? At least the British government had acted quickly, she said. If they hadn't come down on the side of Zanzarim immediately and refused point-blank to recognise the new republic, perhaps Dahum's de facto existence might have become a foregone conclusion. Alacrity was not normally a virtue of Her Majesty's governments, Bond thought – there would be more at stake here than preserving the rule of international law.

'Do you want a pudding?' Bond asked, lighting a cigarette.

'I'd rather have a proper drink somewhere,' she said.

'Excellent idea, Ogilvy-Grant. Let's go back to the Excelsior.'

Blessing drove them to the hotel, Bond looking out of the window at the garish cinema of the night-time city that was Sinsikrou. Blaring high-life music seemed to come from almost every house, and multicoloured neon tubes appeared to be the illumination of choice. Dogs, goats and hens searched the storm drains for titbits; naked children stood in doorways staring at the passing cars, entranced; off-duty soldiers swaggered through the roadside crowds, Kalashnikovs and SLR rifles slung over their shoulders. And every time they stopped at a traffic light or when the gridlock of cars slowed them to walking pace, street-hawkers would appear at their windows trying to sell them combs and biros, dusters and cheap watches.

The bar at the Excelsior was surprisingly busy.

'It's a very popular place,' Blessing said, spotting an unoccupied table at the back of the room. 'Especially since the war began.' They sat down and Bond ordered himself a large whisky and soda and a gin and tonic for Blessing.

The air conditioning was on and working and the chill was welcome after the humid, loud night outside. Not that it was any quieter in here, Bond thought, looking round the room. A lot of white men, some in assorted uniforms, not many Zanzaris.

'Who are they?' Bond asked Blessing, indicating the men in uniform.

'The pilots – they fly the MiGs. East Germans, Poles, a few Egyptians. They're on a thousand dollars a day – cash. Very popular with the ladies.'

Bond had noticed the prostitutes. They sat at the bar or sauntered suggestively among the crowded tables. Beautiful black women with bouffant wigs – modelled on American pop stars, Bond thought, as one of them caught his eye and beckoned him over with a flap of her glossy taloned fingers.

The chatter of conversation was loud and already raucous – everyone drinking heavily. The air smelt of booze, sweat and cheap perfume – redolent of sex and danger. There was a kind of frontier recklessness about the atmosphere, Bond thought, and recognised its allure. These pilots had been out dropping bombs and napalm on Dahum. The temptations offered in the bar at the Excelsior would be hard to resist.

He looked at the men. Ex-Eastern bloc air-force pilots, all on the older side – retired, superannuated, cashiered – earning good money as mercenaries fighting in a nasty little African war . . . $1,000 a day – after three months you could quit, take a couple of years off, build a house back home, buy a smart foreign car.

He ordered another round of drinks from a touring waiter, leaned closer to Blessing and lowered his voice.

'I reckon we can safely talk in this din,' he said. 'What's your plan?'

'I did a quick recce last week when I knew you were coming,' she said. 'The only way into Dahum is by road, or, rather, by road and water. The main highway's impossible – jammed with non-stop military traffic.' She sipped at her drink. 'I think you have to be driven as far south into the delta as possible. Then a local fisherman – I've made contact with one man – will take you through the swamps and the creeks by boat.'

'Is that realistic?' Bond wondered.

'There's no front line as such,' she said. 'And there's constant smuggling of food and supplies into the heartland. It's a labyrinth, a huge network of waterways and streams and creeks. That's one reason why the war's gone on so long.'

'Who'll drive me south? Christmas?'

She looked at him and smiled. 'I thought I would,' she said. 'I speak Lowele. You'd need a translator, anyway. It'll all look very plausible if we're stopped and questioned.'

'Sounds good to me,' Bond said, feeling oddly relieved. 'How long will it take to reach the delta?'

'We'll have to travel on back roads – meander south. I reckon two or three days' driving. Two nights.'

Bond turned the ice cubes in his whisky with a finger, enjoying the sensation of being in Blessing's capable hands as she outlined the plan further. They would stay in local rest-houses, then contact would be made with the fisherman, who would be well paid on Bond's safe delivery into Dahum. Blessing would head back to Sinsikrou and wait until she heard from him.

'Or not,' Bond said. 'I may not come back this way.'

'Of course. As operational necessities dictate.'

'When should we head off?'

'Whenever you want,' she said. 'It's your decision.'

'Let's not wait around,' Bond said. 'How about tomorrow?'

'No problem. I'll have everything ready first thing in the

morning. Come over to the office and we'll hit the road. One thing,' she added. 'I would travel light. Just one small bag or a rucksack or something. You may have to hike a bit once you get into Dahum.'

Bond had been thinking about that, feeling the heart-thump of excitement that gripped him whenever a mission was imminent and all the cosy securities of everyday life were about to be cast aside. He took out his cigarette case – empty. Blessing saw this and reached into her handbag for her pack of Tuskers.

'You'll have to go local,' she said, offering the pack. Bond took a cigarette.

'You're Bond, aren't you?' a slurred male English voice said.

Bond turned. A drunk white man swayed there gently. He was wearing a crumpled pale blue drill suit with darker blue sweat patches forming at the armpits. His jowly face was flushed and sweating. Bond recognised him from the press briefing at the barracks: a fellow journalist – one who'd asked a question.

'That's right,' Bond said, flatly. He wanted this encounter to end. Now.

'Geoffrey Letham, *Daily Mail*,' the man said. 'You're with APL, aren't you? Saw you were a new boy today so I checked the accreditation list.' He leaned forward and Bond smelled the sour reek of beer. 'D'you know old Thierry? Thierry Duhamel?'

'I'm working out of London,' Bond said, improvising. 'Not Paris.'

'No, Thierry's in Geneva. Head office. Everybody at APL knows Thierry. He's a bloody legend.'

'I've only just started. I've been in Australia the last couple of years. Reuters,' he added, hoping this would shut the man up. Blessing leaned forward with her lighter and clicked it on, as if to signal that the conversation was over. Bond turned away from Letham and bent his head to light his cigarette. He sat back and exhaled. But Letham was still there, staring at Blessing as though in a trance of lust.

'Hello, hello, *hello*,' he said, with a caricature leer, and then turned to Bond. 'Pretty little thing. After you with her, old chap.'

Bond saw the offence register on Blessing's face and felt a hot surge of anger flow through him.

'Send her round to room 203 when you're done with her,' Letham said, out of the side of his mouth. 'They can go all night, these Zanzari bints.'

Before Blessing could say anything Bond stood up.

'Actually, could I have a discreet word, outside?' Bond said, laying his cigarette in the ashtray and, taking Letham's arm by the elbow, steered him firmly through the crowded bar. 'Man to man, you know,' Bond said, confidentially, in his ear.

'Got you, old fellow,' Letham said. 'Forewarned is forearmed in the young-lady department.'

They stepped out of a side door into the warm darkness of the night, loud with crickets. Bond looked around and saw the back entrance to the bar – dustbins and stacked empty crates – and led Letham towards them.

'She's not expensive, is she?' Letham said. 'I refuse to pay these Zanzari hookers more than ten US.'

Bond turned and punched Letham as hard as he could in the stomach. He went down with a thump on his arse, mouth open like a landed fish, gaping. Then he vomited copiously into his lap and fell back against the wall making breathy whimpering noises.

'Mind your manners,' Bond said, though Letham wasn't listening. 'Don't speak to respectable young women like that again.'

Bond strode round to the front of the hotel and into the lobby, where he found a porter.

'There's a drunk Englishman been sick – at the back behind the bar,' Bond said, indicating. 'I think you should chuck a couple of buckets of water over him.' He slipped a note into the porter's hand.

The porter smiled, eagerly. 'We shall do it, sar,' he said and hurried off.

Bond returned to the noisy bar and joined Blessing at their table, ordering another whisky on the way.

'Sorry about that,' he said. 'He won't bother us further – he's not feeling very well.'

'My knight in shining armour,' Blessing said. 'Did you administer retribution?'

'Powerful retribution,' Bond said, draining his whisky. 'I despise those types – pond life. They need to be taught a sharp lesson from time to time. Shall we go? Busy day tomorrow.'

Bond silently walked Blessing to her car. He felt the tremors of adrenalin slowly leave him and smiled, imagining Letham being gleefully doused by buckets of water. A cooler breeze had got up and a fat yellow moon had risen above the poolside apartment blocks.

Bond gestured at the moon, wanting to break the silence between them.

'Doesn't quite seem the same,' he said, 'now that we've been up there. Lost something of its allure.'

'I don't agree,' she said. 'It seems to belong to us more, now – not some distant symbol.'

'*La lune ne garde aucune rancune*,' Bond said.

'Who's that?' Blessing said.

'Can't remember. Something I learned at school as a boy.'

'You've a very good accent,' she said.

'I spent a lot of my childhood in Switzerland.'

'Classified information, Commander Bond.'

They had reached her car.

'You didn't need to do that, you know,' Blessing said, opening her car door and turning to him. 'Creeps like that don't bother me. I know how to deal with them.' She shrugged. 'But thank you all the same. I appreciate it.'

'I'm sure you do know how to deal with them – but he was getting on my nerves.'

They looked at each other.

'Goodnight, James,' she said and slipped into the driving seat.

'See you tomorrow at the office,' Bond said, closing the door for her. 'Nine o'clock.'

·7·

ON THE ROAD

After his breakfast – a pint of freshly squeezed orange juice, scrambled eggs, bacon and fried plantain – Bond wandered out to the front portico of the hotel and, after some requisite haggling, bought a bag. It was a grip of black leather with the Zanzarim flag – a banded quincolour of red, white, yellow, black and green – appliquéd to the side. It was unlined and smelled strongly of recently cured leather. The handles were long enough to be slipped over his shoulder if required.

Back in his room, Bond packed with some thought, deciding to wear an olive-green safari jacket over khaki trousers with suede desert boots on his feet. Into the Zanzarim grip went three dark blue short-sleeved Aertex shirts, three pairs of underpants and socks, a rolled up panama hat in a cardboard tube, his anti-malaria pills and his pigskin toilet bag. It was odd and a little unsettling not to have a gun on him: he felt strangely undressed, almost wilfully vulnerable. He decided to leave all his other clothes in his suitcase – and he'd deposit that in Blessing's office for her to ship home at some stage. He who travels lightest, travels furthest, Bond supposed, and that included weaponry. Into a war zone with a can of talcum powder and some aftershave. He walked down to reception with his suitcase and his new grip, ready to check out and settle his bill. Having done that he had an idea and went into the bar and bought a bottle of Johnnie Walker whisky. For medicinal use – you never knew when it might be needed.

Christmas dropped Bond off at the OG offices where he found Blessing standing on the roof of a cream-coloured Austin 1100 with a pot of black paint in her hand. She was painting the word 'PRESS' on the roof in two-foot-high letters and Bond saw, as he circled the car, that the passenger side of the windscreen and the rear window had been similarly inscribed in letters of white sticky tape.

'Couldn't we get a better car?' Bond asked, thinking that this was the sort of vehicle a mother might use to pick up her kids from school or collect the groceries.

'It's perfect,' Blessing said, stepping down. 'We don't want anything showy – we don't want to attract too much attention. We'll just trundle off and no one will notice us.'

Bond helped her load two jerrycans of petrol, two spare tyres and a fifty-litre plastic container of water into the boot. They said goodbye to Christmas, who was going to man the office phone in their absence, and without more ado they climbed into the 1100 and set off, Blessing at the wheel for the first leg of the journey.

She handed Bond a map of Zanzarim with their meandering route south picked out. Bond saw that they would be moving haphazardly from village to provincial town to village again, always a good distance from the main transnational highway. When they set out and had quit the outskirts of Sinsikrou they immediately turned off into the countryside. Bond stared out of the window at the dusty bush, the unfaltering savannah scrub with its occasional trees. However, as they drove on, the vegetation grew steadily thicker until the view from the window was obscured by forest. The roads they travelled on were all tarmac but badly eroded with dangerous, deep potholes. They passed through hamlets and villages of mud huts roofed with grass thatch or rusty corrugated iron, each village with its little cluster of rickety roadside stalls selling bananas, peppers, cassava and various fruits. Seeing Bond's white face at the window of the car as it flashed by provoked shouts and cries of excitement or derision from the villagers – or perhaps they were just pleas to stop and buy something. Bond couldn't tell. He felt the real Africa engulf him, realising that Sinsikrou had nothing to do with the Zanzarim that they were now motoring through. On the roads the only other traffic they encountered was ancient lorries and buses, the occasional cyclist and mule-drawn cart.

They made good progress and at lunchtime they stopped in a more sizeable town, Oguado, and found a roadside bar where they could enjoy a cold drink. Bond ordered a Green Star and Blessing a Fanta and they ate some kind of peppery, doughy cake known as dago-dago, so Blessing told him. It didn't look much, Bond thought, like a beige doughnut with no hole, but it was surprisingly spicy and tasty.

He took over the driving and they headed on through constant scrubby forest, then, at one stage, they passed through a vast plantation of cocoa trees that took them half an hour to traverse.

It was hot and the sky hazed over to a milky white. They saw no military vehicles and encountered no roadblocks. Bond remarked on this: you'd hardly believe this was a country in the grip of a two-year civil war, he said, that just a couple of hundred miles to the south half a million people were starving to death.

'It's Africa,' Blessing said with a shrug. She gestured at the village they were passing through. 'These people may have a transistor radio or a bicycle but their lives haven't really changed in a thousand years. They probably don't even know their capital is called Sinsikrou.'

Bond swerved on to the laterite verge to avoid a six-foot pothole. The road ahead was completely straight and the view so unendingly monotonous he wondered if he was in danger of falling asleep. He pulled on to the verge again and said he needed to relieve himself. As he stepped, carefully, a few yards into the forest he soon lost sight of the car. The air was filled with noises – frogs, bird, insects – and he suddenly felt a sense of immense solitariness overwhelm him, yet everywhere he looked there were signs of non-human life: columns of ants at his feet, a trio of magenta butterflies exploring a sunbeam, some angry screeching bird on a high branch, a lizard doing press-ups on a boulder. This specimen of *Homo sapiens* emptying its bladder was just another organism in the teeming primeval forest. He was glad to walk back to the road and the car – feeble symbols of his species' purported domination of the planet – and to smoke one of Blessing's potent Tuskers before she offered to take over the driving for the final stage of the day's journey to their first destination, the Good Companion rest-house on the outskirts of a small town called Kolo-Ade.

These rest-houses were another just-surviving relic of Zanzarim's colonial past. The Good Companion had been built in the 1930s – a solid large airy brick house with a wide veranda and sitting room, dining room and kitchen on the ground floor and eight bedrooms on the floor above – created for the travelling administrators and functionaries who ran the colony in days gone by. The place was showing clear signs of its age – the paint was flaking and the concrete floors needed rewaxing – but it was clean and simple in its efficiency. Bond's room had a bed with a mosquito net suspended above it and a wooden stand with an enamel jug and ewer. There was a WC at the end of the corridor.

He and Blessing sat on the veranda – they were the only guests – watching the bats swoop and swerve in the brief African gloaming as the sun set in its sudden blood-orange termination. They drank whisky and water and smoked steadily to keep the mosquitoes at bay. Blessing showed him on the map how far they had travelled – they had covered some 200 miles on these back roads, she reckoned. The next day's drive would see them enter the fringes of the Zanza River Delta, where they could expect roadblocks and inevitable delays. The soldiers often kept cars waiting for hours in order to up the fee for being allowed to motor on.

Bond savoured this moment on the veranda as they sat and chatted. He had a powerful sundowner in his hand and the heat was leaving the atmosphere as the cool of the tropical night advanced. He felt at ease – and he was also enjoying the company of a beautiful young woman, he realised. Blessing had changed into an embroidered, tie-dyed dress of many hues of vermilion and rose that had the effect of making her look more exotic and

African – or was that just the result of their journey into the interior of Zanzarim, Bond wondered, recalling her cool sci-fi beauty of the previous evening. He could tell, moreover, that she wore no brassiere under the dress – he could see her pert breasts shiver as she flicked her hand to shoo away a fluttering moth. He found himself imagining her naked, wondering what her youthful firm body might be like beneath the— Stop right there, Bond! – he issued the stern instruction to himself. Don't go down that road.

A white-haired toothless old man, the manager of the Good Companion, called them in for their evening meal: fruit salad, followed by a tough steak with fried cassava. Bond decided to forego the sago pudding with raspberry jam offered as dessert and called for another whisky. They had been driving for a good eight hours today, Bond realised, and he was feeling tired.

So was Blessing, Bond saw, as she yawned widely, and they both agreed it was time to turn in. They climbed the stairs to their bedrooms and parted on the landing.

'I think we should start at dawn tomorrow,' Blessing said. 'I'll knock on your door.'

'Fine,' Bond said and resisted the urge to kiss her goodnight. 'See you in the morning.'

He lay in his bed under the gauze tent of his mosquito net listening to the night noises beyond the shuttered windows – the tireless crickets, the whooping owls, burping toads and pie-dogs yapping in Kolo-Ade's outskirts. One more day's driving, Bond thought, another night in a rest-house and the infiltration into the shrinking heartland of Dahum. He felt the prickle of the adrenalin rush but also a rare sense of foreboding. The drive through the lonely interior of Zanzarim had reminded him of the problems, not to say the enormity, of the task that faced him. As his surroundings had grown more primitive and elemental so, it seemed, whatever strength, capability and powers he possessed appeared more insubstantial and weak. What was it about Africa that unmanned you so? he wondered, turning over and punching the hard kapok pillow into a more amenable shape for his head – why did the continent so effortlessly remind you of your human frailties?

When Blessing knocked on his door it was still dark. Breakfast was a mug of Camp coffee and some toast and marmalade and when they set off the light was growing pearly and the air was wonderfully cool. They made good progress in the morning but, just as they were contemplating their lunch break, they met their first roadblock. There was a queue of around two dozen cars on either side of an armoured personnel carrier that had parked itself across the road. Half a dozen soldiers, in the now familiar patchwork uniforms, lazily scrutinised identity cards and searched the belongings of resigned and unprotesting motorists.

A young officer ambled down the line of cars towards them, attracted by the 1100's self-described press status. He looked smarter than the other soldiers and was wearing a lozenge-camouflaged blouson and trousers and had a moss-green beret on his head.

'Stay there,' Blessing said, and stepped out of the car. Bond watched her talking to the officer in Lowele. From time to time she pointed back at Bond, clearly the topic of their conversation.

Then they both returned to the car. The officer looked in the window at Bond, smiling. Bond smiled back.

'Morning, Captain,' Bond said, elevating his rank by two pips.

'Pleased to assist you, sir,' he said and snapped a salute.

Blessing climbed into the car, started the engine, did a three-point turn, then drove back the way they had just come.

'We'd have been there all day,' she said. 'I told him you were late for an interview with Major General Basanjo – he's the commander-in-chief of Zanza Force. The officer said we were heading in the wrong direction.' She glanced over at him and grinned. 'Plan B?'

'Over to you,' Bond said, quietly impressed with Blessing's powers of improvisation. He tried to ignore the little spasms of sexual interest he was suddenly feeling for her, watching her muscles tauten and flex in her slim brown arms as she turned the wheel of the car, seeing the glow of perspiration on her throat, noting the contour-hugging tightness of the T-shirt she was wearing. Keep your mind on the job, he told himself.

They turned off the road at the next junction and headed east for the transnational highway. They made slow progress for an hour or so once they reached the highway as they were constantly waved off the road to give military vehicles right of way. During one of their enforced pauses Bond counted a convoy of over forty army lorries, packed with troops. At another stage, further down the road, they passed five tank-transporters with what looked like brand-new Centurion tanks sitting on them. A low-level flight of MiGs, heavy with napalm canisters, screeched past, ripping through the air with a sound like tearing linen. Everything Bond saw said 'major offensive looming': it was as if Zanza Force was preparing for the final thrust into the rebel heartland. He said as much to Blessing but she was more sceptical.

'They've got all the arms and men, sure,' she said. 'But these new troops are conscripts – badly trained and nervy. They only advance if given free beer and cigarettes. And those tanks are useless in the delta. They don't like the terrain and all the key bridges are blown.'

Then, as if someone had been overhearing them, they passed a line of parked flatbed trucks loaded with the cantilevered sections of Bailey bridges. As they drove by Bond saw white soldiers in what he thought were British Army fatigues.

'Slow down,' Bond said, craning his head round to catch a final glimpse. 'Could they be British? Royal Engineers?'

'There are some "military advisers" out here,' Blessing said. 'I met three of them at the airport the week before you arrived.'

Bond sat back, thinking. If he was right about those soldiers being British then this urgency, this hands-on military aid, also had an oblique bearing on his mission. The British government was clearly keen for this war to end as soon as possible. Why? Bond wondered. Conceivably, he thought, British 'military advisers' could also be manning those tanks . . .

Bond took over at the wheel after a snatched lunch at a road-side food-shack – more beer and dago-dago. He became aware of the landscape changing as they drove south into the river delta – small lakes and stagnant pools of water began to appear on either side of the highway, great expanses of reed beds and more palm trees and mangroves.

Blessing told him to turn off the highway and follow the signs for a small town called Lokomeji on whose outskirts their next rest-house, Cinnamon Lodge, was situated. It was late afternoon by the time they arrived. Blessing dropped him at the portico-ed entrance and drove on into Lokomeji to rendezvous with the local fisherman who would guide Bond into Dahum.

Cinnamon Lodge was virtually identical in structure and layout to Good Companion and belonged to the same colonial era. Standing on his bedroom balcony Bond could look across the dense low-lying forest that made up the Zanza River Delta. From his vantage point he could see the late afternoon sun glinting silver on the creeks and channels that wove their way sinuously through the vegetation. They were perched right on the edge of the huge delta, Bond could see from the map. Port Dunbar was only forty miles away – as the crow flies – but it might as well have been 400 such was the impenetrability of the marshy forest with its maze of watercourses lying in between. The air felt heavy and moist and, in the far distance, he could see a thin column of smoke rising, hanging in the air, dense as a rag, as if reluctant to disperse into the atmosphere. Another flight of MiGs ripped by, heading north this time, wing racks empty. Mission completed, and no doubt their pilots were looking forward to another evening in the bar of the Excelsior Gateway, Bond thought. It seemed like another world.

He was sitting on a cane chair on the veranda with his second whisky on the go when he saw the headlights of the 1100 sweep into the gated compound. Blessing seemed pleased. The fisherman – named Kojo – would meet Bond tomorrow evening at 6 p.m. by the wharves at Lokomeji and take him out, ostensibly for a spot of night fishing – looking for Zanza carp. Lokomeji sat on the edge of a small inland lagoon that merged into the tracery of creeks and inlets that wormed their way through the forest. Kojo was familiar with every twisting inch of the waterways, Blessing said; he'd been fishing at Lokomeji, man and boy, and knew exactly where to put Bond safely ashore in Dahum.

'Good,' Bond said. 'So what'll we do tomorrow? Maybe we could go back to the highway – I wouldn't mind checking out those British soldiers.' He smiled. 'I am a journalist, after all – might make a good story.'

Blessing advised caution. 'We should stay put,' she said. 'The whole of Lokomeji knows there's an Englishman staying at Cinnamon Lodge. You're a rare bird here. Talk of the steamie.'

Bond was amused by the Scottish expression, no doubt picked up from her father, but she was right of course. He thought of the whole empty day ahead of them tomorrow, confined to Cinnamon Lodge, and rather wished he'd brought his unfinished Graham Greene with him. Still, he considered, another twenty-four hours in Blessing's company was hardly purgatorial.

They were alone in the dining room once again, Cinnamon Lodge's only guests, and were served a surprisingly tasty, peppery fish stew with dago-dago dumplings. Bond even ate the pudding – baked bananas with a rum and butter sauce. After supper they drank more whisky on the veranda from Bond's bottle of Johnnie Walker.

'You'll make me tipsy,' Blessing said. 'I'm not used to whisky.'

'Best drink for the tropics,' Bond said. 'It doesn't need to be chilled. You're meant to drink it without ice, anyway. Tastes the same in Africa as it would in Scotland.'

They went upstairs together. Something had changed in the

mood between them, Bond sensed – perhaps the evening wasn't quite over yet. He decided to kiss her on the cheek as they said goodnight.

'I know you're the head of station,' he said, 'and I probably shouldn't have done that, but you did well at that roadblock today. Quick thinking.'

'Thank you, kind sir,' she said, a little sardonically. 'I have my uses.'

Bond lay in bed thinking about the plans for the following night – the crossing of the lagoon and trusting this man, Kojo, to deliver him safely. And what then? He supposed he would make his way to Port Dunbar and introduce himself as a friendly journalist, provide himself with new accreditation, and say he was keen to report the war from the Dahumian side – show the world the rebels' perspective on events. Again, it all seemed very improvised and ad hoc. He wasn't used to such—

Blessing knocked on his door.

'James, I'm really sorry to disturb you, but only you can help me with this.'

'Just coming.'

Bond pulled on his shirt and trousers and opened the door. Blessing stood there in a long white T-shirt that fell to her thighs and was looking at him a little sheepishly.

'There's a lizard in my room,' she said. 'And I can't sleep knowing that it's there.'

Bond followed her down the corridor to her room. To his vague surprise it was larger and better furnished than his and it had a ceiling fan that was turning energetically, causing the gauze of her mosquito net to billow and flap gently. Blessing pointed: high up on the wall by the ceiling was a six-inch, pale, freckled gecko – motionless, waiting for a moth or a fly to come its way.

'It's just a gecko,' Bond said. 'They eat mosquitoes. Think of it as a pet.'

'I know it's a gecko,' she said. 'But it's also a lizard and I have a bit of a phobia about lizards, I'm afraid.'

Bond took a wooden coat-hanger out of the cupboard and a towel that was hanging from a hook by her jug and ewer stand. With the end of the hanger he flipped the gecko off the wall, catching it in the towel and balling the material gently around it. He stepped out on to the balcony and let the gecko scuttle off into the night.

'A lizard-free zone,' Bond said, closing the balcony doors behind him. Blessing stood by her bed, the angle of the bedside light and the shadows it cast revealing the shape of her small uptilted breasts under her T-shirt. Bond knew what was going to happen next and everything about Blessing's expression confirmed that she did, also.

He crossed the room to her.

'Thank you, James Bond,' she said. 'Licensed to catch lizards.'

Bond took her in his arms and kissed her gently, feeling her tongue flicker into his mouth.

'As station head in Zanzarim it's important I get to know visiting agents,' she said and slipped her T-shirt off. She let Bond take in her nakedness for an instant and then lifted the mosquito net and slid into bed. Bond shucked off his shirt and trousers and climbed in beside her. He pulled her body against his and kissed her neck and breasts. She was tiny and lithe in his arms, her dark nipples perfectly round, like coins.

He looked into her eyes.

'Ah, the old lizard trick,' he said.

'A girl can only work with the materials at hand.'

'I'm going to miss you in Dahum, Blessing Ogilvy-Grant,' he said, as he rolled on top of her and felt her knees part and lift to accommodate him. 'Expect to see me back in Sinsikrou before you know it.'

'I can't wait.'

After they had made love – with an urgency and physicality that surprised them both – Bond fetched his bottle of whisky from his room. They lay naked on the top of the bed, drinking and smoking, talking softly and reaching out to touch each other until they arrived at a new pitch of arousal and they made love again, this time more deliberately and knowingly, prolonging their climaxes with all the expertise of familiar lovers. Afterwards, Bond lay still while Blessing fell asleep, curled at his side, his arm round her narrow shoulders, her arm thrown across his chest. The regular whirr of the ceiling fan blanked out all other noises and, for a moment, before sleep overtook him, Bond allowed himself to float on a sea of simple sensuality, spent and happy, the warmth of a beautiful young woman beside him, giving no thought at all about what might await him tomorrow.

·8·

THE MAN WITH TWO FACES

Bond flinched and woke, thinking Blessing's elbow had moved and was digging into his throat. But whatever was causing the pressure was cold and hard. Bond gagged reflexively and opened his eyes. The man's face that loomed above him in the darkness was zigzagged with olive-green camouflage paint. The gun pressing hard into Bond's windpipe made it impossible to speak.

'Don't try to say anything, big boy.'

Bond sensed other hands reach in beneath the mosquito net and grab Blessing. She managed a half-cry before she was stifled and dragged out of bed. The light went on.

'Get up.' The mosquito net was flipped aside.

Bond sat up slowly, rubbing his throat.

Blessing stood in shock, head bowed, shivering, arm across her breasts, a hand covering her groin. Six soldiers in camouflage uniform in mottled greens and greys and brown stood in the room – they looked like giants facing her, bulked out with their packs and ammunition. Five of them were black. The man with the automatic pistol – a big Colt 1911, Bond noticed – was white.

'Move, sonny,' the white man said. The accent wasn't precisely

English – more like East African or South African, Bond thought. Bond stood up and went to Blessing, putting his arm around her and making no attempt to conceal his nakedness.

'Aw, Adam and Eve,' the white man said.

The other soldiers chuckled, enjoying the show, covering Bond with their Kalashnikovs. Bond noticed that sewn on their shoulders were small flags – a rectangle halved horizontally, black and white, and in the upper white band was a red disc. The flag of the Democratic Republic of Dahum.

'Look, I'm a British journalist,' Bond said. 'She's my translator.'

'British special forces, more like,' the white man said. There was something wrong with his face, something glinting in one eye, but Bond couldn't see exactly what it was because of the zigzag paint stripes.

'Get dressed,' the man said to both of them. 'Then pack up your stuff.'

Bond pulled on his shirt and trousers, shielding Blessing as she put her clothes on as quickly as possible. She seemed calmer once she was dressed, and Bond gave her as reassuring a look as he could muster before he was escorted down the corridor to his room by two of the other soldiers. He put on his desert boots and safari jacket and packed away the rest of his things in the Zanzarim bag. Back in Blessing's room he showed the white man his APL identification and his accreditation from Zanza Force.

'Good cover,' the man said, unimpressed. Closer to him, Bond could see that half his face looked different from the other, normal, half. The glinting that Bond had spotted was caused by tears – his left eye didn't blink and tears flowed unchecked from it – tears that he wiped away with a constant motion of his thumb or dried on his cuff. There were two small round scars below his left eye – bullet entry wounds – that looked like a stamped umlaut and the contours of the left-hand side of his face were strangely dished, the cheekbone missing. Some awful trauma to his face had left him in this state, obviously.

Bond and Blessing were ushered downstairs – no sign of the manager or the staff of Cinnamon Lodge – and out into the warm darkness of the night. Bond glanced at his Rolex – it was just after four in the morning. They were led out of the compound and down a pathway to a small creek. Bond feigned a stumble, dropped his bag and as he stooped to pick it up, bumped up against Blessing.

'They're from Dahum,' he whispered.

'That's what I'm worried about.'

Then they arrived at the water's edge where a twelve-foot fibreglass dory was moored. Bond was shoved up to the front and Blessing told to sit in the stern. Bond acknowledged the Dahumian soldiers' discipline and good training. They moved confidently and briskly about their business with very little conversation. He heard one of the men say 'We are ready, Kobus.' So he was called Kobus, Bond noted – Kobus short for Jakobus. The man with half a face or, rather: Kobus, the man with two faces.

Kobus cast off the dory and sat down in the stern beside Blessing. The other men picked up short paddles and swiftly, silently, propelled the dory down the creek and out into the wider expanse of the lagoon. Bond could see a few lights burning in Lokomeji – no rendezvous with Kojo tomorrow – and it began to dawn on him that Kobus and his men must have come specifically to snatch him, thinking he was one of the British military advisers for Zanza Force. Bond smiled ruefully to himself – it would have been quite a coup if he had been. Blessing had said everyone in Lokomeji knew he was staying in Cinnamon Lodge – word had spread. So Kobus and his men had seized their opportunity and sneaked out of Dahum on a kidnap mission.

Paradoxically, this analysis made Bond feel marginally more relaxed. There was nothing on his person or in his belongings that would identify him as a member of a special-forces team. For once he was hugely relieved that he wasn't armed. Perhaps when the Dahumian authorities realised that he appeared to be what he was claiming to be – a journalist working for a French press agency – they would hand him and Blessing over to civilian authorities in Port Dunbar. It was something to hope for.

They crossed the lagoon surprisingly quickly and entered one of the winding watercourses. Bond heard the dry whisper of the soft night wind in the tall reeds that lined the channel and sensed rather than saw the overarching bulk of the mangroves and other trees. The men paddled on, tirelessly, and soon the sky began to lighten as dawn neared and with it Bond became aware of a mounting nervousness in the soldiers as they glanced around watchfully and muttered to each other. They clearly didn't want to be caught out on the water in daylight. Then Bond heard the rhythmic judder of a helicopter's rotors as it took to the air and the distant sound of diesel engines revving. They must be passing through the Zanza Force lines that surrounded Dahum's diminishing heartland.

Soon they reached a ramshackle cribwork jetty and they disembarked. The dory was hauled ashore and covered with palm leaves. Then the small column moved down a forest path to a clearing where a canvas tarpaulin had been erected as shelter, draped with camouflaged netting. Bond was ordered to sit down beneath it at one end and Blessing at the other. Kobus took both their bags away and their hands were tied behind their backs. One soldier was left to guard them and Bond saw Kobus posting lookouts on the trails that led into the clearing. As the sun began to rise, he heard the sporadic *crump, crump* of heavy artillery being fired.

Kobus came in and squatted by Blessing and began to interrogate her, but he kept his voice low and Bond couldn't hear his questions or her replies. Then Bond saw him stand up, look round and wander over to him.

He had removed the zigzag stripes from his face and Bond was able to see the full damage – the tear-fall from the unblinking eye and the saucer-deep declivity where his cheekbone should have been made Bond think that half his upper jaw had gone as well. He searched Bond roughly, taking his passport, his APL identification and his remaining wad of dollars. He also pocketed Bond's cigarette lighter and his Rolex.

'I'll want them back, one day,' Bond said. 'So look after them.'

Kobus slapped his face.

'Don't be a cheeky bugger,' he said.

'Kenya? Uganda?'

'Rhodesia,' Kobus said, with a knowing smile. He nodded over to Blessing. 'Your girlfriend tells me that you're in the SAS.'

'No, she didn't,' Bond said calmly. 'Look, I'm a journalist. I met her in a bar in Sinsikrou. She's smart, beautiful and speaks fluent Lowele and I needed a translator. I was meant to be interviewing General Basanjo today. I thought she'd be useful and we might have a bit of fun on the way, you know? Then you went and spoiled everything.'

Kobus slapped his face again, harder. Bond tasted salty blood in his mouth.

'I don't like your attitude, man. I'll get you back to Port Dunbar where I can do some serious work on you and find out exactly who you are. One thing's for sure – you're no journalist.' He stood up and left. Bond spat out some bloody saliva and looked over at Blessing. She was lying on the ground, curled up, turned away from him.

The day crawled by in the steaming heat beneath the tarpaulin. They were temporarily unbound and given some water and a plate of cold beans. Bond could hear the irregular detonations of artillery all day and at one stage two MiGs streaked over the clearing at very low level setting up a squawking and a squealing amongst the riverine birds that took a good five minutes to die down, such was the sky-shuddering guttural roar of the jets.

As dusk approached the men began to pack up the camp – the tarp and the netting were taken down and rolled up and any bits of litter were collected and buried. Bond and Blessing were untied and given another drink of water. Kobus swaggered up to them, smoking, and Bond felt a sudden craving for tobacco.

'We're walking out of here, OK?' Kobus said. 'If one of you tries to run I'll shoot you down and then I'll shoot the other. I don't care. Just don't be clever. Clever means death for you two.'

When it was dark they marched into the forest in single file,

Kobus leading, followed by Blessing, Bond at the back of the small column with one soldier in the rear behind him. Bond felt grimy and sweat-limned, itches springing up all over his body. He fantasised briefly about a cold shower then ordered his brain to stop and concentrate. The path they were on was well trodden, Bond could see in the moonlight, and the forest around them was full of animal and insect noises that rather conveniently disguised the sound of their passage, the clink of buckles on machine gun, the dull thump of shifting harness, the tramp of boots on the pathway. Bond could see his Zanzarim bag lashed with a webbing belt on to the rucksack of the soldier in front of him. The fact that it hadn't been abandoned or thrown away he found somehow reassuring, as if it betokened a future for him, however short-lived.

They walked for about an hour, Bond guessed, before Kobus halted them. He signalled them to crouch down where they were and wait. Bond turned to the soldier behind him.

'What are we waiting for?'

'Shut you mouth,' he said simply.

Bond peered ahead – there was a lightening in the general gloom that would signal a gap in the trees and by craning his neck Bond could see the moonlight striking on what seemed like a strip of asphalt. Then Kobus waved them forward to the very edge of the treeline and Bond was able to get his bearings.

They had reached a road – a typical two-lane, potholed stretch of tarmac with wide laterite verges on each side. This section ran straight with no curves and the light of the moon afforded a good view a couple of hundred yards in each direction. Kobus obviously planned to cross it and pick up their forest path on the far side. However, they sat there in silence another five minutes or so, waiting and listening. Bond calculated that the distance to the other side was no more than thirty yards, maximum, before you reached the dark security of the forest again. It was the middle of the night, for God's sake, Bond said to himself – what could be so problematic about crossing a road?

As if in answer to his question, Kobus stood and ran briskly at a crouch across the road without pausing and disappeared into the vegetation on the other side. They waited another five minutes. Then he heard Kobus shout an order: 'Femi! Dani! Bring the girl, chop-chop!'

Two of the soldiers stood up, one of them took Blessing's arm and began to jog across the road.

The night erupted in gunfire.

Bond saw the tracer looping a split second before he heard the detonations. There was the usual sensory delay – the lazy flow of glowing light-flashes picking up speed – and then the road surface disintegrated under the impact of the heavy-calibre machine-gun bullets. Blessing screamed and fell to the ground. One of the soldiers seemed literally torn apart, shredded by the impact of a dozen rounds, while the other was spun around in a mad pirouette before Bond saw one of his arms flail off and go tumbling into the undergrowth end over end.

On hands and knees Blessing scrabbled back into cover and Bond grabbed her.

'You all right?' he shouted. The yammering noise of gunfire ripped through the night.

'Yes,' she sobbed. 'I'm not hit.'

Kobus was screaming orders at his men, firing back up the

road where the machine guns were. The other three soldiers had opened up with their AK-47s. Leaves and bits of branches were falling on them as the machine guns hosed the sides of the road, raking the forest verge.

This was their moment.

Bond took Blessing's hand and drew her slowly back into the darkness. One yard, two, three. The soldiers were too intent taking cover or returning fire. Bond backed them off the path and deeper into the undergrowth. Ten seconds, twenty – they were completely hidden, out of sight. He heard Kobus shouting and then the noise of one soldier blundering down the path.

'They gone, Boss!'

Bond drew Blessing still further into the leafy obscurity.

'Where are we going?' she said, panic in her voice.

'Say nothing,' Bond hissed at her.

Then enormous explosions sent shockwaves through the trees – mortar bombs – brief flashes of brilliant, scalding light. There was a scream from one of the soldiers. Bond grabbed Blessing's hand more firmly and turned, moving as fast as he could, forcing a way through the bushes and the branches, running away from the road and the firefight.

Now there was more firing coming from another direction on their flank. A random spraying of the forest as another group of soldiers appeared to be coming up from the rear.

'Lie down,' Bond said, 'they'll never find us.'

He dragged Blessing off her feet and pressed her down into the dry leafy mulch of the forest floor.

'Keep your eyes down, don't look up.'

Someone would have to stand on them to discover them, Bond

reasoned, listening to the chaos of the night, the shouts of men, the staccato rattle of machine guns. It was crazed firing, soldiers loosing off at shadows – staying still and prone was the only solution. Shots thunked into tree trunks near them, ripped through foliage overhead, and every now and then there was another brief flash of light washing through the forest as another mortar shell was lobbed in their general direction.

He could hear men thrashing through undergrowth not far from them. Kobus? Or was that the Zanza Force ambush?

Blessing gripped his arm, fiercely.

'James – we've got to get out of here, now!' she whispered harshly at him. 'They're going to find us.'

'No! Don't move – listen, they're moving away.'

He felt her fist pounding on his restraining hand.

'Let me go!'

'Blessing – no – we're safer here—'

She snatched her hand away.

'I'm not going to die here!' she screamed at him. She was uncontrollable, panicked out of her wits. She stood up and ran into the dense gloom of the surrounding trees.

'Blessing!' Bond shouted – and someone, hearing the noise, began to loose off quick bursts of fire in his direction. Bond fell to the ground and crawled away as fast as he could, rolling into a hollow and clawing dead leaves over him. Blessing had first lost her nerve, then lost her head and made a run for it. Fool! Bond thought. Then he heard her scream, shrill and terrified, and a long chatter of gunfire before she screamed again and it was choked off. Bond pressed his forehead into the earth, feeling sick, breathing shallowly and waiting. Slowly the spatter of gunfire diminished and grew more distant. A lot of shouting seemed to be coming from the direction of the road and then he heard a metallic rumble from the tracks of some kind of armoured vehicle approaching.

He lay there motionless, counting the seconds, the minutes. He saw the beam of torchlight through the trees and heard the excited voices of Zanzari soldiers – whoops and shouts. For a brief second he thought about surrendering himself to them but realised that any figure emerging from the trees would be cut down instantly. Best to stay put. Had they taken Kobus? he wondered. Maybe he was dead? He heard the vehicle start up again and move off.

The forest quietened, and then the insects and the animals began their interrupted squeaks and chatterings again. Bond sat up, slowly: he could smell smoke and cordite but there were no sounds of any human presence that he could distinguish. He pushed himself backwards in the darkness until he came up against the bole of a tree. He hugged his knees to him and closed his eyes, trying not to think about what had happened to Blessing. There was nothing more to do but wait for dawn.

·9·

JAMES BOND'S LONG WALK

At some stage in the night Bond had fallen asleep in his sitting position against the tree, his forehead resting on his knees, his arms locked around his shins. At first light he woke and, very slowly, stretched his legs out, massaging his thigh muscles back to life and taking his time to rise to his feet. He windmilled his arms and ran on the spot for a minute or two to get his circulation going. Then he pushed cautiously through the undergrowth until he found the pathway and advanced slowly up to the road. There was a crude confetti of shredded leaves everywhere, as if some violent storm had passed, but not a body to be seen, all casualties carted away. The road surface was scarred and torn with bullet strikes and there were two drying pools of blood, humming with flies, where the two soldiers had been hit by the first fusillade.

He cast around half-heartedly up and down the road, not expecting to find Blessing or any trace of her. Brass cartridges glinted everywhere on the ground and he found a bloodstained pack with a few rounds of ammunition in it. Otherwise there was little sign of the firefight and its victims.

He stood in the middle of the road feeling the heat of the

rising sun on his face. What to do? Which direction to take? He turned northwards – that was where the Zanza Force fire had come from. If he walked up the road in that direction surely he'd reach the advancing columns of the main army . . . Bond forced himself to think about his options for a while, kicking at bits of the shattered road surface. He could, he supposed, realistically abort his mission, after what he'd been through. M would surely understand. But there was unfinished business and he felt an obscure sense of guilt over what had happened to Blessing. If he'd only held on to her more forcefully, even knocked her out . . . Was she dead? Was she safe in the hands of Zanza Force? Or perhaps Kobus and his men had recaptured her.

Bond looked around him. Kobus's plan had been to cross this road and continue on the forest path they had been walking along. Perhaps that was the option to choose . . . he had no food, no water, no weapon. He could last a couple of days, he reckoned, perhaps longer if he could find something to eat or drink. Bond thought – Kobus knew exactly where this path was heading and that it was the route to follow. Bond made up his mind: he crossed the road and walked into the forest.

He walked for two hours, he calculated, then stopped and rested. It was hot and clammy and he had been bitten by many insects but at least the path was shaded by the tall trees it meandered through. Bond looked up at the high canopy of trees above him, the branches like twisted beams in some giant deformed attic. He set off again. The path remained surprisingly well trodden and occasionally he came across evidence of human passage – a bottle top, a shred of indigo material, a foil wrapper from a chocolate bar. At one stage he found a butt from a hand-rolled cigarette with some shreds of tobacco left – and he cursed the loss of his lighter. There was enough tobacco to provide a good couple of lungfuls of smoke. Bond was about to throw it away when he saw that it wasn't tobacco in the cigarette at all. He sniffed – marijuana or some other kind of potent weed. Was this a hunters' path, he wondered, some traditional route from village to village, from tribal land to tribal land, or, more likely, was it used by Kobus and his men to mount raids and incursions behind Zanzari lines?

He moved on, noting that there were fruits and berries of every hue and size on the plants and bushes that bordered the pathway, but he didn't dare try one and, for such lush and green vegetation, there was no visible water source. He found a smooth round pebble and popped it in his mouth and sucked on it, coaxing some saliva flow to ease his increasingly parched throat.

He rested up again at midday, the sunbeams that penetrated the canopy now shining down directly on the path, and waited until the afternoon shade encroached. He thought he was heading vaguely south, though the path did take many illogical jinks and turns. He came across a gym shoe (left foot) with a flapping sole and a label-less tin with an inch of rainwater in it. He was about to swig it down when he saw that it was hotching with pale yellow larvae.

By dusk he was feeling tired and footsore and uncomfortably thirsty. He found a large ash-grey tree with great buttressing roots and settled down snugly between two of them. Darkness arrived with its usual tropic speed and, to distract himself from his cracked throat and his hollow stomach, he forced his mind to concentrate on matters far from the Zanza River Delta. He debated with himself over the respective merits of the Jensen FF and the Interceptor II, trying to calculate if he had enough ready cash to make the deposit required for an eventual purchase. Then he wondered if Doig and his team had finished redecorating his Chelsea flat. He had instructed Donalda to supervise the work in his absence and issue cheques as required. It would be a bonus to go home to an effectively transformed flat after this job was over, he thought, and he was particularly looking forward to his new shower – then he laughed at himself. He was lost in a tropical rainforest wandering along a path somewhere between two warring armies. The reality sank in and with it came the questions about Blessing and her fate. Blessing whose lithe slim naked body he could see in his mind's eye, their night of intimacy so violently interrupted nearly forty-eight hours ago. He felt bitter and remorseful – but what more could he have done? He had his own survival to focus on now.

He turned up the collar of his safari jacket and thrust his hands in his pockets. He was not the repining kind – he felt absolutely sure tomorrow would prove better than today.

Some fluting bird-call woke him at dawn and he set off again without more ado, his throat swollen and sore, his tongue dry as a leather belt. After about half an hour he noticed the forest was starting to thin. There were clearings of blond grass, the giant trees diminished – lower, scrubbier varieties beginning to dominate. He also lost his shade and felt the sun start to burn. He took off his safari jacket and buttoned it over his head like an Arab kufiyya. Sweat began to drip from his nose and chin.

And then the path simply disappeared. The ground beneath

his feet was cracked and arid with tufts of wiry grass – as if the path were a forest creature and this scrubby orchard-bush was not the sort of environment it liked.

Then he saw the pawpaw tree.

It was about ten feet tall and had a solitary ripe fruit on it. He grabbed its rough trunk and gave it a vigorous shake, then butted it with his shoulders, making it whip to and fro and, as the pawpaw was shaken free and fell, he caught it safely in both hands.

He sat in a patch of shade and dug his thumbnail into the yielding skin, breaking off a portion of the fruit. He flicked away the soft, swart seeds and sank his teeth into the warm orange flesh. It was moist and sweet and Bond felt his throat respond and ease as he swallowed avidly. He closed his eyes and suddenly he was transported to the terrace of the Blue Hills Hotel in Kingston, Jamaica, where it was his habit to eat two halves of a chilled pawpaw for breakfast, drizzled with freshly squeezed juice from a quartered lime. He would have happily killed for a cup of Blue Mountain coffee and a cigarette. His impromptu memories of those days and that life brought a thickening to his throat – then, cross with himself for this expression of emotion, he wolfed down the rest of the pawpaw with caveman hunger, eating the seeds as well and scraping the skin free of any lingering shred with his teeth.

It was extraordinary how good he felt having eaten something at last. The morning sun was still clearly in the east so he knew in what direction the south lay. He headed on with fresh purpose. Two hundred yards from the pawpaw tree he came across a rudimentary track for wheeled vehicles. He followed the track and it led him to a dirt road where there was an ancient bleached sign that read 'Forêt de Lokani', some forgotten legacy from the former French colonial days. But where there was a road sign, Bond realised, there must be some kind of traffic. His spirits lifted and he strode down the road with new enthusiasm.

He rounded a bend and saw the thatched conical roofs of a small village half a mile further on. He found a heavy stick to use as a makeshift weapon and advanced cautiously down the road towards the mud huts. There was no smoke rising from cooking fires; the cassava fields were withered and neglected. Bond walked into the village sticking close to the mud walls of the houses. There were about twenty dwellings clustered round a big shade tree. On some of the huts the thatch had been burnt away and one or two had demolished walls, as if hit with some kind of ordnance. As he stepped into the beaten-earth meeting area beneath the tree Bond saw three badly decomposed bodies – a woman and two men – a shifting miasma of flies humming above them. Bond skirted them, moving through the alleyways between the houses looking for water – some well or trough. There must be a stream or a river nearby, he reasoned, from where water could be easily carried – no African village was far from water.

Then in a doorway he saw a small boy sitting, leaning weakly against the door jamb. A small boy as skeletal as an ancient wizened man. Naked, his ribs stretching his slack dusty skin, running sores on his stick legs, his head huge, almost teetering on his thin neck. Flies explored his eyelids and the corners of his mouth. He stared at Bond listlessly, barely interested, it seemed, in this apparition of a white man standing in front of him.

Bond crouched down, disturbed and unsettled.

'Hello,' he said, with a token smile, before realising how stupid he sounded.

Something moved behind the boy and another skull-faced child appeared, staring at him, dully. Bond stood and went to peer into the mud hut but an awful smell made him recoil, rake his throat and spit. It seemed full of the corpses of children. Nothing was moving inside. Starved into this kind of fatal inertia, Bond supposed: crawl away to some shade and wait to die. This was the fate of the weak and forgotten in the shrinking heartland of Dahum.

Bond left the village feeling helpless and depressed. It had been like witnessing some surreal version of hell. What could he do for those two kids? They'd be dead before nightfall, like all the others lying in that infernal room. His powerlessness made him want to weep. Perhaps there was another village further down the road; perhaps help could be sent from—

Then, miraculously, he saw a figure up ahead – a very skinny young man in a tattered pair of shorts. The young man shouted at him and then threw a stone. It kicked up a puff of dust by Bond's feet. The young man shouted at him and threw two more stones.

'Hey!' Bond shouted. 'Come here! Help!'

But the figure turned and sprinted away, disappearing from view behind a copse of thorn trees. Bond gave chase but stopped as he rounded the copse. Here was the water source for the village – a small creek dammed to form a shallow pool. The skinny young man seemed to have vanished into thin air, like some kind of sprite or vision. Bond wondered if he had been hallucinating, but he didn't care any more – he waded out into the centre of the pool and sat down, soaking himself, scooping up mouthfuls of warm cloudy water with his cupped hands. He could press on now, and perhaps see if there was any way of getting some help for those children. He lay back and submerged his head, closing his eyes, feeling weak with relief. When he surfaced a moment later he could hear the distant sound of a car changing gear. His long walk was nearly over.

Bond stood by the side of the dammed creek, his sodden clothes dripping, in a sudden stasis of indecision. No, he couldn't just walk on. He made his way back to the village and found an empty calabash and a large tin that had once contained powdered milk. Returning to the creek he filled them both with water and carried them to the mud hut with the dead children. The little boy had disappeared – crawled back inside, Bond hoped, and he set the two containers down carefully at the threshold. Then he heard a cracked shout from behind him.

A stooped old man stood there at the entry to the meeting square, leaning on a staff. He was incredibly thin, his arms and legs like vanilla pods, wearing a tatter of rags. Bond approached slowly as the old man berated him with hoarse incomprehensible curses. He had a small head with a powdering of grey hair, a collapsed face with white corpse-stubble. He was like something from a myth – or a symbol of death, Bond thought – and his red eyes blazed at Bond with a weary venom.

Bond pointed at the hut with his two water containers placed in front of the door.

'Children – pickin – inside. Help them.'

The old man shook his fist at Bond and continued with his spitting maledictions.

Bond pointed at the doorway again and as he did so saw two tiny claw-hands reach out and drag the powdered-milk tin inside. Now the old man grasped his stave and giddily, powerlessly tried to hit Bond with it. It thwacked painlessly against his leg.

'Help those children!' Bond admonished the old man for a final time and turned and strode out of the village, his head in a swoon of pressure, feeling as if he'd taken part in some atavistic dumb-show – a stranger's encounter with death on the road – all the ingredients of some dreadful folktale or legend. He concentrated. He had heard a car, he would be saved – unless the malign spirits of this place were still tormenting him.

·10·

WELCOME TO DAHUM

Bond's ears had not been deceiving him. There was indeed a road at the end of the dirt track leading from the village, the usual potholed frayed tarmac ribbon, along which the odd car raced at full speed as if fleeing from some natural disaster or catastrophe. Two flew past him without stopping. Then there was nothing for half an hour and Bond felt his clothes drying in the hot sun. Finally a third car came into view – a Volkswagen Beetle which slowed as Bond flagged it down and the door opened. Like the other cars that had passed, Bond noticed this one had a large red cross painted on the bonnet.

A sweaty grey-haired man was at the wheel. He watched in candid astonishment as Bond slid in beside him.

'Where you go?' he said.

'Port Dunbar,' Bond replied.

'I go drop you at Madougo. I fear too much for the MiGs.'

'Is that why you have red crosses on your car?'

'Yes. Maybe they think we are ambulance.' The man glanced skywards, as if expecting a MiG to appear at any moment. 'If they see one car they come and shoot you. Bam-bam-bam. They don' care.'

Bond told him about the village and the dying children.

'They all die,' the man said.

'No. There are two alive. Maybe more, I couldn't tell.'

'All village are dead,' the man insisted. 'Everybody go to Port Dunbar.'

Bond kept on and extracted a promise from the man that he would report the presence of starving children in the village of Lokani, or whatever name it had. Perhaps something would be done.

Madougo turned out to be another semi-destroyed hamlet of mud huts on the roadside but this time there were signs of life. There was, amazingly, a stall set up on the laterite verge, tended by a toothless old mammy. Bond was dropped here and the VW turned off down a track and sped away. The mammy had a small bunch of unripe bananas, a shrivelled pawpaw and a bottle of Green Star beer. Some stubborn undying commercial instinct made her come to her stall in Madougo and pretend life was going on as normal. And maybe she was right, Bond thought, as, using sign language, he bartered his safari jacket for the bottle of beer. He sat on a wooden stool in the shade cast by her stall and drank it slowly. It was sour, warm and gassy, an ambrosial liquor of the gods.

A few people emerged from the shattered huts, stared at him and went away. The beer had gone to Bond's head and he felt woozy and sleepy, exhausted from his two-day hike through the forest. The occasional car stopped and he was scrutinised but never spoken to. This dirty, unshaven white man lounging in the shade of a roadside stall in Madougo would be the subject of much speculation, Bond reasoned. The bush telegraph would do its business – all he had to do was wait; he would be sought out, he was absolutely sure.

It took longer than he thought but in the heat of mid-afternoon he heard the tooting of a car on the road, heading north. Bond shook himself out of his torpor and stood up to see a dusty black Mercedes-Benz station wagon drive through the village and pull on to the verge by the stall.

The door opened and Kobus stepped out. He was wearing jeans and a blue checked shirt. He took off his sunglasses.

'Mr Bond,' he said, with a brief dead smile. 'Welcome to Dahum.'

As they drove south, Bond decided to remain cautiously taciturn, despite Kobus's crude attempts at amiability, as if there were no history between them. After all, this was a man who had thrust a gun in his throat, struck him twice in the face, who had threatened him with death and had stolen all his possessions. Kobus's endeavours at small talk were forced and unnatural, as if he were being paid to be agreeable while everything in his nature rebelled against it. Bond said nothing: he knew Kobus's pleasant formalities and empty smiles counted for nothing.

So they drove on, for the most part in this mutual silence, Kobus interrupting from time to time to ask him to check the sky from Bond's side of the car for sign of any MiGs.

Kobus was obviously aware of the chill between them and, half an hour later, made another semi-reluctant effort to try and break it down. He turned and conjured up another of his awkward smiles. When he smiled he showed both top and bottom rows of teeth – small teeth with gaps that resembled the radiator grille of a cheap car.

'I forgot to say – the name's Jakobus Breed. Call me Kobus, man – everyone does.'

'I'm James Bond. As you know. Call me Mr Bond.'

Kobus took this as a signal that all was now well and began to chatter.

'You walked out of the Lokani forest after two days, Bond. I'm damn impressed, I got to tell you. You're good – for a journalist.' He failed to keep the tone of scepticism out of his compliment. 'Smoke?'

Now this did moderate the chill in their relations, somewhat. Bond gladly accepted one of Kobus's proffered cigarettes. He lit it and inhaled.

'Is this a Tusker?'

'Nah. It's a Boomslang – they make them in Dahum. A boomslang's a snake. It bites but it doesn't kill.' He chuckled and wiped a dripping tear away from his bad eye. 'You get a taste for them – you'll never smoke a Tusker again.'

Bond drew on his Boomslang, feeling the powerful nicotine hit. He remembered Kobus slapping his face.

'No hard feelings,' Kobus said, as if reading his thoughts. 'I had a job to do: snatch the SAS guy, they told me. How was I to know any different?'

'Try using your intelligence,' Bond said.

'Hell, do they love you in Port Dunbar,' Kobus pressed on, ignoring him. 'The government boys jumping up and down: Agence Presse Libre. We haven't had a Frenchie in town for months. When I showed them your ID they crapped all over me. How could you lose him, you stupid douche-bag?' Kobus gave an odd barking laugh, like a seal. 'Then word comes down this lunchtime. An Englishman has just walked out of Lokani forest. I said – that's Bond, that is. Jumped in the car and here we are.' He glanced over again and a tear tracked disconcertingly down from his bad eye. 'Glad you made it. That crazy fucking firefight on the road. Somebody set us up.'

'What happened to the girl?' Bond asked.

'Never saw her, man. I swear. I thought she was with you.'

'She panicked and ran. I heard her scream. Twice. I lost her.'

Kobus grimaced. 'Let's hope she died in the bush. If those Federal boys got her, then . . .' He sniffed. 'She'd be better off dead, believe me. I've seen what they do to women.'

Bond felt that weary heart-sink, that heaviness of loss.

'I looked for her in the morning,' he said. 'But there were no bodies left behind.'

'Pretty girl,' Kobus leered. 'How was she in the sack? A real goer, I'd bet.'

Bond registered this glimpse of the old Kobus, the brutal gun-for-hire, not this purported pseudo-comrade he was being offered, and stubbed his cigarette out in the dashboard ashtray. He didn't want to be friends with Kobus Breed.

They drove on in silence, as if Breed sensed Bond's new sombre mood. There was very little traffic on the road to Port Dunbar. At one stage Breed pulled over to the side in the shelter of a tree convinced he'd heard a MiG. They both sat and listened for a couple of minutes but there was no sound of jet engines, so they motored on.

Eventually, they came to the outskirts of Port Dunbar. They

passed through two roadblocks – Breed was waved on – and drove down the main boulevard into the city. Bond looked around him – it appeared to be a typical, bustling provincial capital, even though there were many soldiers on the streets. Otherwise it seemed bizarrely normal; police directed traffic at crossroads, the roadside food stalls were busy with customers, street-hawkers harassed them when they stopped and, as they passed a church, Bond saw that there was a wedding party emerging. Port Dunbar gave no sign of being a beleaguered, besieged city. Bond noticed that on the roofs of the higher buildings – office blocks and department stores – there were batteries of ground-to-air missiles.

'What're they? SAMs?'

'Dead right,' Breed said. 'But they're all dummies. Knocked up by the local carpenters in a couple of hours. No, we got one real S-75 SAM site in the central square and one at Janjaville. Two months ago they shot down a MiG. Now the MiGs don't come near Port Dunbar. Those boys don't want to lose their wages.'

Bond thought of the pilots he'd seen drinking in the bar of the Excelsior.

'So they just shoot up cars on the road,' Breed went on. 'Chalk it up as a kill – military vehicle. Money for old rope, man.'

'How did you get your hands on S-75 missiles?'

'Present from our pet millionaire. He pays for the Janjaville flights as well.'

Pet millionaire, Bond thought, filing away the information for later. Breed was turning off into a compound. He showed his pass to a guard at the gateway and they drove into a courtyard surrounded by neat white two-storey buildings.

'Welcome to the DRD Press Centre, Mr Bond,' Breed said.

It turned out that the Press Centre was a former Methodist primary school converted by the Dahum government after the secession as a comfortable base for foreign journalists and a location where the daily SitRep briefing took place. Forward planning, Bond thought – they knew they needed friendly propaganda. Once again he was impressed by the organisation and efficiency. He signed in at reception where his new accreditation was waiting for him, and Breed showed him upstairs to his room. There was even a private bar that was open from 6 p.m. to midnight. The only problem was, Breed said, that it wasn't like the early days of the war when the place was heaving; now there were hardly any journalists – just three, apart from Bond: an American, a German and another Brit. 'A freelance,' he said, with a sneer.

Breed opened the door to Bond's room. There was a bed, a table fan, a chest of drawers and a desk and a chair. Sitting on the bed was Bond's Zanzarim bag. Breed gave him back his passport, his APL identification and his Ronson lighter and Rolex watch.

'You took a lot of money off me as well,' Bond said.

'I lost that in the firefight, unfortunately,' Breed said, dabbing at his eye with his shirtsleeve cuff. 'Must've fallen out of my pocket. Sorry about that.'

'Yeah, sure.'

'See you,' Breed said, bluntly, moving to the door. Then added, remembering he was meant to be amiable now, 'Oh, yeah. Let me know if I can help with anything.'

He left and Bond unpacked his bag. He checked that

everything was there – his shirts, his underwear, his panama hat and his pigskin toilet bag. He unzipped it – everything in its place. He took the panama out of its tube and unrolled it, pulling and tweaking it back into its hat-shape. Then he slipped out the cardboard lining of the tube and unpeeled the twenty new $20 bills that were rolled neatly around it in the interstice. His own idea for a hiding place – Q Branch would be proud of him. He was solvent again.

He gathered up his razor, soap and shaving cream and went down to the shower room at the end of the corridor and cleaned himself up thoroughly – a long shower, a hair wash and a close shave. Then he changed into a clean shirt and began to feel human again. He slipped his Rolex back on his wrist. Ten past six. The bar would be open – time for a drink.

The journalists' bar at the Port Dunbar Press Centre served beer, gin, whisky and various soft drinks. Bond changed $20 at reception for 380,000 Dahumian sigmassis and went back to the bar, where, entirely alone, he drank two large whisky and sodas with untypical speed. He also bought a packet of Boomslangs and, with his whisky in front of him on the table and a cigarette lit, felt his mood improve. The mission was full-on, all systems 'go' once more, he realised. He had infiltrated himself into Dahum, his cover was solid and his special equipment was intact. The fact that he had almost died, that Blessing Ogilvy-Grant, Zanzarim head of station, was almost certainly dead, and that he'd spent forty-eight hours lost, walking through virgin forest, seemed almost irrelevant, somehow. He could hear M's voice in his ear:

'Just get on with it, 007.' So he would – phase two was about to commence.

A young man in his late twenties, wearing a crumpled, grubby linen suit, wandered shiftily into the bar. He had a patchy beard and long greasy hair that hung to his collar. He gave a visible start of surprise on seeing Bond and came over, his eyes alive with welcome.

'Hi,' he said. 'I'm Digby Breadalbane – the freelance.' He had a weak handshake and a slightly whiny London accent.

'I'm Bond, James Bond. Agence Presse Libre.'

'Oh, they'll love you here,' Breadalbane said with some bitterness. 'They love anything French, this lot.' He sat down. 'I've been here three months but because I'm freelance they don't rate me.' He leaned closer. 'Thank God you've arrived. There's just a Yank and a Kraut and me, the Anglo – it's like a bad joke, isn't it? – the foreign press in Port Dunbar.' He rummaged in a pocket for a cigarette but the pack he found was empty. Bond offered him a Boomslang and asked him what he'd like to drink. A beer, Breadalbane said, thanks very much. Bond signalled the barman and a Green Star was brought over. Clearly the beer in Zanzarim didn't distinguish between rebel and federalist.

Breadalbane continued his moaning for a while and Bond dutifully listened. Then the two other journalists appeared, both older men in their fifties. They introduced themselves – Miller Dupree and Odon Haas. Dupree looked fit and had a close-cropped *en brosse* haircut like a marine. Haas was corpulent and his grey hair fell down his back in a ponytail. He also had many strings of beads around his neck and wrists, Bond noticed. Both of them asked him if he knew Thierry Duhamel.

'Ah, Thierry,' Bond said, forewarned by his encounter with Geoffrey Letham. 'He's a legend.' They all agreed on this and that was an end to the matter.

Bond fired questions at them, asking them about the war from the rebels' side and the situation in Port Dunbar. They all confirmed that the city was surprisingly safe – and efficiently run. Postal services worked; public servants were paid; only when you went beyond its precincts did things change – the random danger and meaningless chaos of the civil war reasserted its dominance. No one knew where the front lines were, or where the opposing forces were manoeuvring, or might attack or mysteriously retreat. Bombing and artillery were completely indiscriminate: one village might be razed, another left untouched. Janjaville airstrip was the place to visit, they said. Once you saw what happened there – with the flights arriving after dark – then you could begin to make some sense of this conflict.

Bond was intrigued and, to his vague surprise, found himself enjoying the worldly company of his new 'colleagues'. He bought round after round of drinks with his copious supply of sigmassis and encouraged them to talk. Dupree and Haas were ageing socialists writing for left-wing magazines in their respective countries. Still avid for the cause, they unequivocally supported Dahum's right to secede from Zanzarim. Bond was pleased to note how secure his APL cover was and he began to think that perhaps this mission was not as haphazardly planned as he had once thought. Perhaps this mission was achievable, in spite of everything – all he had to do was find a way of getting close to Brigadier Adeka. Perhaps his new 'friend' Kobus Breed was the man to help him out there.

·11·

SUNDAY

Bond had an uneasy sleep, despite all the whisky he'd consumed with his new colleagues. His dream-life was full of the clamour of the firefight in the forest and Blessing's terrible panic, all merging with images of the dead children in the hut in Lokani, stirring, rising, pointing their bony fingers at him in reproach.

At first light he went and had a cold shower and forced himself to do half an hour of callisthenics – star-jumps, press-ups, running on the spot – to clear his mind and make him feel alert. He strolled down to the bar – now functioning as a dining room – and ate the breakfast that was provided: orange juice, an over-cooked omelette and watery coffee. He had lit his first cigarette of the day when a young man came into the room and walked over to him, smiling broadly.

'Mr Bond, good morning, sir, I am Sunday. I am your assistant.'

I am your minder, Bond thought. Dupree and Haas had told him about the Ministry of Interior minders that they were provided with. Not for Breadalbane, of course, to his shame and chagrin. These minders also provided transport and accompanied you everywhere.

Sunday was in his early twenties, short and muscle-bound

with a cheerful, easy manner and a near-constant smile. His car was a large but bashed-about cerise Peugeot 404. One headlight was missing and there was a neat row of bullet holes punched along the left-hand side.

'The MiGs do this,' Sunday explained. Then laughed. 'But they miss me.'

First stop on their agenda was at the Ministry of the Interior – housed in a former community centre with a chequerboard tile facade, and a lobby filled with empty pinboards. He had a meeting with the Minister of the Interior herself, a handsome, serious-looking woman called Abigail Kross, who had been Zanzarim's first woman judge after independence. Her brother was Minister of Defence in the Dahumian government and, during their conversation, Bond gained a clear impression of the absolute strength of Fakassa tribal loyalties – loyalties and bonds that seemed far stronger than anything equivalent in Western Europe.

Abigail Kross smiled at him.

'I'm counting on you, Mr Bond, to make sure your French readers fully understand our terrible situation here,' she said. 'If the French government could recognise Dahum then everything would change. I know they've been close to this decision – perhaps one more gentle push . . .'

Bond was diplomatic. 'I promise you I'll report what I see – but I have to say I'm very impressed so far.'

'You'll see more today,' she said. 'Our schools, our civil defence, our militia training.' She looked at him shrewdly. 'This is not about stealing oil, Mr Bond, this is a new country trying to shape its own destiny.'

And so Sunday dutifully took him to a school, to the central hospital, to the barracks and a fire station, to underground bunkers and experimental agricultural enterprises. Bond saw workshops where local blacksmiths reconstituted crashed and wrecked cars into hospital beds and office furniture. More intriguingly he saw there was a burgeoning defence industry fabricating their own hand grenades and anti-personnel mines from the most humdrum materials. By the end of the day's touring around, Bond was exhausted. He had deliberately taken notes – acting the journalist – but something about the desperation inherent in all these activities had depressed him. This was a country – barely a country – clinging on to its existence with its fingernails, desperate to survive through its talent for improvisation and inspired gimmickry. But Bond had seen the forces massing against them and knew how doomed and forlorn their efforts were. A hand grenade forged from bits of an old sewing machine and a lawnmower wasn't going to stop a Centurion tank or a canister of napalm dropped from a low-flying MiG.

'Take me back to base, Sunday,' Bond requested after half an hour of watching smartly uniformed schoolchildren marching to and fro with wooden rifles over their shoulders. 'Oh, yes,' he added. 'I want to go to the Janjaville airstrip tonight. Can you arrange that?'

'We get you special pass,' Sunday said. 'They will issue it at Press Centre.'

They drove back through Port Dunbar's busy but ordered streets. Sunday leapt out of the car and opened the door for him.

'You know what you can do for me, Sunday,' Bond said. 'I need a jacket, a bush jacket, lots of pockets.' He handed over a few thousand sigmassis.

'I get one for you, sir,' Sunday said. 'One fine, fine jacket.'

Bond went to the Press Centre's administration office where a young lieutenant provided him with the special pass that would allow him entry into Janjaville airstrip.

'While we have Janjaville, there is hope,' he said, with evident sincerity.

It sounded like a slogan, Bond thought, something to shout at a rally – but the man's self-belief made him even more curious to see the place and what went on there. He suspected that the placid near-normality of life in Port Dunbar meant that the real target of Zanza Force's efforts would be directed at the airfield. Janjaville seemed the strategic key to the whole war. He reminded himself of the strategic key to his mission.

He smiled at the lieutenant.

'I'd like officially to request, on behalf of the Agence Presse Libre, an interview with Brigadier Adeka.'

'It's impossible, sir,' the lieutenant said. 'The brigadier does not talk to the foreign press.'

'Tell him we're a French press agency. It could be very important for Dahum in France—'

'It makes no difference,' the lieutenant interrupted. 'Since the war began we've had over one hundred requests for interviews. Every newspaper, radio station, TV channel in the world. The brigadier does not give interviews to anyone.'

Bond went back to the bar, perplexed. Perhaps he'd have to try gaining access through Abigail Kross. Breadalbane was sitting in the bar and asked if there was any chance that he could borrow some money, running out of funds and all that. Bond gave him a wad of notes and bought him a cold beer.

·12·

JANJAVILLE

Sunday's Peugeot bumped over potholes as it approached the perimeter fence of Janjaville airstrip. He had switched off his one headlight as there was a strict blackout imposed. Here and there at the side of the road were little flasks of burning oil providing a dim guiding light – enough to know you were on the right track. Bond looked at his watch. The journey had taken forty minutes, east out of Port Dunbar.

At the gate Bond showed his pass and they were waved through. The perimeter fence was high and heavily barbed-wired, Bond saw, as Sunday parked up behind the airstrip buildings. There was a concrete blockhouse with a towering radio mast and wires looping from it to a mobile radar dish that spun steadily round on its bearings. There was a corrugated-iron hangar, and a few low wooden huts made up the rest of the airstrip's buildings. On the grass by the blockhouse several dozen soldiers sat patiently waiting beside a row of assorted lorries and trucks, all empty.

Bond was wearing the bush jacket Sunday had acquired for him – in fact it was an army-surplus combat jacket with a patched bullet hole in the back and the Dahum flag sewn on its right shoulder – the red sun in its white plane casting its black shadow below. Had it been stripped from a corpse, Bond wondered, cleaned and resold at a profit? He didn't particularly care.

Bond stepped out of Sunday's car and looked around. The runway was closely mown grass but there seemed to be orthodox landing lights, though currently extinguished. In front of the hangar were three Malmö MFI trainers painted in camouflage green and black – single-engined, boxy-looking aircraft with oddly splayed tricycle undercarriages that had the effect of making them look as if they were about to fall back on their tails. Technicians were working on them and Bond saw the spark-shower of oxyacetylene. To his eyes it looked like they were attaching .50-calibre machine guns on to pylons beneath the wings.

'This will be our new air force,' Sunday said with manifest pride. 'Madame Kross, she ask for me to introduce you to Mr Hulbert Linck. Please to follow me, Mr Bond.'

Bond walked with Sunday towards the hangar. As he drew near he saw that there was a very tall European man supervising the work on the Malmös. Sunday approached him, gave a small bow and indicated Bond standing a few paces away. Very tall indeed, Bond realised, as the man turned to look at him. Six foot six, perhaps, like a basketball player, and he had all the lanky awkwardness and ungainliness of the very tall. He was in his fifties and his thinning, fine white-blond hair was blown into a kind of hirsute halo by the evening breeze. He wore faded jeans and canvas boots, his shirt had a tear at the elbow. He looked more like some crazed inventor than a shrewd international businessman and multimillionaire.

Sunday introduced Bond, respectfully. 'Mr Bond from Agence Presse Libre.'

'Hulbert Linck,' the tall man said, in good English with the faintest accent that Bond found impossible to place: Swedish? German? Dutch? He shook Bond's hand vigorously. 'At last, the French are here.'

Bond saw, in the glow from the engineers' lights, the shine of a zealot's near-madness in Linck's eyes. He immediately began talking rapidly.

'When will the French recognise Dahum? Perhaps you can inform me. We've all been awaiting the news from the outside world.' He put his thin hand on Bond's shoulder. 'Everything you write will be vitally important, Mr Bond. Vitally.'

'I'll do my best,' Bond said, changing the subject. 'These are Malmös, aren't they?'

'Bought cheap off the Swedish air force,' Linck said. 'We're converting them for ground attack. When we can strike back from the air the whole context of this war will change. You wait and see.' Linck talked on excitedly, outlining his plans. It was as if the Zanzarim civil war and the survival of Dahum were a personal problem of his own. Dupree and Haas had told Bond of Linck's unswerving support – he had spent millions of dollars of his fortune (his was a pan-European dairy empire, originally: butter, milk and cheese) recruiting and paying white mercenaries, chartering planes, buying illicit military materiel in the shadier locales of the world arms' market, all to keep this fledgling African state alive. There was no rationale, Bond supposed, looking at the man as he spoke and gesticulated, it was a 'cause' pure and simple. It gave him something to live for – it was Hulbert Linck's personal crusade. Bond had asked Haas where Linck was from and had received no precise answer. Nobody seemed to know his early history in any detail. Rumours abounded: that he had made his first fortune smuggling foodstuffs in the black market during the chaos of post-war Europe; that he was the bastard son of an English aristocrat and an Italian courtesan. He had a Swiss passport but was resident in Monte Carlo, Haas had told him; he spoke excellent German and French but no one really knew for sure where he was from – Georgia, someone had said, or one of the Baltic states, perhaps; Haas had even heard rumours about Corsica and Albania. His companies were all based in Liechtenstein, apparently.

Bond looked at him, closely – was the white-blond hair dyed? he wondered suddenly. Another ruse. Were the slightly deranged mannerisms – the wide-eyed enthusiasms, the carelessness about what he wore – more examples of a very clever and duplicitous mask? Everything about him, to Bond's eyes, seemed slightly bogus and worked-up. He realised that for someone like Hulbert Linck the more speculation about his origins, the more wild guesses thrown about, the better the disguise.

Suddenly a bell rang briefly from the blockhouse and Bond sensed a quiver of readiness from those waiting around the Janjaville strip.

'Excuse me, Mr Bond,' Linck said and loped off.

The runway lights were switched on, delineating the grass strip with dotted lines of blue and, seconds later, Bond heard the growing roar of aero engines.

Then out of the darkness he saw landing lights appear and into the blue glow cast from the runway a Lockheed Super

Constellation swooped, touching down heavily, bouncing, then great clouds of dust were thrown up as the four propellers went into reverse, slowing its progress so it could turn off and wheel round on to the piste in front of the hangar.

Bond had flown in Super Constellations in the 1950s, when they, along with the Boeing Stratocruiser, were the apogee of airline glamour. They still had a remarkable look about them, Bond thought, watching this one come to rest and the cargo doors in its side open. The three tail fins, the four radial engines, the unusually high undercarriage and the curved slim aerodynamics of the fuselage all gave it a particular degree of beauty for an aeroplane. This one was elderly, its paint finish patched and blistered and there was no airline logo in evidence, no trace of where, or from whom, Linck might have chartered it. Arc lights were switched on and the soldiers and the lorries rushed forward to unload its cargo.

Bond watched, his mind busy, as the plane was unloaded in minutes, the four propellers still turning. He saw boxes of ammunition, mortars, bazookas, heavy machine guns, food, powdered milk, crates of Scotch whisky and gin, drugs, spare tyres and what looked like household goods – air conditioners, stainless-steel sinks, a couple of coffee tables – all passed down the chain of soldiers' hands from the cargo doors to the waiting lorries and trucks that, once loaded, sped off into the night. Bond looked on, amazed. Then, just as the doors seemed about to close, he saw Kobus Breed run from a building and climb the steps to the plane, handing over a small package to someone inside. The doors were shut, Breed descended and the steps were wheeled away. It wasn't entirely one-way traffic, then, Bond thought to himself. Breed was now talking to Linck – like two familiars, Bond noticed. Linck clapped him on the shoulder and Breed headed off into the darkness.

'The planes come two, three, four times a night,' Sunday said.

'Where from?' Bond asked, turning back to Sunday.

'Dahomey, Ivory Coast, Mali – we don't know for sure.'

Bond looked at the tall figure of Linck, as the Super Constellation revved its engines and turned to taxi back to the runway. It hadn't been on the ground for more than fifteen minutes, Bond thought, watching Linck waving enthusiastically at the taxiing plane as if he were bidding farewell to parting relatives.

'Mr Linck, he control everything,' Sunday said.

With an accelerating roar of its Wright radial engines the now empty Super Constellation barrelled down the Janjaville runway in a blue-tinged cloud of dust and took off into the night sky. The landing lights were extinguished and all that could be heard was the diminishing drone of the engines as the plane climbed to cruising height. Bond walked back to Sunday's Peugeot, impressed: this rearguard action had real potential, he could see.

·13·

GHOST WARRIORS

Bond spent many hours the next day sitting in an anteroom outside Abigail Kross's office hoping for an appointment. When she eventually saw him she seemed distant and preoccupied and her apology was perfunctory. Bond asked if she could use her authority to arrange an interview with Brigadier Adeka. She said that would be impossible. The brigadier had a lifelong distrust of the press and never spoke to journalists. Bond played the French card – 'Agence Presse Libre would see it as an honour to be able to speak to the brigadier exclusively' – but in vain.

'Perhaps you could talk to Jakobus Breed,' Madame Kross then suggested. 'He supervises the foreign military advisers.'

'I'm already familiar with Mr Breed,' Bond said, savouring the euphemism. Then he added, 'I met the brigadier's brother in London,' hoping that this claim would give him a little more credence. 'He wanted to pass on a message to his brother.'

'Gabriel Adeka is no friend of Dahum,' Abigail Kross said, her smile fading permanently. 'His name will open no doors here, Mr Bond. Especially not with his brother.'

Bond left her, thinking hard. Madame Kross was a woman of

intelligence and integrity, Bond recognised, but her absolute intransigence seemed almost perverse to him. Why wouldn't the brigadier speak to the foreign press? Propaganda was a highly effective weapon when it was well deployed. Something strange was going on here. Perhaps Hulbert Linck was the man to approach next – maybe he could apply some pressure.

Back at the Press Centre, Bond sent a telex to the fake APL address he had been given and that went straight to Transworld Consortium in Regent's Park. He wrote bland stuff about plucky little Dahum defying the odds, soldiering on gallantly, but Bond knew that the subtext would let M know he was 'in country'. He added a postscript that he was making every effort to interview Brigadier Adeka but 'operational difficulties' made it seem unlikely that it would be granted. He also mentioned that the chief executive of OG Palm Oil Export and Agricultural Services was currently indisposed. Blessing's fate would at least be investigated now.

He spent another bibulous evening with Dupree, Haas and Breadalbane and learned from Haas that anyone could book a seat on an empty outbound flight on the Super Constellation for $100. The actual port of Port Dunbar was completely block-aded and the only way out of the country was by air – or over-land, if you were prepared to risk your neck beneath the watchful eye of the MiGs.

Bond climbed upstairs to bed in a bad mood, wondering if he should just pay his $100, quit Dahum and admit failure. It went against his nature, but he couldn't see how there was any way he could get close to Adeka, short of storming his headquarters. And he had a horrible feeling that this military stalemate might leave him stranded in Dahum for weeks or months, like Digby Breadalbane.

He was woken before dawn by an urgent knocking on his door. It was Sunday, in a state of real excitement.

'We have a scoop, Mr Bond. There has been a small battle and we have defeated the enemy. I thought you might like to see it.'

Bond dressed as quickly as possible and Sunday drove him north out of Port Dunbar on increasingly minor roads. As they bumped along through the pearly, misty light Bond wondered if this was a simple propaganda exercise – something staged for him, the gullible newly arrived journalist, who would duly report it as a Dahumian feat of arms. His mood was still sour – he wasn't expecting much.

After an hour's drive, they turned off the metalled road and entered an area of mangrove swamp and winding creeks. The road they drove along was built up above the watercourses on a kind of revetted embankment. Then they began to pass jubilant Dahumian troops returning from the front and in the morning sky they saw smoke curling up above the treeline.

The village they arrived at had been burnt out and destroyed weeks previously: shattered mud huts, charred roof timbers and leafless trees signalled a napalm strike. Bond and Sunday left the Peugeot and walked through exuberant milling Dahumian soldiers towards the giant shade tree at the village's centre. Here they found Breed and half a dozen other white mercenaries standing round eight Zanzari soldiers' corpses laid out in a row. A little way off at another entrance to the village was a still smoking, upended armoured personnel carrier, a hole punched through its side – perhaps, Bond wondered, from a bazooka or an anti-tank gun unloaded from the Super Constellation the night before.

Breed turned to meet him, wiping away a tear. He was wearing a grey T-shirt with 'HALO' printed on the front and his bashed kepi was pushed back on his head at a rakish angle. He was exhibiting his usual shifting cocktail of moods – at once jovial, wired and sinister.

'Yah, we know they were coming so we just waited up here in the village,' Breed said. 'Bang-bang – got these fellas and the others just ran away. We're gonna chase them back to Sinsikrou.'

He shouted orders and some soldiers shinned up into the shade tree with lengths of rope that they secured to the branches and let fall. Then Breed had a man bring him a clinking, heavy sack and from it drew out what looked like giant fish hooks, six inches long, with a large eye. Breed attached the dangling ropes to the hooks and then, to Bond's shock and surprise, he thwacked the sharp end in and under the jaws of the dead soldiers, like a stevedore walloping a bale hook into a sack. He tugged sharply at the hook to make sure its grip was secure under the jawbone.

'Pull away, boys,' he shouted.

The men in the tree hauled on the ropes and the dead bodies were lifted aloft by their jaws. Like so many fishing trophies – like marlin or bluefin, Bond thought – on a dock after a successful fishing expedition.

'Stop!' Breed shouted when the dead men were three feet off the ground. 'Secure them there!'

The ropes were lashed to the branches and the dead men hung there, twirling gently. Bond had seen lynched men before but these bodies looked different, unusually dehumanised by the hooks and the forced jut of their lower jaws and the tearing stretching strain on their necks that were taking the full weight of their bodies. He thought as they hung there that they looked like ghoulish sides of beef in a butcher's chill room, the dangling arms and legs all the more obscene because of the unnatural angle of the head with the giant hook through the jaw.

Breed looked on with an eerie, satisfied smile on his face.

'That's a good haul,' he said. 'The more the merrier. One isn't enough, you need a cluster, like. Once I strung up more than thirty. I tell you it—'

'Why do you do it?' Bond interrupted.

'Because it freaks them out when they see this,' Breed said, cheerfully, lowering his voice as he spoke to Bond. 'I leave them all over the forest, hanging from trees. Scares the shit out of the Zanzaris – bad juju.'

'Where did you learn that little trick?' Bond asked, concealing his disgust.

'Down in Matabeleland in '66,' Breed said. 'I used to string up the ZIPRA terrs we caught like this.' He smiled. 'What do you say in French? *Pour encourager les autres.*'

Bond turned away from the dangling bodies, feeling nauseous, and went to join Sunday, who looked equally distressed.

'Does he do this all the time?' Bond asked Sunday.

'Yes. He like it too too much.'

'I don't like it,' Bond said. 'It's revolting.'

'I go 'gree for you, sar,' Sunday said. 'They are just soldiers, like our own men.'

Bond looked over to see Breed striding around and shouting

at the Dahumian troops, forming them into a rough column of about 200 men. They were charged and energised by their victory, armed with an odd variety of weapons – AK-47s, SLRs and ancient World War Two Lee–Enfield rifles. They all had machetes at their waist in leather scabbards or thrust through their belts. Every one of them, Bond noticed, despite their patchwork uniforms, had the red, white and black flag of Dahum sewn on to their right shoulder.

'Bring him on,' Breed shouted and from behind a ruined hut a witch doctor appeared. Bond couldn't think of any other word to describe him. His face was painted white with lurid green circles around his eyes. A great mass of shells and beads was wrapped around his neck and wrists setting up a coarse rattle as he shuffled forward in a half-dance. He was bare-chested and wore a thick dry grass skirt that fell to his ankles and he carried a gourd and a long horsehair fly whisk. He shuffled up and down the column of men – who stood there rapt and rigid – and as he went he drank from the gourd and spat out the liquid through his clenched teeth in a fine spray into their faces and flicked their chests and groins with the fly whisk, chanting all the while in a low monotone. When he had sprayed and touched them all he screamed shrilly, three times, stepped back, made a weird sign of benediction over them and shuffled off behind the house again.

'Take 'em away, Dawie,' Breed shouted at one of the other white mercenaries and the men wheeled around and, beginning a chant, started to jog out of the village in pursuit of the rest of the Zanzari soldiers fleeing back up the road to what they hoped was safety.

Breed whooped encouragement at them. 'I just love that,' he

said to Bond, taking out a pack of Boomslangs and offering it to Bond. They both lit up.

'Great show, isn't it?' Breed said. 'That fetish priest is worth a thousand men. They won't fight without his blessing.'

'What does all the mumbo-jumbo mean?' Bond asked.

'He makes them immortal, you see,' Breed said. 'If they die today they come back as spirits and continue the fight. You can't see them but they're fighting beside you.' He chuckled. 'Now they're fearless, those boys. They even want to die – to become a "ghost warrior". Amazing.' He dabbed at his weeping eye. 'If they catch those Zanzaris it'll be quite a picnic, I tell you.' He turned away. 'Let's head back,' he said. 'I just wanted you to see this – good copy for your newspapers, eh?'

Bond was happy to leave the village and its shade tree with its hanging fruit of dangling corpses.

'We'll pull back,' Breed said. 'Mine the embankments. They're attacking us all over the place at the moment – but there'll be no way through here.'

They walked back towards the Peugeot.

'I want to speak to Adeka,' Bond said. 'Can you help?'

'You must be joking,' Breed said. 'Even I can't get to see him.'

'How do you communicate?'

'Most of the time I get these written orders. Reinforce there. Destroy that bridge. Move more men there. Repel this attack. Fall back and regroup. He seems to see the big picture, Adeka. It's uncanny, man. And he distributes all the ordnance from the Janjaville flights – you get what he gives you. He seems to know what he's doing – for a black brigadier.' He smiled at Bond. 'Fancy a drink?'

He didn't wait for a reply and led Bond over to a US Army jeep with a canvas canopy and a tall whippy aerial. In the back was an impressive-looking, many-dialled radio set and a young man in an over-large tin helmet sat there listening to the traffic. Breed reached into a knapsack and brought out a bottle of schnapps. He fished around some more and came up with two cloudy shot glasses. He set the glasses down on the jeep's bonnet and poured them both a drink. Bond didn't feel like drinking with Breed but perhaps some hard liquor was required after what he'd witnessed in the village.

'*Proost*,' Breed said, and they both knocked back the schnapps in one. Bond felt his throat burn. Strong stuff. Breed topped them up.

'So,' Bond said. 'Matebeleland, 1966 . . . Rhodesian African Rifles?'

'No. Light Infantry. The good old RLI.' Breed pointed at the two scars on his cheek. 'I got shot in the face by a ZANLA terr. Thought he'd killed me. I was six months in a hospital in Salisbury then I was invalided out of the army. Lucky for me Hulbert Linck came by recruiting. Five thousand US a month in any bank in the world you choose. Hard to resist. So me and a few of my RLI mates signed up for Dahum. They're a good bunch of guys, though, the Dahum grunts. When the juju man fires them up they'll fight till they drop.' He grinned. 'That's why, in spite of everything, we're winning. We've got bigger balls than the Zanzaris.'

Bond said nothing. Breed poured another schnapps.

'What do you think, Bond?' he suggested. 'There's a little club in town – nice atmosphere, good music, European alcohol, very obliging girls. They like us white boys fighting for their country. Want to meet there tonight?'

Bond did not want to go out on the town with Kobus Breed. Not in a thousand years.

'Actually, I'm not sure I can make it. Copy to file.'

Breed's finger tapped the Dahum flag on Bond's jacket.

'You could pass for one of us.'

There was an audible crackle of static from the radio in the jeep and Breed turned to see what was going on. The operator was intent, concentrating, nodding.

'It's for you, Boss.'

Breed strode over and put on the headphones. As he listened he looked progressively more serious.

'Yah. OK – roger that.' He took off the headphones and wiped his eye.

'What's up?' Bond asked.

'A pretty major shit-storm. All this stuff we did here today was a feint. There's another Zanza Force column moving on the airstrip.' He gestured at the radio, 'That came from Adeka.'

'Himself?'

'No. But relayed from him. I got to move, man. This is serious.'

'Mind if I tag along?' Bond suggested, spontaneously.

Breed looked at him, a little askance. When he spoke his voice was heavy with scepticism.

'You ever been in combat?' Breed asked.

Bond smiled, tiredly. 'You ever heard of World War Two?'

·14·

THE BATTLE OF
THE KOLOLO CAUSEWAY

Bond stood with Breed on a small bluff and looked through binoculars at the view. A little bit of orientation and a few glances at Breed's map had made everything fairly clear.

The village of Kololo, the main Dahumian strongpoint guarding this eastern approach towards Janjaville, had been lost, abandoned. Some huts in the village were on fire – apparently there had been a MiG airstrike. The troops that had been manning it had fled the village and had retreated across the 200-yard causeway that ran above a great swathe of swampland and had regrouped on the far side, barricading the road with logs and oil drums, ready to repel any new advance out of the village along the causeway.

Bond could see that the village was thick with Zanza Force soldiers and he could spot one Saracen armoured car with a roof turret sheltering by the gable end of a mud hut that was close to the road leading to the causeway. He suspected they were waiting for the MiGs to return before they continued their advance. He remembered Blessing's remarks about their lack of military zeal.

'Well, at least there's only one direction they can attack from,' Bond said. 'But that barricade will last twenty seconds in the face of that Saracen.' He turned to Breed. 'You don't have enough men.'

Breed had explained the problem. Eighty per cent of the Dahumian army faced the Zanza Force advance astride the trans-national highway that led to Port Dunbar. That's where the tanks were, and the artillery. It was a stand-off that could be maintained forever, each army waiting for the other one to blink. Consequently most of the action in these later stages of the war consisted of skirmishes as Zanza Force units explored other routes into the rebel heartland. Breed and his flying columns were able to confront and repel any of these secondary thrusts – they were more aggressive in their soldiering and they had the power of the fetish priest and his juju on their side, whereas the Zanzari soldiers could only be persuaded to muster on the promise of free beer and cigarettes. Bond had seen the consequences with his own eyes that morning. Dahum's hinterland was now so small that sufficient troops could be rushed here and there to repel any new attempt at incursion. Except today they had been caught out – Breed's mercenaries and two heavily armed companies were chasing fleeing Zanzaris through the forest. And in the meantime Kololo had fallen.

Breed took the binoculars from Bond.

'I suppose we could try and blow the causeway,' he said vaguely, peering out over the swamp.

'That's no good. You have to retake Kololo.'

'Oh yeah, good idea. Why didn't I think of that? That's easy, man.'

'You have to be on the other side of the causeway. Dug in back in the village.' Bond gestured at the troops huddling behind their barricade. 'Look at your guys. Wait until the MiGs get here. They'll blow you away.'

Breed turned and looked at him resentfully.

'So what do you suggest, General?'

Bond shrugged. 'It's not my war – you're the one getting the big pay cheque. But you're going to be in real trouble if you let them get established this side of the causeway.'

Breed swore and spat on the ground. Bond could see he was worried.

'Have you any second line you could defend back up the road? Another creek, a bridge?'

'No,' Breed said. 'We could fell some trees, I suppose.'

'Then you'd better get your axes out,' Bond said, reclaimed the binoculars and surveyed the panorama in front of him again. There was no way around the swamp that the causeway traversed. On the Dahumian side of the swamp he could see that a deep artificial gully had been dug – probably some old flood-prevention device. An idea was forming in his head. He might be able to apply some useful advantage here, he thought. This situation might just be the opportunity he was waiting for.

'I've got an idea,' Bond said. 'But I need to know what firepower we have.'

He and Breed slithered down from the bluff to the makeshift positions occupied by the soldiers who had fled Kololo. Bond saw at once that any resistance would be purely token. The Saracen alone would brush them aside and then the troops following the armoured car would have a field day.

Bond surveyed the offensive possibilities. There were two 4.1-inch mortars with a couple of boxes of bombs and one heavy .50-calibre machine gun. Then he saw about a dozen galvanised buckets with curious bulbous lids on them.

'What're they?' Bond asked.

Breed sneered. 'They're our Dahumian home-made piss-poor landmines. They call them "Adeka's Answer".'

'Do they work?'

'They go off with a hell of a bang. Huge percussion – burst your eardrums, make your nose bleed, maybe up-end a small vehicle. Saracen'll drive right over it.' Kobus sneered. 'You've got a big charge of cordite. I told them to fill the rest of it with nails and bolts – cut people up – but nobody listens to me.'

'They may just be perfect,' Bond said, thinking, remembering.

'So what do we do, wise guy?' Breed said, with heavy mockery. He was increasingly worried, Bond could see. Any move that threatened Janjaville meant the end of the war. 'Go on, genius. What do we do?'

'If I tell you,' Bond said, 'there's one condition.'

'I don't do "conditions",' Breed said.

'Fine. All the best of luck to you and your men.' He turned and began to walk away.

'All right, all right. What condition?'

Bond stopped and Breed approached.

'If I show you how to get back into Kololo,' Bond said, 'then you have to get me a meeting with Adeka.'

Breed looked at him – Bond could practically hear his mind working.

'You can get us back in that village?' Breed said. 'You guarantee?'

'You can't guarantee anything in a war zone. But I think this will work.'

Breed looked down at the ground and kicked at a stone. Bond could tell he was reluctant to ask for help, as if it signalled some lack of military expertise in himself, showed some fundamental weakness. He spat again.

'If you get us back in that village Adeka will want to marry you.'

'We don't need to go that far,' Bond said. 'A meeting, face to face, will be fine.'

'It won't be a problem,' Breed said. 'I promise you. If you get us back across the causeway you'll be a national hero. But if you fail . . .' He didn't finish.

Bond concealed his pleasure at this concession. 'We won't fail if you do exactly what I say.'

'Where do we start?'

'We retreat,' Bond said. 'In panic. As they say in French: *reculer pour mieux sauter*. Take a step back to jump higher, you know.'

Breed looked at him, darkly. 'You'd better know what you're doing, man.'

'Maybe you have a better idea,' Bond said, amiably.

'No, no. Over to you, Bond. This is your party.'

Bond managed not to smile and began to issue instructions to the non-commissioned officers. He sent teams of men to bury the bucket bombs in the irrigation ditch. He then positioned and precisely sighted the mortars, taking his time, calculating distances as best he could and adjusting the calibration on the sights minutely.

'Don't touch them,' he said to the mortar teams. 'Even after you've fired and you think the range is wrong. Just keep firing, understand?'

Then he had the heavy machine gun taken up to the bluff and set it down where it had a field of fire over the whole causeway. He gave Breed precise instructions and checked on the village again through the binoculars. The troops were gathering. The Saracen had moved away from the protection of its gable-end and was now close to the entrance to the causeway – obviously they weren't going to wait for any air strike.

'We'll let the Saracen through,' Bond said. 'It'll be going hell for leather. Have some men waiting to engage it further up the track. Then, when we "retreat" we'll re-form in the trees and be ready to race across the causeway when I give the word.'

'You seem very confident,' Breed said.

'Well, it worked the last time I tried it,' Bond said.

'When was that?'

'1945. The principle being that, in a battle, confusion can be as important as an extra regiment.'

'Who said that? The Duke of fucking Wellington?'

'I did, actually,' Bond said with a modest smile. 'Now, here's exactly how I expect everything to happen.'

At midday the sound of the Saracen's revving and manoeuvring carried across the marsh to the Dahumian positions. It was hot and steamy. Bond was standing by the rudimentary barricade and ducked down as the first fusillade of bullets began to come their way. The Saracen roared on to the causeway, its .30 Browning machine gun firing wildly as the turret traversed left and right, a massed column of troops surging behind it.

'Right,' Bond shouted. 'Everybody run!'

The defending Dahumians took him at his word. With histrionic display they stood up, waved their arms and abandoned their positions with alacrity, pelting down the road away from the causeway, seeking the protection of the forest trees. Leaving the barricade unguarded and undefended.

Bond sprinted back to the mortar crews. Breed was up at the bluff behind the machine gun. Through his binoculars Bond saw the Saracen accelerate, blasting through the log and oil-drum barrier, spraying the forest fringe with its machine gun. Behind it the Zanza Force troops raced forward over the causeway. It looked like a walkover.

'They are comin', sar,' said the lance corporal who was manning the first of the mortars.

'Wait,' Bond said. He wanted most of the men across the causeway before there was any retaliation.

'OK, fire!' He waved up at Breed.

There was a dull *whump* as the first mortar bomb took off into the air. A split second later the other followed. The bombs exploded some way behind the advancing Zanzaris.

'Keep firing,' Bond said to the baffled mortar crew. 'Don't stop.' He ran off and scrambled up through the undergrowth to where Breed was blasting away with the machine gun.

Bond could see that his ally 'confusion' was already contributing to this firefight. The advancing troops had already slowed, disoriented by this barrage of harmless explosions to their rear. Breed, on Bond's instructions, was also firing at the rear of the troops' advance, raking the causeway with his heavy-calibre bullets, chewing up great gouts of earth and dust. More bombs exploded as the mortars kept up their rate of fire.

'OK. Turn the gun on the rear ranks.'

Breed swivelled the gun and worked the bullet impacts closer to the shifting static mass of Zanzari soldiers. One or two of them were cut down. Others flung themselves in the swamp. There was a collective race to get off the causeway as the troops desperately began to search for cover from this baffling assault from behind.

The irrigation ditch lay there invitingly. The perfect place to keep your head down. Men began to pour and slither into the security its depth provided.

Further up the track Bond could hear firing and explosions as the Saracen was engaged. The irrigation ditch was packed with cowering men as Breed kept up his fire, hosing bullets along the ditch's edge. Now, Bond thought, all we need is 'Adeka's Answer'.

The first of the bucket bombs exploded and Bond felt the shockwave even up on the bluff. That detonation set off a chain reaction and the others exploded in a Chinese firecracker of eruptions along the irrigation ditch.

'Breed – get your boys across the causeway and into the village.'

Bond didn't want to think about what had happened in the ditch. He could hear the screams of wounded men and a great billowing pall of smoke and dust obscured the view.

On Breed's signal – a green flare – the Dahumians in the forest began to stream across the causeway towards Kololo village. There was some sporadic firing as they advanced but the debacle on the far side of the causeway must have been very visible to whatever troops had remained behind.

Breed was on his feet with the binoculars.

'Yes, they're running away,' he said. 'True to form. Big bunch of girls.'

Bond looked down at the irrigation ditch as the smoke cleared. Stunned and wounded soldiers were staggering and crawling out of it, being rounded up by Breed's men.

'Don't kill them,' Bond said. 'A nice large group of prisoners might be a useful bargaining chip, one day.'

'Whatever you say, Mr Bond,' Breed chuckled, wiping his eye on his cuff, and then looking at him with something that might just have been respect, Bond thought. Score one for the Agence Presse Libre.

'Remember my condition,' Bond said. 'Remember your promise. I got you back into Kololo – so get me to Adeka.'

·15·

GOLD STAR

Bond sat in the bar of the Press Centre, drinking his second whisky and soda, his mind full of the battle that he'd directed and won. One hundred and eighty-two prisoners had been captured and the Dahum army was back in Kololo, dug in and secure in its fortified bunkers. Breed had been exultant and had promised him a face-to-face meeting with Adeka within twenty-four hours. If that were the outcome then a momentary reverse in the Zanza Force advance would have been well worth it. There was every chance that the larger objective might be achieved. *Reculer pour mieux sauter*, indeed.

To be honest, Bond had to admit that he hadn't thought much about what he was doing once the urgency of the situation was apparent and the beautiful clarity of his plan had seized him. All that had concerned him was how best to execute it. And it had been incredibly exciting: the gratification of seeing mental concepts vindicated so completely in a small but classic wartime encounter between infantry units – one so skilfully turning defence into attack and eventual victory. The Battle of the Kololo Causeway could be usefully taught at military academies, he thought, with a little justified pride.

Digby Breadalbane came diffidently into the bar, saw Bond and strode over and sat down – looking for a free drink.

'How was your day, James?' he asked.

'More intriguing than I expected, Digby,' Bond said, circumspectly, and offered to buy him a beer.

Breadalbane seemed chirpier than usual as he sipped his beer, foregoing his usual litany of moans and complaints.

'How long do you think this war will last?' he asked.

'Who knows?' Bond shrugged.

'I mean, it's not going to end next week.'

'You never can tell.'

'No, it's just that I've decided to stay on, no matter what, and see things out to the bitter end. I expect you and the others will fly out on a Constellation when the end is nigh. I can't afford the fare, so I thought if I witness the fall of Port Dunbar then that'll be my scoop. You know – the sole eyewitness.'

'It would make your reputation, Digby,' Bond said, his face straight. 'You'd be famous.'

'I suppose I would, wouldn't I?' Breadalbane said, liking the idea.

'And if you could get slightly wounded, even better.'

Bond saw Sunday poke his head around the door and beckon to him.

Bond stood and dropped a few notes on the table.

'I bet you'd get a salaried job out of it as well,' he said. 'Have another on me.'

He crossed the room to Sunday leaving Breadalbane to his dreams of journalistic glory.

'Please to come with me, sir,' Sunday said. 'We have to leave now.'

'Where are we going?'

'I'm not permitted to say.'

Sunday drove Bond out of Port Dunbar, heading south towards the harbour. Then they turned off into a high-walled compound containing three private houses all linked by covered walkways. As they parked, Bond noticed that Sunday seemed cowed and oddly apprehensive.

'I wait here for you, Mr Bond.'

Bond stepped out of the car and, at the door to the main building, was met by a young bespectacled man in a white coat.

'Mr Bond? I am Dr Masind. Please follow me.'

He sounded Indian or Pakistani to Bond, who obediently followed him through the house – that had clearly been converted into some kind of clinic: clean, brightly lit, nurses hurrying to and fro – and out on to a walkway, leading to a separate house, guarded by two armed soldiers and with, Bond noticed, a tall thin radio mast towering above it.

They went upstairs and Bond was asked to wait in a corridor. After about five minutes, a young officer, a colonel, emerged and introduced himself. He was smart, slim and dapper, his dark green fatigues neatly pressed. He had a small pencil moustache, like a matinee idol.

'I'm Colonel Denga,' he said, speaking with the slightest accent. 'I want to thank you for what you did for us today.'

'It was very spur-of-the-moment. As you know I'm just an APL journalist – but the situation did call for fairly drastic action,'

Bond said. He was aware that his self-effacingness could be counterproductive and he was conscious of Denga looking at him shrewdly.

'Not every journalist can dictate and control a battle on the spur of the moment . . .'

Bond smiled. 'I didn't say I was inexperienced. I'm older than you, Colonel. I served with British commandos in World War Two. You learn a lot, and fast.'

'Well, wherever your expertise originates – we're very grateful. Please – go in.'

He opened a door and Bond stepped through into a dark room, with only one light burning. A man was lying on a hospital bed with a saline drip attached to his neck. He was terribly gaunt and thin, his hair patchy and grey. He gestured to Bond to come closer and spoke in a weak, semi-whispering voice.

'Mr Bond – I am Brigadier Solomon Adeka. I wanted to thank you personally for what you achieved at the Kololo Causeway.'

Bond stared, astonished, taking in every detail. Adeka was obviously gravely, terminally ill – that fact apparent from his drawn face and his dead eyes. Some kind of aggressive cancer, Bond supposed. Adeka reached out a quivering hand, all bones, and Bond shook it briefly. There was no grip at all.

Adeka signalled to Colonel Denga – who had slipped into the room behind Bond – and the colonel stepped forward, reached into his pocket and drew out a slim leather case.

'You'll probably laugh,' Adeka said, 'but I wanted you to have some symbolic evidence of our gratitude. The Republic of Dahum salutes you.'

Bond took the case from Denga and opened it. Inside, on a

bed of moulded black velvet, was an eight-pointed gold star hanging from a red, white and black silk ribbon.

'The Gold Star of Dahum – our highest military honour.'

Bond was both surprised and oddly touched. 'Well . . . I'm very grateful,' he said slowly. 'Very flattered. But I don't feel I'm really—'

But then Adeka began to cough, drily, and Bond saw how his frail body was wracked with the effort as it quivered and shook beneath the blankets.

'We should go,' Denga said, quietly.

'Goodbye, Brigadier,' Bond said, not wanting his farewell to sound final but knowing he would never see the man again – and knowing also that his mission was now effectively over. He turned and left the room.

He sat in silence as Sunday drove him back to Port Dunbar. He felt a human sadness, he had to admit, that Adeka's life was ending so early, and at the same time a gnawing sense of unease that he had been sent here precisely to achieve that object – to make him 'a less efficient soldier'. No need for that now.

'Is everything OK, sir?' Sunday said, cautiously, aware of his sombre mood.

'Yes,' Bond said. 'I've just been given a medal.'

'Congratulations,' Sunday said, cheering up. 'Do you want to go to Janjaville? There are five flights tonight. Two already come and go.'

'No thanks,' Bond said. 'Take me back to the Press Centre. It's been quite a day – I need another drink.'

Bond went straight to the bar and bought a bottle of whisky. He intended to sleep well and soundly tonight and he knew whisky to be an excellent soporific. There was no sign of his colleagues but he didn't mind drinking alone. He sat down and poured himself a generous three fingers of Scotch. Then the door to the bar opened and Geoffrey Letham walked in.

·16·

A VERY RICH MAN

All five members of the foreign press corps in Port Dunbar were invited to Brigadier Solomon Adeka's state funeral, three days later. The journalists stood in a loose, uneasy group at the rear of the dusty, weed-strewn cemetery that adjoined Port Dunbar's modest cathedral – St Jude's – as a guard of honour carried Adeka's coffin to the graveside. Through a crackling PA system Colonel Denga gave a short but passionate eulogy, outlining Adeka's virtues as a man, a patriot and a soldier, describing him as the 'first hero of Dahum' and saying emphatically that the struggle for freedom would continue – this brought cheers and applause from the large crowd that had gathered beyond the cemetery walls – and that the people of Dahum should draw their inspiration, their courage, their endurance from the memory of this great man.

A firing party raised their rifles and delivered a ragged six-shot volley into the hazy blue sky as the coffin was lowered.

Bond looked on in an ambivalent state of mind and then became aware that Geoffrey Letham was sidling over in his direction. They had greeted each other curtly the other night, not shaking hands, and Bond had swiftly taken himself off to his room with his bottle of whisky. He had managed to avoid him subsequently, having Sunday fill his days with endless rounds of official sightseeing. However, there was no escaping him now, as Letham appeared at his shoulder, mopping his florid face with a damp ultramarine handkerchief.

'I say, Bond,' he whispered in his ear, 'Breadalbane tells me you met Adeka just before he died. What was all that about?'

'Nothing important.'

'What was he like?'

'Under the weather.'

'Most amusing. Why did he want to meet you? I was told he refused to speak to the press. I'd come to Dahum expressly to interview him. The *Mail* was going to pay him serious money.'

'I've no idea,' Bond said.

'All very curious, I must say.' Letham gave an unpleasant smile. 'In fact, you're a very curious man, Bond. For a journalist of your age and alleged experience, no one seems to have heard of you. You and I must have a little chat about it one day.'

'I don't speak to the press, Letham, hadn't you heard?'

Bond wandered away, wondering if Letham was issuing some kind of covert threat. He had arrived on a Super Constellation flight, having left Sinsikrou after his encounter with Bond and travelled to Abidjan in Ivory Coast. There, he'd paid Hulbert Linck to be flown in, posing as a friend and supporter of 'plucky little Dahum'. Initially Bond was more irritated than perturbed by Letham's surprising presence – he could deal with dross like Letham effortlessly – but what was disturbing him now was that nothing in Dahum had changed with the death of Adeka. It had been announced in a black-bordered edition of the *Daily Graphic* – Dahum's sole newspaper – but the expected collapse of morale in the army and population had not taken place. The junta had simply announced that Colonel Denga was the new commander-in-chief of the Dahumian armed forces. The king was dead – long live the king.

Bond saw Kobus Breed talking with a group of his fellow mercenaries. He wandered over and called his name and Breed turned to greet him.

'Hail the conquering hero,' he said, not smiling.

Bond ignored this and asked him how he and his fellows had taken the news of Adeka's death.

'Well, it was a bit of a kick in the crotch,' Breed said with a shrug. 'But, you know, Denga's as smart as a whip. Learned everything at Adeka's knee. And, hey,' he grinned, 'we've got an air force now. The Malmös are ready for their first mission. Everyone's in good heart – and of course we still have our secret weapon.'

'What's that?'

'Tony Msour.'

'Who is?'

'Our juju man. Our fetish priest. Makes our boys immortal.'

'Oh, yes, of course.'

Bond walked back to the Press Centre from the cemetery, thinking hard, composing in his mind a telex message to M at Transworld Consortium. He could let M know that Adeka had died – though surely that news had broken by now – and point out that Adeka hadn't in fact been the vital key to Dahum's survival as everyone in London had supposed. What more could he do? he wondered. Perhaps he should book a $100-seat on the next Constellation out.

Bond duly sent his telex and received a swift and brief reply from Agence Presse Libre. 'Suggest you stay in Port Dunbar until hostilities cease. Have you any idea when that might be?'

Bond detected M's hand in the message's ironic terseness. He could read the subtext: his mission was not over, that much was clear.

Two days later the foreign press corps was invited to reassemble to witness the first attack by the Dahumian air force on a key Zanzarim army position – a substantial bridge over one of the many tributaries of the Zanza River. Bond happily allowed Breadalbane to travel with him in Sunday's Peugeot. They set off well before dawn and after a two-hour drive along bumpy minor roads they arrived, as the sun was rising, in a village called Lamu-Penu, a half-mile from the targeted bridge. There were no villagers in evidence, just 300 well-armed Dahumian soldiers drawn up in a long column, waiting for the fetish priest. Hulbert Linck was there in a Land Rover equipped with a radio that gave him contact with the Janjaville strip. The fetish priest arrived and proceeded to 'immortalise' the troops, spraying liquid from his magic gourd through his bared teeth at them, and flicking at them with his horsehair whisk. Bond looked over at Letham, who was trying to suppress his hilarity, his shoulders rocking, small snorts coming from his nose and throat.

Then Linck called in the Malmös and ten minutes later they flew low over the village, waggling their wings in salute to great cheers and exultation from the massed troops waiting to follow them in. Seconds later came the sound of their machine guns as they strafed the bridge defences and, with whoops and yells, led by Breed and his men, the soldiers jogged off to do battle.

It was all over in fifteen minutes and the journalists were duly called up to the bridge to bear witness. Clearly Zanza Force's aptitude for swift and sudden retreat had prevailed again, Bond thought. He paced around, thoughtfully, looking at the marginal damage – some burst sandbags, discarded equipment, the odd bloodstain on the tarmac – and ran into an exhilarated Hulbert Linck.

'Look what we can do, Bond, with three little aeroplanes. Wait until the ship arrives.'

'What ship?'

'We're going to run the blockade at Port Dunbar,' Linck said, tapping the side of his nose. 'Don't worry – I'll keep you informed.'

Bond went in search of Breed to see if he could shed more light on this mysterious ship and its cargo. He found him stringing up three Zanzari corpses – the only fatalities of the air strike – busying around them with his ropes and his fish hooks, hauling the bodies up by their jaws into the trees above the road that approached the bridge and the river.

'Linck told me about the ship,' Bond said.

'Did he?' Breed said, impressed. 'It's meant to be a deadly secret. He must think you're one of us – now you've won your medal.'

'So, what's with this ship?'

'Big cargo vessel. Got some serious stuff on board. Going to change everything.' He cuffed away a tear and turned to his men in the trees. 'Take 'em up a bit higher, boys. Up! Up! Heave-ho! We want everyone to have a good view.'

On the drive back to Port Dunbar, Bond began to feel a debilitating sense of impotence. What was he meant to do in this situation, for God's sake? Hulbert Linck was a one-man arms industry coming to the rescue of embattled Dahum – and what was this 'serious stuff' Breed mentioned? Bond wondered if there was any way he could immobilise Linck, somehow take him out of the equation . . . But how to get to him? And then there was still the Dahum army, fighting on efficiently under Colonel Denga—

The sound of a car horn being tooted angrily behind them interrupted his thoughts and Sunday pulled in promptly.

A glossy black Citroën DS swept by, curtains drawn in its rear windows.

'Who the hell's that?' Breadalbane asked.

'That's Tony Msour,' Sunday said. 'Very rich man.'

Bond remembered where he'd heard the name before: Kobus Breed's juju man. Bond watched the Citroën roar down the road, its hydropneumatic suspension coping effortlessly with the potholes. Nice cars. The nudging intimations of an idea were beginning to nag at him.

·17·

THE $50 PEUGEOT

Bond said he needed a private word with Sunday so Breadalbane left them in the car and slouched into the Press Centre alone.

'Have I made mistake?' Sunday asked, full of apprehension.

'No, no – I just want to ask you a few questions.' Bond smiled, keen to reassure him. 'For example: how much would you sell this car for – in US dollars?'

Sunday thought for a moment. 'Twenty dollar – but for you, Mr Bond, I say fifteen.'

'All right – but I'll give you fifty for it,' Bond said, enjoying the look of joyful astonishment registering on Sunday's face. 'But I also need you to get me a few other things. I want a hat – like the one Mr Breed wears – and a belt, a webbing belt. Oh yes, and two litres of drinking water and a small sharp knife.'

'I get them for you, sar.'

Bond counted out $50 and handed the notes over.

'Bring the car tonight, at six-thirty. I won't need it until then.' Bond raised a warning finger. 'Don't tell anybody, Sunday. This is our little secret.'

*   *   *

At lunch in the Press Centre Bond pocketed a bottle of ketchup and, in the lavatory later, emptied it and washed it out thoroughly. Back in his room he unzipped his pigskin toilet bag and prepared his solution of talcum powder dissolved in aftershave. He screwed the lid on tightly and shook the bottle until the liquid was clear. He took the lid off again and sniffed – completely odourless.

At six Bond went down to the bar and ordered a whisky and soda while he waited for Sunday to arrive. Dupree and Haas were in a corner playing chess but there was no sign of Breadalbane. Bond drained his drink and was on the point of going outside to wait for Sunday when Letham came into the room and, seeing Bond, made straight for him.

'Can I have a word, Bond?'

'I'm afraid I'm busy.'

'You said you worked in Australia before this job. Reuters.'

'That's right.'

'Funny – none of my Reuters friends in Oz can remember you.'

'I was a bit of a loner – got to go.'

Letham touched his elbow, looked like he was going to grab his arm and then thought better of it.

'Sydney or Melbourne?'

'It's really none of your business, Letham, but the answer is both.'

Bond left, annoyed with himself for being goaded by Letham into answering. He shouldn't have told him anything.

Sunday was parked outside the front door, sitting on the bonnet of the Peugeot. He handed Bond the car keys.

'Not yet – I need you to drive me somewhere, Sunday. Did you get everything?'

He had and, in the car, Bond tucked his trousers into his desert boots, buckled the webbing belt round his combat jacket and put on the soft, peaked kepi that was the headgear of choice for most of the mercenaries.

'How do I look?' he asked Sunday.

'Like soldier, sar.'

'Excellent. Do you know where Tony Msour lives?'

'Everybody know. Big, big house on the road to Janjaville.'

'Right. Take me there.'

It was completely dark by the time they reached Tony Msour's house, a large concrete villa with a balcony circling the first floor, set behind high breezeblock walls with a sliding metal gate. Bond could see the black Citroën DS squat on its haunches outside the front door. Sunday parked by the gate and Bond said he would take over from here. Sunday gave him the keys and set off walking jauntily on the road back to Port Dunbar.

There was an intercom on the gate and Bond pressed the button.

'Yes?' a crackling voice said after Bond had rung a second time. 'Who there?'

'Kobus Breed,' Bond said. 'It's very urgent.'

The buzzer sounded and Bond slid the gate back and stepped into the compound. A light above the front door came on and a couple of chained dogs barked angrily at him. The door opened and Tony Msour stood there in a string vest and a pair of loose mauve cotton trousers. He was smoking a small stumpy cigar. It was strange seeing him in his civilian persona, Bond thought, minus the white face and the green circles round his eyes. In fact he was a handsome man with fine features and very dark skin – more Nilotic or Nubian than Fakassa. He had two little vertical tribal scars under his eyes. Bond gave a loose salute.

'Where be Breed?' Msour said, a little suspiciously.

'He sent me. They're trying to recapture the bridge at Lamu-Penu.'

'Jesos Chrise.'

'Exactly. Breed's rushing men up. He needs you – fast.'

Msour thought for a second. 'It will be one hundred dollars.'

'Of course. Breed said the money wasn't a problem. There's real trouble up there.'

Msour dashed back into the house and emerged minutes later with a shirt on and a large kitbag – containing his beads, skirt, gourd and whisk, Bond supposed – and followed Bond out to the Peugeot. Msour chucked his kitbag in the back and climbed into the car beside Bond.

'I don't like to doing this at night, you know. That is why I go charge you extra, extra.'

'I quite understand,' Bond said and started the engine, roaring off down the road towards Port Dunbar at high speed. After five minutes they passed through a large plantation of oil palms and Bond slowed, keeping his eyes open for the turning he'd spotted earlier on the way out. He turned off the road on to a dirt track that led into the plantation, the one headlight of Sunday's Peugeot illuminating the serried trunks of the palm trees.

'Where you dey go?' Msour asked.

'Short cut. We're in a hurry,' Bond said and then turned off the track and drove into the plantation itself, bumping along the avenue of palm trees.

'You done go craze, man!' Msour shouted.

'Shit. Wrong turning,' Bond said. 'Sorry.' He stopped the car, put the gear lever into reverse and then punched Msour full in the face, knocking his head back so heavily against the window-pane that it smashed with a tinkle of glass. Msour cried in pain and Bond reached across him, opened the door and kicked him out of the car. Bond leaped out and ran round to find Msour on his hands and knees, shaking his head as if he couldn't believe what had happened to him. Bond stood above him and brought the edge of his hand down full force on to the exposed nape of his neck with a karate chop. Msour was flattened, face in the dirt, poleaxed, out cold.

Bond opened the boot and dragged Msour's limp body over, tipping him into the space. Msour made no sound as Bond rolled him on to his back and forced his mouth open. He unscrewed the cap on his ketchup bottle and filled Msour's gaping mouth with some of the solution. He sat him up and heard the fluid go down with a reflex gurgle then repeated the process. He should be comatose for at least forty-eight hours, according to Quentin Dale of Q Branch. Then Bond added the kitbag and the two litres of water Sunday had provided in a plastic container and slammed the boot shut, locking it. He took the clasp knife Sunday had brought out of his pocket and punctured all four tyres. The Peugeot settled with a hissing wheeze of escaping air. Then with a rock he smashed the windscreen and the remaining windows. Finally he kicked dents in the bodywork and threw handfuls of dirt and leaves over the car.

He looked around. He was in the heart of the plantation far from the road and the dirt track. It was doubtful that anyone would casually come across the Peugeot here – if they did there was little to scavenge; it looked like an old wreck. And even if Msour came round in a day or so and shouted and banged on the lid of the boot it was highly unlikely he'd be heard. Bond was hoping for two or three days, at least. With a little luck Msour might be missing for even more.

He walked back to the track and, turning, saw that the Peugeot was invisible. He set off and after five minutes regained the road to Port Dunbar. He tossed his hat and webbing belt into a deep ditch by the roadside, untucked his trousers from his boots and flagged down the first taxi he saw, asking to be taken to the Press Centre. A good night's work, he thought – $50 well spent – time for a drink, a bite to eat and then bed. He just wished it could be as easy to deal with Geoffrey Letham. The Letham problem nagged at him – he realised it would be for the best if he could find a solution to that issue as well.

·18·

ONE-WAY TICKET OUT

Bond kept very much to himself the next two days. He stayed in his room writing up an account in encrypted plain-code of everything that had happened to him (the narrative looked like notes for an article set in rural France: he was a woman, Blessing a man, the war a complex property deal). It would mean nothing to any other reader but for him it would function as an important aide-memoire for his eventual report to M, given that absolutely nothing about this mission had really gone to plan.

On the first morning, Sunday reappeared in an ancient woodwormed Morris Traveller that he had bought for $10. They set off in it for a day trip to the blockaded port of Port Dunbar – which, because of the copious silting of the Zanza River Delta, was now some ten miles to the south of the city itself. Bond wandered along its empty quays and wharves, its giant rusty cranes and derricks standing sentinel over empty tracts of water, listening to the far-booming surf beyond the harbour. He knew that out at sea the two ex-Royal Navy frigates that comprised the Zanzarim Marine Force were patrolling the Bight of Benin looking for blockade runners. And further out at sea, waiting for its moment, was Hulbert Linck's cargo vessel full of 'serious stuff' that might just change the course of this war.

Bond stood on the dockside looking out at the horizon feeling himself in a strange kind of limbo, thinking that everything would change – or that nothing might change. He thought of Tony Msour unconscious in the boot of the Peugeot hidden in the midst of an oil-palm plantation – what effect would his mysterious absence have on events? It was an act of audacious inspiration that might have no consequence at all, or else it would materially alter everything. It was all in the balance – he had played his best cards, now he could only wait and see.

As one day dragged into the next he began to feel that time was a curious irrelevance. He had his room in the Press Centre, he was fed, he could buy a drink. Somewhere to the north of the city, on the forest roads and tracks, across creeks and marshy expanses, by collapsed bridges and mined causeways, Zanzarim soldiers confronted Dahumian ones, everybody waiting – waiting to see what might happen next.

Then the first symbol of that possible change arrived in the late afternoon of the second day after the abduction of Tony Msour. Suddenly, the city's air-raid sirens sounded and for the first time Bond sensed something crack in the ordered discipline of the population of Port Dunbar. It wasn't panic but it was fearfulness, anxiety, and the streets became full of people running, frantically looking for shelter. He thought he could hear the distant roar of jet engines and a SAM missile was fired – more in hope than expectation – from the battery in the central square. Then, after twenty minutes the all-clear sounded. Breadalbane said that a MiG had been shot down but no one believed him.

The next morning Kobus Breed came to see him at the Press Centre. Bond was surprised.

'You booked your passage out?' Breed asked.

'Not yet,' Bond said, carefully. 'Why do you ask?'

Breed lowered his voice, as if he might be overheard. 'I might need your expertise,' he said. 'We've got a massive Zanza Force build-up on the main highway. We've seen heavy armour – Centurion tanks. And the artillery shelling has gone up two hundred per cent. Something big's about to happen.'

'Look,' Bond said. 'Kololo was a one-off. You're the brave soldier being paid five thousand dollars a month to fight for Dahum, not me.'

'We could always arrange something.'

'I'm not a military man any more,' Bond said. 'You're on your own.'

'And our bloody fetish priest has disappeared,' Breed said. 'Can you believe it? Picked up by a "white soldier" three days ago.'

'One of your guys?'

'Absolutely no.'

Bond shrugged. 'Can't you get another fetish priest?'

'You must be joking. He's the only one they believe in.'

It was enough of a sign for Bond – equilibrium had gone – or was going fast. That evening he drove out to Janjaville and paid Hulbert Linck $100 to fly out on a Super Constellation the following night.

Linck looked at him shrewdly.

'Do you know something we don't, Mr Bond?'

'I've been summoned home,' Bond said, resignedly. 'Personally,

I'd love to stay on. See your famous running of the blockade. See your ship come in. I'm missing the big story.'

'The sooner the better,' Linck said, looking worried. 'There's a big Zanza Force push coming. We've got eight flights due in tonight.'

He turned and looked at the Constellation as it was being unloaded. As a truck backed away the wash of its headlights momentarily illuminated the nose of the plane. Bond peered closer – and was astonished to see, stencilled just below the cockpit, a sign that he had last observed in Bayswater, London: AfricaKIN.

He glanced at Linck but he was giving nothing away. What was this all about, Bond asked himself? And then thought – perhaps it was a former AfricaKIN charter; someone had simply forgotten to remove the logo. But it was another coincidence – and here in Dahum Bond was very suspicious of coincidences. What connection could Gabriel Adeka have with Linck and his blockade-running? Some sort of subterfuge? Were they using AfricaKIN funds? Exploiting its good name . . . ?

'Well, good luck to you,' Bond said, his mind still turning with the implications. 'See you tomorrow night.'

Bond slept badly. He kept hearing, in his half-sleep, urgent knocking on his door. Convinced it was Blessing he went to open it twice. Of course it was all in his troubled imagination. At dawn he woke to hear the distant sound of explosions and again the air-raid siren went off. This time a solitary MiG streaked low over the city, just above the rooftops, shattering the morning peace – too low and too fast to loose off a SAM.

Another indication, Bond thought, as he packed up his few

belongings and emptied the remains of his coma-inducing drugs down the toilet. He had lunch with Breadalbane who told him that Dupree, Haas and Letham had gone up to the front to see if this news of a Zanza Force thrust was genuine or not.

Bond told him he was booked out on a flight that night and he could see the news disturbed Breadalbane.

'But why?' he asked, uncomprehendingly. 'You're going to miss everything.'

'I just think it's time to go,' Bond said and offered him the loan of $100 if he wanted to leave also.

'Can't do that,' Breadalbane said. 'No, no. I have to stick it out. Have to. Otherwise why have I spent all these months here?' He thought for a while. 'Actually, the loan would be very handy, all the same – if you could spare the cash.'

Dupree and Haas came back in the afternoon in a state of shock. There had been a massive breakthrough on the transnational highway – Centurion tanks crossing rivers on improvised bridges had outflanked Dahumian defences. More worryingly, there was panic and mass desertion by the normally steadfast Dahum troops – all resistance, all morale suddenly gone.

'No juju man,' Haas said. 'Breed is going insane. He shot three of his own men for deserting. Even the mercenaries are talking of leaving now.'

By late afternoon the heavy detonation of artillery shells was audible in central Port Dunbar and columns of black smoke were rising from the northern outskirts. The streets of the city emptied as if in response to some silent order. Sunday drove Bond out to the airport in sombre mood.

'We done lose this war, Mr Bond. It finish. We don't want fight no more.'

They motored out to Janjaville past columns of dishevelled soldiers retreating on the airstrip, where some sort of final defensive ring was being formed. Bond noted the new trenches, barbed wire and gun emplacements but there seemed little sign of martial spirit among the troops. He saw officers striking men with bamboo batons and the soldiers looked frightened and resentful. No one wants to be the doomed rearguard, Bond realised. In the distance the sound of gunfire and explosions grew ever louder as the Zanzarim army advanced into Port Dunbar.

Janjaville airstrip had never been busier. Two DC-3s and a Fokker Friendship were parked in front of the hangar and, as Bond arrived, he saw Linck's Malmös take off and head east, away from the fighting, their mercenary pilots all too aware of what was impending.

Bond said a heartfelt farewell to Sunday and gave him the remains of his dollars. He told Sunday to go to the oil-palm plantation the next morning. 'You'll see the Peugeot there, off the track'. He gave more specific directions. 'There's a man locked in the boot. I want you to let him out. Don't say anything. You were just passing by.'

'I don't know you, sar.'

'Exactly. It'll be our secret.'

They shook hands and Bond wished him good luck.

Bond confirmed that his place was secure on the flight, due to leave in an hour. He encountered Hulbert Linck, who was agitated and fretful. 'How could this have happened?' he kept repeating, rhetorically. 'A week ago we were in total control. Total control.' To Bond's eyes Linck seemed untypically distressed, all his old confidence gone, as if there was something more at stake than the fate of Dahum, something that touched him personally.

'That's the fortunes of war for you,' Bond said, conscious of the scant comfort in this lame adage. He said goodbye to Linck and walked over to the Quonset hut that did duty as a departure lounge.

Soon Haas and Dupree joined him, complaining that the price of a seat on the Constellation had now risen to $500, and then the mercenaries began to arrive, awkward in their civilian clothes, their guns and swagger left behind. They looked edgy and uncomfortable, having no desire to be subject to the full-blooded retribution of the Zanzarim army.

Bond stood by the window watching the families and retainers of the Dahumian junta board one of the DC-3s and the Fokker Friendship. And then came the members of the government themselves – he saw Abigail Kross and Colonel Denga amongst them. The die was cast now. He watched both planes take off and realised that the Republic of Dahum was officially rudderless – he wondered if the terrified soldiers manning the perimeter knew that they were now on their own.

Just as he was beginning to worry vaguely that their own departure might not take place he saw the Constellation swoop in, land and taxi round to its usual position in front of the hangar. However, this time the engines were cut. The plane was empty, Bond supposed. And once again he saw the AfricaKIN logo on the nose – and it was a different Constellation from the one he'd seen the night before, traces of an old airline livery marking it out as another aircraft. What had Gabriel Adeka to do with these last perilous flights in and out of the shrinking Dahum heartland? Why this overt connection? Bond turned away from the window, questions yammering in his head. Was it some final gesture of solidarity between the Adeka brothers? A sign that Gabriel had heard of Solomon's death and had stepped in? Or simply some futile, symbolic despatch of aid before the war ended . . . ? He wandered back to rejoin Haas and Dupree, thinking there was no point in further speculation. Once he had safely left Dahum he could investigate further.

The mood in the Quonset hut was increasingly tense. The sound of small arms was now audible – the pop and chatter of machine guns – and from time to time nervous sentries triggered bursts of aimless fire into the darkness of the night. Bond sat apart, taking in the images of almost-chaos of a small country about to forcibly lose its brief identity forever. Its government had fled; its highly paid foreign mercenaries – about to flee – were passing themselves off as civilians; a few hundred frightened and reluctant troops had been ordered – at gunpoint, no doubt – to keep the airstrip open until the last rat had left the sinking ship and they could all throw their guns away and go back home.

He was not pleased to see Letham arrive. He was wearing a white linen suit with a raffish navy bandana at his neck and he actually asked Haas to take a photograph of him standing beside the armed soldier guarding the door. His new picture by-line, Bond assumed. Ace foreign correspondent Geoffrey Letham reporting fearlessly from the world's crisis zones. Bond saw him look over in his direction and was grateful when he didn't approach. He and Letham had nothing more to say to each other – and, with a bit of luck, would never see each other again after tonight. There were minor satisfactions to register about the fall of Dahum, he considered.

A crew member came in from the Constellation and all the mercenaries were invited to board. Bond heard the engines spark and fire up, generating their throaty rumble. The four journalists joined the back of the queue.

Haas looked round, his face was sweaty. 'They seem to be getting closer,' he said.

'Did you see Breadalbane before you left?' Bond asked. 'I lent him some cash – thought he might have changed his mind and decided to join us.'

'I told him,' Dupree said. 'I said that with all the mercenaries gone he'll be the only white man in Port Dunbar. Not a good idea, I said. A most uncomfortable situation. I thought he'd be here.'

Bond was about to reply when three soldiers pushed their way in, all carrying AK-47s, swathed in bandoliers of bullets and somehow looking more capable and alarming than the demoralised men manning the defences. They wore the soft, peaked kepis that the mercenaries favoured. Everyone went quiet.

'Who is James Bond?' one of the soldiers called out.

Bond stepped forward. There was no hiding place here.

'I am,' he said.

'Come with us. The rest of you please to board the plane.'

Bond picked up his grip, feeling his mouth dry, suddenly. What was this – had Msour been found and somehow identified him? He followed the three soldiers out of the Quonset hut, glancing back over his shoulders to see the others striding energetically across the grass towards the Constellation, its four engines now turning in a shimmering blur in the airport lights.

'What's going on?' Bond asked, feigning minor irritation – he was feeling concern mount in him. 'I need to be on that plane.'

'Someone wants to talk with you,' the soldier said.

Perhaps it was Linck, Bond thought, though his worries didn't subside. The last DC3 was still there, its propeller blades now beginning to revolve slowly as the generator fired up the engines, the exhausts coughing out smoke. Perhaps Linck wanted them to fly out together. But Bond recognised the symptoms – he was trying to put a benign gloss on serious alarm. It never worked – something was wrong here.

Bond was being led towards the concrete blockhouse of the control tower, he saw. A door in the side was opened and he was ordered in. He found himself in a windowless cement cell with a neon tube in the ceiling casting an unkind glaring light.

'Excuse me. What's happening?' he asked, still managing to preserve his tone of mild irritation. 'Can you tell me? Who am I meant to meet?'

One soldier left, to fetch the person who wanted to talk to him, Bond supposed. The other two stood by the closed door, hands resting on the AK-47s slung across their fronts.

Bond paced slowly to and fro, affecting unconcern, but his mind was hyperactive. Something must have gone very wrong – but what? No clever strategy suggested itself.

Two minutes went by, then five. The only thing that reassured Bond was that the idling motors of the Constellation hadn't changed pitch. It must still be in position, waiting for the final passengers to arrive before taking off.

Then Kobus Breed came through the door. He was wearing a light blue seersucker suit and a yellow tie. Bond almost laughed – he looked so different. Bond noticed that he held one hand behind his back.

'Kobus, hello,' he said. 'You look very smart. What's going on?' Breed's thick neck didn't suit a collar and tie, Bond thought. It looked like a bad disguise.

Breed wasn't smiling any more. 'What's going on is that you're a devious bastard, Bond.'

'No more devious than you are,' Bond said. 'We all have our strategies for survival. Look at you.' He gestured at Breed's new clothes. 'Very man-about-town, all of a sudden.'

'Yah. But your strategy's just been discovered. What did you do with Tony Msour?'

'I don't know what you're talking about.'

Breed let the hand that was behind his back swing into view. He was holding one of his big fish hooks.

'I don't have time to piss around with you, Bond. This hook's got your name on it. I'm going to let you swing from the control tower – a special welcome for Zanza Force. But, before I kill you I just want you to know that I know what you did and I know who you are. Your fellow journalist, Letham, was most helpful. Seems nobody in the entire world of journalism has ever heard of you.'

'Letham is scum. I wouldn't believe anything he says.'

Breed stepped up to him and punched him in the face. Bond ducked and Breed's fist slammed into his left temple. He went down. Breed kicked him heavily in the ribs and Bond felt one stave in.

His vision blurred. He heard the noise of the Constellation's engines grow more shrill as the revs were increased. Bond hauled himself to his feet, swaying, a sharp pain in his side.

'Look, Breed, whoever told you I—'

He stopped, completely astonished. It was as if he'd seen a vision.

Blessing Ogilvy-Grant had stepped quietly into the room.

'We've got to go,' she said sharply to Breed.

'I've got unfinished business with Mr Bond, here,' Kobus said. He dropped his hook with a clang and took a small automatic out of his inside pocket.

Bond was experiencing a kind of accelerated revelation, an unwelcome one, a massive and dramatic reorganisation of everything he thought he knew.

'Better not mess around,' Blessing said. She looked at Bond but her eyes were cold, lifeless. 'We've no time.'

'OK, I know,' Breed said. 'Let's take the lover out of lover-boy – before I string him up by his jawbone.'

He aimed his automatic at Bond's groin and pulled the trigger.

In that split second Bond turned and the bullet thunked into his right thigh just below the hip with a splash of blood as it exited. Bond felt the hot tear in the meat of his muscle and went down, heavily, spinning with the impact, feeling more pain in his rib. He sensed his trousers dampening with the blood flow.

Hulbert Linck shouted from outside.

'We leave in ten seconds!'

Blessing snatched Breed's gun from him.

'Stop fooling around!' she snarled and fired.

Bond felt the punch as the bullet hit him in his chest and he fell back.

He heard the door slam shut and sensed his consciousness begin to leave him, encroaching shadows gathering at the edge of his vision. He tried to sit up but his hand slipped in the spreading pool of his own blood and he fell back to the floor again. Best not to move, he told himself as the room went steadily dark, best to stay very still. The last thing he heard was the sound of the Constellation taxiing to the end of the runway and the roar of its engines as it took off, fading, fading, fading . . .

PART THREE

GOING SOLO

·1·

CARE AND ATTENTION

James Bond stood a little shakily under the hot shower, both hands gripping the chrome rails on either side of the stall. He closed his eyes, letting the water run over his face, hearing the sharp patter of the spray on the sheets of plastic that were taped over his dressings on his thigh and chest. It was his first shower in almost five weeks. It felt like the first shower of his life, so intense was the pleasure he was taking in it. He managed to wash his hair with one hand – still holding on with the other – and then turned off the water and stepped out. He'd forgotten his towel – left on the end of his bed in his room.

The door opened and Sheila McRae, the nurse he liked best, came in, his towel in her hand.

'Just in time, eh, Commander?'

Bond stood there naked, dripping, as Sheila checked the plastic protection over his dressings. She chattered away.

'It's a wee bit chilly this morning but at least it's no raining. Aye, they're all fine.'

She helped Bond on with his dressing gown after he'd dried himself and Bond reflected on the curious, intimate non-intimacy that existed between nurse and patient. You could be standing there, naked, as your bedpan was emptied or a catheter was inserted in your penis, chatting to the nurse about her package holiday in Tenerife as if you were passing time at a bus stop waiting for your bus to arrive. They had seen everything, these nurses, Bond realised. Words like prudish, embarrassed, shocked, disgusted or ashamed simply weren't in their vocabulary. Perhaps that was why people – why men – found them so attractive.

Sheila was in her late twenties with an animated, fresh prettiness about her. She had thick unruly blonde hair that she found difficult to pin up neatly beneath the little starched white bonnet that topped off the nurses' uniforms here. She had two children and her husband was a welder at the Rosyth dockyards. She had told Bond a great deal about herself over the weeks of his recovery. The covert nature of this wing of the sanatorium meant that all the conversational traffic tended to be one-way.

They walked back slowly along the corridor to Bond's private room, Bond still limping slightly. He had a drain in his thigh wound, a corrugated rubber tube emerging from the muscle with a clamp at the end. When he slipped back into bed it would be connected to a glass Redivac suction jar with two erect antennae that flopped limply when the vacuum was spent. He had developed a perverse dislike for the suction jar but there was still some infection in the thigh wound and the drain still dripped. However, his chest had healed remarkably well, the entry and exit wounds now two puckered rosy coins, new additions to the palimpsest of scars his body carried.

He was in a military sanatorium located in a discreet corner of a large army base to the south of Edinburgh. There were six private rooms in his wing all reserved for soldiers, sailors and airmen with serious health issues requiring twenty-four-hour intensive care. Or, to put it another way, rooms reserved for military personnel who needed to keep their injuries secret – almost all of the patients were from special forces.

'Oh, yes, I forgot to tell you,' Sheila said as they reached his door. 'You've got a visitor.'

Bond stepped into his room and to his astonishment saw M standing there looking out of the window. He turned and smiled. He was wearing a heavy brown tweed three-piece suit. He was so out of context that Bond felt it was like seeing Nelson's Column on a village green.

'James,' he said. 'You're looking extremely well.'

They shook hands.

'It's very good of you to come all this way to visit me, sir,' Bond said, feeling a great upwelling of affection for this elderly man, all of a sudden.

'Oh, I didn't come to see you. I've got a few days' shooting in Perthshire. Thought I'd kill several birds with one stone.' M chuckled, pleased with his joke. 'Got anything to drink?' he asked.

'They give you a bottle of sherry to help with your appetite but I wouldn't recommend it. Wouldn't even cook with it. I haven't touched a drop.'

'Thought as much,' M said and took a half-bottle of Dewar's whisky out of his pocket and placed it on Bond's bedside table.

'I was going to bring grapes and chocolate but I thought you'd prefer this,' M said. 'I do hope you won't get into trouble.'

Bond went into his bathroom and found a tooth-glass. He washed out a teacup and poured a fair-sized dram for them both.

'*Slangevar*,' M said and clinked his glass against Bond's cup. 'Here's to your speedy recovery.'

Bond took a cautious sip of his whisky. It was the first alcohol he'd drunk since Dahum. He felt its wondrous, comforting warmth bloom and fill his throat and chest.

'Perfectly, magnificently therapeutic,' he said and topped them both up.

'When will they let you out?' M asked.

'In a week or two, I think. Getting stronger every day.'

'Well, take a month's leave when they do,' M said. 'Get properly fit again. You deserve it. It's not every day a man can say he ended a war.'

'And I even got a medal,' Bond said, a little sardonically.

'And you've earned the gratitude of Her Majesty's Government.' M fished his pipe out of his pocket. 'Can I smoke in here?'

Bond said he could and lit a cigarette himself.

'I know you'll write a full report, eventually,' M said, 'so there's no need to go through the whole business now. But you may have some questions for me.'

Bond did, indeed. 'How did I get out?' he asked. When he'd regained consciousness he was tied down on a gurney in a Royal Air Force transport plane heading for Edinburgh. None of the various doctors who'd treated him since then could give any explanation of what had happened to him.

'You were found by a journalist called Digby Breadalbane,' M said. 'He was making for the airstrip himself but got held up in the chaos – panicking troops, deserters, total disarray. By the time he arrived the last plane had left. Once the planes had gone no defence was offered and the Zanzari army overran the airstrip in minutes. Still, there were a few bullets flying around so this Breadalbane fellow went to take shelter in the control tower and found you, unconscious, lying in a pool of blood.'

Bond took this in, nodding. Digby Breadalbane, his guardian angel . . .

'Actually there was a rather good article by him in the *Observer* last Sunday. "Death of a Small Country". You should read it – no mention of you, of course.'

So Breadalbane had his scoop after all, Bond thought.

M plumed smoke at the ceiling light. 'Fortunately some of our special forces were with the Zanzarim army.'

'Ah, yes, the "advisers", of course.'

'Yes . . . They patched you up as best they could and put you in a helicopter for Sinsikrou. Twenty-four hours later you were on your way here.'

'I was lucky,' Bond said, feeling a little disturbed at all these contingencies that had randomly conspired to save him.

'Lucky 007,' M said with an unusually warm smile.

Bond thought back to that night at the Janjaville airstrip and the chilling look in Blessing's eyes as she'd levelled the gun at him and pulled the trigger. Lucky, yes . . . Her shot had hit him high on the right side of his chest, in under the collarbone and out at the shoulder. The right lung collapsed but no other internal damage.

'Any news of Ogilvy-Grant?' Bond asked.

'He's very well and living in Sinsikrou and wondering why you never made contact.'

'*He?*'

'Edward Benson Ogilvy-Grant, fifty-one years old, ex-Royal Marine captain, head of station in Zanzarim.'

'The Ogilvy-Grant I dealt with was a young woman.'

M looked shrewdly at him. 'Yes. You were well duped. And you didn't follow procedure.'

'I did follow procedure.' Bond resented the implication. 'Q Branch told me Ogilvy-Grant would make contact after I arrived. And she did.'

'It seems she may have been Ogilvy-Grant's secretary. Her real name is Aleesha Belem.'

'Jesus Christ.' Bond shook his head. 'Which would explain how she knew all about me.' He paused. 'But she was damn good – really good . . . So, who was she working for?'

'We don't know. But a lot of people are interested in Zanzarim.'

Bond thought of Blessing's clever duplicities: the perfect shabby office; Christmas, the driver; her own carefully constructed biography – the Scottish engineer father, her Celtic colloquialisms, Cheltenham Ladies' College, Cambridge, Harvard . . . And the lovemaking, of course. At least M didn't know about that.

'Could she have been working for the Dahum Republic?' Bond asked.

'Could be . . . Did you come across a man called Hulbert Linck?'

'Yes,' Bond said. 'A one-man arms dealer – single-handedly trying to arm, protect and save Dahum. A man of no fixed abode, it seems.'

'Shady character,' M said.

'There was something bogus about him, as if he was acting a part.'

'Be that as it may, he's disappeared. So has she. Perhaps someone killed them.'

Bond topped up his whisky – M declined. 'There was a man called Kobus Breed – a mercenary from Rhodesia,' Bond said. 'A psychopath, but a clever one. She was working with him, I now think. Perhaps he killed her.'

'We can't find Mr Breed, either. But no, it wouldn't have been his show. Somebody else was pulling the strings. Still, they may have got out of Dahum but at least they lost everything.' M smiled. 'Thanks to you. You can't be very popular with that lot – don't expect a Christmas card.'

M stood up and put down his glass, searched his pockets absentmindedly then lifted his hat and coat off the hook on the back of the door.

'Call in when you get back from your holiday,' M said. 'Go somewhere nice and relax. You've had a hell of a time and you're lucky to be alive. Get yourself really fit and well – be self-indulgent.' He patted Bond's shoulder.

Bond stood and they shook hands again as they parted. There was a tiny but palpable current of mutual feeling in the room, Bond thought, of barely discernible emotion. For all Bond knew, M only possessed a superior's affectionate regard for him – the respect due to a trusted and prized operative who'd done a good job and had put his life on the line. But, on his side, Bond wanted to show that he was genuinely grateful for this unexpected, informal visit, all the same – that it marked something out of the ordinary, out of the line of mere duty, somehow – but he couldn't think of anything to say without making a fool of himself or embarrassing M.

'Thanks for the whisky, sir,' was all he could manage in the end.

·2·

DONALDA AND MAY

Three days later the ward sister yanked out the rubber tube draining Bond's thigh. It was one of the most unpleasant sensations he could recall experiencing, as if some sinew or vein had been bodily wrenched from his side. His head reeled as she reapplied the dressing and taped it down again. The sister was a rather wonderful woman who treated Bond with pointed egalitarianism – he could have been a duke or a kitchen skivvy and nothing would change in her manner, he knew.

'There you are, Commander,' she said, with an ironic smile, using his rank for the first time. 'A normal human being once more – no tubes hanging out of you.'

After she'd gone Bond went into his bathroom and looked at himself in the mirror above the sink. He was pale and he'd lost weight and the scar on his face stood out more starkly, he thought. He felt well enough but not particularly strong, not his usual self. Still, he couldn't hang around until his physical status quo returned. There was work to be done. He had been thinking hard since M's visit and the unexpected offer of a month's leave. A whole month – what could be achieved in four weeks? As far as M was concerned he had carried off his mission with flying colours, but from Bond's point of view there was a sour taste of bitter dissatisfaction and incompleteness. Two people had tried to kill him – one had tried to maim him in the most brutal way possible; the other was a woman he had made love to in all openness and generosity of spirit, and she had tried to deliver the *coup de grâce* to a man who was already grievously wounded. He couldn't forget those terrible seconds in the control tower at Janjaville airstrip – he would never forget them. To stare death in the face like that, to feel bullets impact on your own vital body . . . You couldn't, you shouldn't, just write that down to experience, walk away with a shrug and congratulate yourself on your luck. Fate and blind chance had conspired to keep him alive. Many people had tried to kill Bond over his career and, more often than not, he had managed to show them the folly of that ambition. M had told him to relax, get well, cosset himself – but at the forefront of his mind he wanted retribution, he wanted to hunt these people down and confront them. He wanted to be their grim nemesis and revel in that moment. What was the point of a month's holiday when this was your frame of mind? No – this was an opportunity to be seized. His superior officer had gifted him a month of repose and idleness. Bond decided instead, with hardening resolve, that these days were going to be put to exceptionally good use.

He pulled on his dressing gown over his pyjamas, and left the private wing, going down to the ward sister's station at the foot of the stairs. He asked if he could make some telephone calls and was directed to a glassed-in cubicle with a pay telephone inside. Once he'd borrowed some change he made three calls:

first to his bank to arrange a transfer of money; then he telephoned Donalda and asked for an address and finally he was put through to his secretary, Minty Beauchamp, and told her he was going on holiday for a month and would be out of contact.

As he lay in bed that night, Bond plotted the nature of his revenge in more detail – revenge on Blessing Ogilvy-Grant (or whatever name she was now going under) and Kobus Breed, the man with two faces. And throw in Hulbert Linck for good measure, he thought, if it turned out he'd been involved in Bond's purported assassination. And as he speculated about what he might do to these people, as and when he caught up with them, he felt peace of mind slowly returning, but he didn't forget that they too, if they were alive, might simultaneously be plotting their revenge on James Bond, the man who had messed up their little war in Africa. Somehow he was sure that they would know he hadn't died in the concrete cell beneath the Janjaville control tower. Any dead Briton found in the aftermath of Dahum's collapse would have made some newspaper or news bulletin, somewhere. No, the absence of comment would be seen as confirmation of his unlikely survival.

In any event, a plan was slowly taking shape in his mind – but it was a plan he had to carry out himself. It could have nothing to do with his role as a Double O operative, M or the Service. It had to be wholly unauthorised – it had to be rogue action. He smiled to himself in the darkness of his room: in a way the fact that it would be unauthorised would make it all the sweeter. He intended to 'go solo', as he phrased it to himself. In the unwritten ethos of the Secret Service he knew that such solo personal initiatives were strictly forbidden.

Punishments for going solo were draconian. Bond smiled to himself – he didn't care. He knew absolutely what he wanted to do.

The next day he dressed in a dark navy flannel suit, white shirt and black tie (his clothes had been sent from Chelsea by Donalda) and went down to administration and informed the duty officer that he was discharging himself. A doctor was summoned who strictly forbade him to leave – he needed at least another week to ten days to recover fully. Bond said he was going to stay with a cousin on his estate in South Uist in the Hebrides and gave a name and address – there was no telephone but he could always be reached by telegram – and took full responsibility for his decision.

Bond sought out Sheila and said goodbye, thanking her warmly and kissing her on the cheek, then a taxi was summoned and he was driven to Edinburgh. In a bank in George Street he withdrew £300 in cash. He next went to an oyster bar off Princes Street where he ordered a bottle of Veuve Clicquot, a dozen oysters and smoked salmon and scrambled egg. At Waverley Station he bought a first-class sleeper ticket to London and boarded the train. He took a sleeping pill and slept all the way through the night as the train thundered southwards. A steward woke him at six in the morning with a cup of strong British Rail tea and two digestive biscuits. Bond ignored the tea – he didn't drink tea – but gladly ate the biscuits.

He booked himself a room in a clean but somewhat decrepit bed and breakfast near King's Cross under the alias of Jakobus Breed and considered his few options. As far as he was concerned everyone would think he was convalescing in the Hebrides for a month. The address he'd given to the hospital and to Minty was that of Donalda's uncle. The key factor, Bond thought, was that nobody knew he was in London. He had plenty of cash and he had plenty of time – somewhere in the city he would pick up the ghost of a trail that would lead him to his quarry and he had a good idea where to start. But first of all he needed some essential equipment and information that were hidden in his Chelsea flat.

Bond sat in a booth at the rear of the Café Picasso on the King's Road, a carafe of Barolo and a plate of spaghetti amatriciana in front of him, his eyes on the door. He'd finished his spaghetti when Donalda entered and he waved her over. She sat down at the table, unable to conceal how pleased she was to see him as they greeted each other.

'The flat's all finished, sir,' Donalda said. 'And they did a grand job. It's a shame you haven't been here to enjoy it.'

'I've been abroad,' Bond said.

'Have you no been very well? You look a bit pale, sir.'

'I got some kind of bug.'

Bond supposed that May had told Donalda the bare minimum about her employer's unusual job. The less she knew and the fewer questions she asked, the better.

'I don't want anyone to know I'm back in London,' Bond said, choosing his words carefully. 'That's why I'm meeting you here – I think someone may be watching the flat.'

'I've seen nobody suspicious in the square,' Donalda said. 'And

I've been popping in every two or three days – just to check, like, and gather up the post.'

'Good. So you could pop in again, now, and unlatch the big window that looks on to the back garden.'

'Yes, of course.'

'Then leave, and come back as usual in a couple of days.'

'All right, sir.' She couldn't help a small smile of excitement at all this subterfuge.

'And your uncle knows what to say if anyone comes looking for me.'

'You've gone to Inverness. Fishing trip.'

'Perfect. Thank you, Donalda.' Bond poured himself another glass of Barolo. 'Do you want a glass of wine?'

'I'll just have one of those wee frothy coffees, if you don't mind, sir.' She opened her handbag and took out some envelopes. 'There's a few bills need paying and I ran out of cheques.'

Bond gave her the necessary cash and ordered a cappuccino.

'What do I do if I need to get hold of you?' Donalda asked.

'Call the usual number and leave a message for me. Then I'll call you back.'

'Fine,' Donalda said and smiled brightly. 'Delicious coffee, here.'

After Donalda left to go to the flat Bond waited ten minutes then walked down the King's Road to the street adjacent to Wellington Square. There was a covered passageway off the street that led to a small mews where the former stables and coach houses had been converted into workshops and tiny flats. It was possible to ascend a flight of stairs and shin over the wall and drop into the garden that belonged to Bond's basement neighbour.

It was an easy matter to gain access to his rear window – there was a stout trellis and a convenient drainpipe. It was a route that Bond had occasion to use from time to time when he wanted to leave his flat clandestinely. His neighbour – a flautist in a symphony orchestra who was often away on tour – was both incurious and happy with the arrangement. He left his spare set of keys with Bond for safe keeping.

Bond stood on the trellis and pushed up the big sash window then, stepping on to a horizontal length of drainpipe, he climbed easily into his drawing room.

The flat still smelled of paint and builder's putty. He needed to smoke a few cigarettes in the place, he thought, make it his own. He went into his study and lifted the false radiator off the wall by the desk. There was an airbrick behind it that pulled out to reveal a small cavity that contained a spare Walther PPK automatic, extra clips of ammunition, some cash, a set of keys to a bedsit in Maida Vale that he rented as a safe house, and a list of crucial telephone numbers and addresses.

Bond was after some essential contacts and he jotted the telephone numbers down that he might need. He slipped the gun and a clip into his pocket and debated about the Maida Vale bedsit. He decided that the King's Cross bed and breakfast was more anonymous – he didn't want to encounter any other occupants in the house and have to start making up stories about his long absence.

He replaced the brick and rehung the radiator and went to look at his new bathroom. Doig and his team had done a good job. The marble tiling was laid faultlessly, the grouting and the mastic professionally smooth, and the new shower's chrome fittings gleamed invitingly behind its plate-glass door. Bond slid it open and turned on the shower: he heard the pump kick in quietly in its concealed housing beneath the bath. Ordered from America, the pump boosted London's water pressure fourfold. He turned the tap off. There would be plenty of time for domestic pleasures later. Still, he thought, maybe he would make himself a cup of coffee and smoke a cigarette in his new streamlined kitchen. He switched off the lights and padded along the recarpeted corridor and pushed the kitchen door open.

Donalda lay face down on the floor, the hair on the back of her head matted with fresh blood. Bond crouched down beside her and for a ghastly second thought she was dead – then she gave a little moan. Bond gently rolled her on to her side and she opened her eyes – and winced.

'Don't move,' Bond whispered. 'Just lie there.'

He took the Walther from his pocket and quickly searched the flat again, finding no one and no trace of intrusion. But someone must have already been inside when Donalda arrived to unlatch the window. Someone looking to see if James Bond had returned from abroad . . . ?

He returned to the kitchen and carefully sat Donalda up. He found a dishcloth, soaked it in warm water, wrung it out, and dabbed the blood off the back of her head where he could see she had a nasty two-inch cut. She still seemed very dazed.

'I think I'm going to be sick,' she said.

Bond managed to grab a saucepan out of a cupboard before Donalda vomited.

'That's good,' Bond said. 'You're always sick after you've been knocked out. It's a good sign.'

He put the pan in the sink and helped Donalda to her feet, sitting her on a kitchen chair. Then he made her a cup of tea.

'What happened?' he asked. 'Did you see or hear anyone?'

'No. I came in – everything was just as I'd left it. I put the post on the hall table, unlatched the window, came in here and everything went black.'

'Must have been in here behind the door, hoping you wouldn't walk in. Then left.' Bond was thinking: they know where I live. They entered with a key. This was no burglar casually thieving in a Chelsea flat. At least they didn't kill Donalda.

He looked at her as she sat there shivering, both hands cupping her mug of tea, drawing off the warmth. Then she wiped away a tear. The gesture reminded him – Kobus Breed? Could it have been Kobus Breed in his house? As he speculated, Bond felt an unreasoning fury mount in him, not so much at this violation of his personal space but at the fact that Donalda – his Donalda – had been so brutally attacked. Do not prey on my people, Bond said to himself, the consequences for those who do tend to be fatal . . .

He told Donalda he was going to call a taxi to take her to hospital, where her head wound could be examined, cleaned and stitched. She was to say only that she had slipped and fallen – and then to go home and rest in bed for a full twenty-four hours. Then he had a better idea – he called May, who said she would be with them in thirty minutes. Bond relaxed: everything would be taken care of now. While he waited, he packed a few clothes in a suitcase, thinking further. So someone was checking on his movements – was James Bond back in his London flat? Any traces of his presence? If he was truly going solo then he wouldn't be returning here, he felt sure, until this business with Kobus Breed, or whoever else it might be, was fully resolved.

May arrived and took over, telling Bond crossly that he looked 'awfy peely-wally' and that he should take better care of himself, eat three square meals a day and so on. Bond agreed, and promised to do his best. She watched him throw his suitcase into the back garden, say goodbye and climb out of his drawing-room window as if it were the most natural way in the world of leaving your house.

·3·

AfricaKIN

The AfricaKIN sign had been removed and the poster had been replaced with a 'TO LET – ALL ENQUIRIES' notice in the grimy window, now barred with a sliding iron grille. Bond stood across from the parade of shops in Bayswater feeling frustrated. This had been his key line of investigation; he recalled the shock he'd experienced on seeing the AfricaKIN logo on the nose of the Super Constellation at Janjaville airstrip. He had felt sure that Gabriel Adeka would – unwittingly or not – be the route to Hulbert Linck and then to Breed, or whoever else was behind the whole plot. Bond paced around. With the AfricaKIN door closed maybe Blessing – or Aleesha Belem – was the person to search for, but where would he begin to pick up that trail?

Then the door to the shop opened and a young man came out – a young black man – carrying a typewriter. He chucked the typewriter on the back seat of a Mini parked outside and was about to climb in and drive away, when Bond stopped him with a shout and crossed the road to introduce himself – without giving his name – as a friend of Gabriel Adeka and a long-time donor to AfricaKIN.

The young man – who said his name was Peter Kunle – spoke

like an English public schoolboy. He let Bond into the shop so he could have a look around. Everything had gone on the ground floor, even the linoleum, leaving just an empty expanse of noticeably clean concrete amidst the general grime, almost as if it had been freshly laid; and upstairs in Adeka's former office there was only a curling yellowing pile of posters that signalled the place's previous function.

'So did Gabriel close everything down when the civil war ended?' Bond asked Peter Kunle, who had followed him up the stairs.

'Oh, no. AfricaKIN still exists. He's just moved everything to America.'

'America?' Bond was astonished.

'Yes,' Kunle said. 'He's set the whole charity up there – AfricaKIN Inc. He's got major backers, apparently, very big sponsors.'

'When did all this happen?' Bond paced around, picking up a poster and dropping it – a starveling fly-infested child, all too horribly familiar now.

'Maybe a few weeks or so ago,' Kunle said. 'Maybe a bit longer, actually. We all had this round-robin letter explaining what was happening.'

'So everything changed just as the war was ending,' Bond said, trying to get a sense of a narrative.

'Yes. The charity now focuses on the entire continent. Not just Zanzarim – or Dahum, as was. You know, famines, natural disasters, disease, revolutions, anti-apartheid. The whole shebang.'

Bond was thinking hard. 'Where's he gone in America? Do you know?'

'I think it's Washington DC,' Kunle said, adding, 'I didn't know Gabriel that well. I used to help out as a volunteer a little in the early days but there was too much harassment. It was quite frightening sometimes.'

'Yes, he told me,' Bond said.

'He forgot that I'd lent him the office typewriter,' Kunle said. 'That wasn't like Gabriel.'

'What do you mean?'

'He was very scrupulous,' Kunle laughed. 'Self-destructively honest. He even offered to rent the typewriter off me – one pound a week. I said no, of course. So it was odd that he just left it here and didn't tell me. I had to ring up the landlord to get the keys and retrieve it.'

'So, it's now called AfricaKIN Inc.'

'Yes . . . I suppose the offer was too good to refuse. Too much money on the table – a bright shiny future. A shabby rented shop in Bayswater hardly impresses.'

Peter Kunle could tell him little more and apologised as he locked up the place. Bond shook his hand and thanked him for his help.

'Sorry – what was your name again?' Kunle asked as he opened his car door.

'Breed,' Bond said. 'Jakobus Breed. Do tell Gabriel I called round if you ever speak to him.'

They said goodbye and Bond wandered off up the road, pondering his options in the wake of all this new information. So: Gabriel Adeka had upped sticks for the USA and reinvented AfricaKIN in Washington DC as a global philanthropic concern overseeing the entire continent. Perhaps it was all perfectly legitimate and full of charitable integrity. He recalled his meeting with Gabriel Adeka and how impressed he'd been with the force of his quiet zeal and humanity . . . But Bond needed to ask him one pressing question: why was his charity's name on the side of an aeroplane delivering weapons and ammunition to a war zone? What had that to do with his African kinsmen? If he couldn't answer the question he might be able to point Bond in the direction of someone who would.

Bond paused to light a cigarette and noticed he was standing outside the cinema where Bryce Fitzjohn alias Astrid Ostergard's vampire film had been playing the last time he'd been here in Bayswater. What had it been called? Oh, yes: *The Curse of Dracula's Daughter*. It seemed like a year ago, not weeks, Bond thought, smiling to himself as he pictured Bryce's unknowing, innocent striptease for him that night he'd broken into her house. Bryce Fitzjohn – yes, he'd be very happy to see her again, one day.

He wandered on, up towards Hyde Park, still ruminating. There was a trail, thankfully, but it led to America, to Washington DC . . . And thereby lay a major problem. He could buy a plane ticket but could hardly use his own passport to travel. He was meant to be convalescing in South Uist, not taking international flights across the Atlantic. One way or another word would get out and he'd be in trouble.

Bond crossed the Bayswater Road and strolled into Hyde Park. What he needed was a fake passport and he needed it fast – in a day, two days, maximum. This was the major disadvantage about going solo – lack of resources. Normally, he'd call Q Branch and have a perfect used passport – full of stamps and frankings from foreign journeys – with his new name in an hour. He thought about the numbers he'd jotted down from the contact list in his flat. No, there was no one who could do a complete job like that in the short time necessary. Bond sauntered on. Maybe he could steal someone else's? He started glancing at passers-by, looking for men of his age who vaguely resembled him and then realised that most people didn't conveniently carry their passport on them, unless they were foreign visitors. Perhaps he'd need to go to an airport. No, it wouldn't be—

He stopped. It had come to him like a revelation. All you had to do was give your brain enough time to work. A solution always presented itself.

·4·

VAMPIRIA,
QUEEN OF DARKNESS

Amerdon Studios was situated on the banks of the Thames between Windsor and Bray and consisted of a large rambling red-brick Victorian country house with a couple of sound stages built on what had been a parterred garden modelled on Versailles. Around the sound stages there was the usual cluster of wooden shacks and Nissen huts that contained storage rooms for props and equipment and the various technical workshops that a modern film studio required.

He told the surly man supervising the visitors' car park that he was Astrid Ostergard's agent and was sent to sound stage number two, where *Vampiria, Queen of Darkness* was shooting.

Bond headed over, briskly, a man with purpose, on important business. A couple of phone calls – one to the distributor of Bryce's last film, *The Curse of Dracula's Daughter*, and then to the office of her talent agent, a company called Cosmopolitan Talent International – had elicited the information that Astrid Ostergard was not available to open Bond's new department store in Hemel Hempstead because she was busy filming *Vampiria, Queen of Darkness* at Amerdon Studios. No, absolutely impossible, thank you very much, Mr Bond, nothing you can say will make any difference, goodbye.

As Bond approached sound stage number two he saw groups of extras in dinner suits and evening dress lounging around chatting and drinking tea out of wax-paper cups. One of them left her folding canvas chair and Bond swiftly purloined the script that she'd neglected to take with her. He asked a fat man coiling lengths of electric cable where he could find the production offices and was directed to a long caravan parked beside the sound stage.

Bond knocked on the open door and a harassed-looking woman glanced up crossly from an adding machine into which she'd been ferociously tapping figures.

'Yes?' she said. Tap-tap-tap.

'Randolph Formby,' Bond said in a patrician accent, holding up his script distastefully. 'Equity. I need to see Astrid Ostergard. She's two years behind on her payments.'

Bond had once enjoyed a short affair with an actress who'd told him that every theatrical, televisual and cinematic door opened when the word 'Equity' was pronounced, such was the power and sway of the actors' trade union. Bond was pleased he'd remembered and curious to see if it actually worked.

'Bloody Astrid!' the woman exclaimed. 'So sorry. Typical. Jesus Christ!' She carried on muttering swear words to herself as she walked Bond around sound stage number two to where a row of caravans was parked.

'Third on the right,' she said. Then, adding nervously, 'There's not going to be a problem, is there? With Astrid, I mean. We're already five days behind.'

'I can't guarantee anything,' Bond said with a thin apparatchik's smile. 'She has to pay her dues.'

The woman left, still muttering, and Bond approached the caravan, designated by a scrawled sign stuck to the side with 'Astrid Ostergard/Vampiria' written on it.

Bond knocked on the door and uttered the magic word: 'Equity.'

Seconds later Bryce Fitzjohn flung open her door. She was wearing fishnet stockings and a red satin bustier that pushed her breasts up and together to form an impressive cleavage. She looked at Bond blankly for a moment and then laughed – loudly, delightedly.

'I don't believe it,' she said. 'James bloody Bond.'

'Hello, Vampiria,' Bond said. 'I'm here to apologise.'

'Come into my parlour,' she said.

Bryce pulled on a silk dressing gown and Bond sat on a bench seat opposite a make-up table and mirror. He took out his cigarette case and offered it, Bryce selecting a cigarette and lighting it herself. She stared at him as she blew smoke sideways, eyes narrowing.

'I still don't know how you got into my house.'

Bond lit a cigarette. 'It was wrong of me, I admit. I turned up for your party and there was no one there. I thought you were playing some kind of a game, winding me up. So I left you a note.' Bond smiled. 'You should get a better lock on your kitchen door. It was child's play.'

'So what are you? A professional burglar?'

'I shouldn't have done it,' Bond continued, ignoring the question, 'so I've come to say sorry and invite you to dinner. At the Dorchester,' he added. 'Tonight, if you're free.'

Bryce crossed her long legs and Bond took her in. She was wearing a dense blonde wig with red stripes in it and he found her powerfully alluring. Nothing had changed, he thought, remembering their first encounters.

'Well, it's tempting, but I can't go up to town,' she said. 'I've an early call tomorrow morning.'

There was a knock on the door. 'We need you now, Miss Ostergard,' a voice said.

Bryce stood up. Bond did so as well, and for a moment in the confined space of the caravan they were close. Bond sensed her interest in him, renewed. They were each other's type, he realised, it was as simple as that. The attraction was very mutual, it had been from the beginning, from those first moments in the lift at the Dorchester.

'I've got to go to work,' she said. 'You know where my house is in Richmond, don't you? There's a nice little place nearby we can go to. See you at eight.'

·5·

IMPORT–EXPORT

Bond slid very quietly out of Bryce's bed and stood there for a moment, looking down on her as she slept deeply, lying on her side, one breast innocently exposed. She was a beautiful mature woman, Bond thought, pulling on his trousers and remembering the last time he'd made love – weeks and weeks ago – and how different in almost every degree his partner had been then. He moved to the door in bare feet and turned the handle slowly, thinking about the rest-house on the edge of the Zanza River Delta with Blessing Ogilvy-Grant in his arms. He smiled with a certain bitterness – that was when all his misfortunes had begun.

He left the bedroom door ajar by an inch and padded downstairs to Bryce's study. He switched on the light and sat at her desk, sliding open the top drawer and taking out her passport. The date of birth pretty much fitted – and he was more than happy to shed a few years. The name was both masculine and feminine. All he needed to do was have the photograph and the gender designation changed – and he had exactly the man in mind who could do that. He would become Bryce Fitzjohn, 'professional actor'. 'Actress' could be easily tampered with. He slipped the passport into the back pocket of his trousers and went through to the sitting room, where he poured himself an inch of brandy into a tumbler and sipped at it, turning his back to the warm embers still glowing in the grate of the fireplace, thinking back agreeably over their evening together.

Bond had arrived on time (in a taxi from Richmond station) and when Bryce opened the door to him she kissed him on the cheek – a good sign, Bond thought – and he smelled the scent of 'Shalimar' on her. She was wearing a black velvet dress to just above the knee with a low scoop neck. Two diamonds glittered at her ears and her thick blonde hair was brushed casually back from her brow. There was a bottle of Taittinger champagne waiting in an ice bucket on a table in the sitting room that she asked Bond to open. They toasted each other as they had done that evening across the dining room in the Dorchester.

'Here's to breaking and entering,' she said.

'Where's this little restaurant of yours?' Bond said. 'We don't want to be late.'

'It's about ten yards away. I thought it'd be nicer to eat at home.'

They both knew exactly what was going to happen later and that knowledge provided a satisfying sensual undercurrent to their conversation as they ate the meal she cooked for him – a rare sirloin steak with a tomato and shallot salad, the wine a light and fruity Chianti, with a thin slice of lemony torta della nonna to follow.

They were both worldly and sophisticated people of a certain age, Bond reasoned, and no doubt her sexual history was as varied and interesting as his. Well, maybe not quite . . . Still, the point was, Bond thought as he looked at her clearing away the plates, that there was no pretence involved here. No artificial wooing or effortful foreplay. They both candidly wanted each other, in the way that men and women know this instinctively, and they were going to bring this state of affairs about with as much fun and seductive expediency as they chose.

They went back through to the sitting room, where Bond lit the fire. They drank a brandy, smoked a cigarette and talked to each other – deliciously postponing the moment they were waiting for. In fact Bond sensed the timbre of her voice change, dropping, growing huskier, as she told him of the disaster of her last marriage – there had been two – to an American film producer with, it turned out, a significant drug problem. He thought it was remembered emotion, but he quickly sensed that the huskiness in her voice was desire: it was a signal, and when Bond stood up and crossed the floor to her and kissed her she responded with an ardency that surprised him.

They made careful love in her wide bed, Bond relishing the smooth ripeness of her body. Afterwards, she sent him down to the kitchen for another bottle of champagne and they lay in bed drinking and talking.

'You say you're a "businessman",' she said, studying his lean form as he lay there beside her. 'Import–export, whatever that means. Yet you've more scars on your body than a gladiator.'

'I had a difficult and dangerous war,' Bond said.

She reached over, her full breasts shifting, and touched the new puckered rosy coin below his right collarbone.

'You're still fighting it, so it seems.'

He kissed her to stop her speculating further.

'I'll tell you all about it one day,' he said. And they began to make love again.

Bryce's alarm clock rang at five in the morning and she slipped out of bed, washed and dressed. Bond dressed also and the unit car that came to pick her up for the studio detoured to the station so he could catch an early train back to London.

She stepped out of the car so they could say their goodbyes discreetly.

'What're you doing this weekend?' she asked. 'I'm only free on Sunday. This film has another three weeks to run at the studio and I'm in every scene.'

'I've got to go to America,' Bond said. 'Just for a week or two. When your film's finished I'll come and take you away somewhere very, very special that only I know.'

They kissed goodbye and Bond whispered in her ear, 'Thank you for last night. Unforgettable.'

'For me too,' she said and squeezed his hand. Then they parted and Bond, with a full heart and a smile on his face, joined the jaded commuters on the platform at Richmond station. As he waited for the train he took Bryce's passport from his pocket and felt a twinge of guilt. But if she was working for another three weeks she wouldn't be going anywhere and wouldn't miss it. When he came back he'd replace it in her desk drawer – she'd never know. His conscience was assuaged somewhat by the fact that he hadn't made love to her just to steal her passport. He had every intention of seeing his Vampiria, Queen of Darkness, again. He had been stirred and affected by her in a way he had almost forgotten was possible. He'd be back – as soon as he'd administered swift and rough justice to the people who had so nearly killed him. Bryce had no idea how inadvertently important she had been to his plans – he'd find a way to show her his gratitude.

At Waterloo station Bond had his photograph taken in a booth, then he made a telephone call – to one of the numbers he'd retrieved from his flat – and took a taxi to Pimlico, to a shabby street of dirty peeling stucco houses aptly named Turpentine Lane. He rang the door of a basement flat and an elderly man in his sixties, wearing a flat tweed cap and smoking a moist roll-up cigarette, answered the door.

'Mr Bond, sir, always a royal pleasure.'

'Morning, Dennis,' Bond said, stepping past him into the flat to be greeted by a noisome smell of cooking.

'Good God, what's that?'

'Cow-heel stew. Bugger to cook – takes three days – but it tastes something marvellous.'

Dennis Fieldfare was a forger de luxe, occasionally called upon by Q Branch when they felt their own expertise wasn't sufficient. Bond had first met Dennis when he'd needed a post-dated visa to Cuba that would have to pass microscopic inspection. It had raised not the slightest suspicion and had been so good that he'd decided to add Dennis's name to his personal pantheon of experts to be called on, as and when.

Bond showed him Bryce's passport and his photograph.

'Swap the picture, change the sex and tweak "actress" for "actor".'

'That's a bloody insult, Mr Bond. A simple-minded child could do that,' Dennis said, professionally aggrieved.

Bond gave him £50. 'But I need it very fast – this evening – that's why I came to you. Keep the original photo safe – I'll want you to change it back in a couple of weeks. And this is strictly between you and me, Dennis.'

'Doddle, Mr B. And I never seen you,' Dennis said, enjoying the feel of the money in his hand. 'Six o'clock all right?'

At six o'clock that evening Bond had his faultless new passport and was now irrefutably Bryce Connor Fitzjohn, actor, eight years younger than he actually was but he had no complaints there. In fact, he was rather pleased by the coincidence. He had used the name 'Bryce' as a pseudonym before, in the early 1950s as an alias for a long train journey he'd made from New York to St Petersburg, Florida. He'd been John Bryce then and it had worked very well. He hoped Bryce Fitzjohn would prove equally effective. He had a feeling the new name would bring him good luck.

From Dennis's Pimlico flat he went directly to the BOAC terminal at Victoria and bought himself a first-class return ticket to Washington DC, leaving Heathrow airport at 11.30 the following day. It was perhaps an unnecessary expense to choose first class but Bond, despite being an exceptionally well-travelled man, was not the happiest of fliers. The more pampered and indulged he was on an aeroplane the less uneasy he felt when any turbulence or bad weather was encountered. Anyway, he thought, if you'd decided to 'go solo' you might as well do it in style.

PART FOUR

THE LAND OF THE FREE

·1·

BLOATER

Bond looked out of the oval window as the plane began its descent into Dulles airport, Washington DC. The sky was clear and as the plane banked steadily round he had a fine view of the capital of the United States of America. The city lay far below him – they were still thousands of feet high – but Bond could pick out the familiar buildings and landmarks: the cathedral, Georgetown University, the Capitol, the White House, the mighty obelisk of the Washington Monument, the Tidal Basin, the Library of Congress, the Lincoln Memorial – such was the clarity of the light and the angle of the sun. The umber Potomac wound lazily round the western edge of the District of Columbia, flowing down to Chesapeake Bay and, beyond it, the undulating hills and woods of Virginia stretched out towards the Blue Ridge Mountains. It all looked neat and ordered from this high altitude but Bond felt a tension building in him as he wondered what retribution was going to be meted out by him in those streets, busy with traffic. He would take his time, plan his campaign scrupulously and without emotion. Revenge is a dish best served cold, he reminded himself.

'Welcome to the USA, Mr Fitzjohn,' the immigration officer said, stamping his passport. 'Business or pleasure?'

'Bit of both,' Bond said. 'But it's the pleasure I'm looking forward to.'

He was cleared in customs and picked up his suitcase, moving into the main arrivals concourse. He had changed all his money into dollars in London and felt the comforting flat brick of notes in his breast pocket, snug against his heart. He had left his Walther PPK in London, deciding that it was both safer and more efficient to arm himself in America, and besides, he had no idea what or how much firepower he'd require on this particular mission.

He wandered through the concourse looking for the car-rental agencies. He wasn't particularly enamoured of American cars but decided that he'd—

'Bond?'

Bond heard his name called out but deliberately didn't turn round – he was Fitzjohn, now. But it came again.

'Bond. James Bond, surely—'

The voice was closer and the accent was patrician Scottish and not aggressive or hostile. Bond stopped and turned, feeling angry and frustrated. Barely minutes on American soil and already his elaborate cover seemed blown – somebody had recognised him.

The man who was approaching him – beaming incredulity written on his face – was very stout, mid-forties, Bond estimated, with thinning blond hair above a round pink face, wearing a light-grey flannel suit with an extravagant, oversized Garrick Club bow tie. Bond had no idea who he was. There was something immediately dissolute about his plump features, the bags under his eyes and the unnatural roseate flush to his cheeks. This was a man who lived slightly too well. The stranger stood in front of him, arms spread imploringly.

'Bond – it's me, Bloater.'

Bloater. Bond thought, but nothing came.

'I think you may be confusing me with somebody else,' Bond said, politely.

'I'm Bloater McHarg,' the man said.

And now the name conjured up some dim resonance. Bond had indeed known someone called 'Bloater' McHarg, about thirty years before, at his boarding school in Edinburgh – Fettes College. The fat man's features began to assume the configuration of a familiar. Yes – Bloater McHarg, last seen in 1941, Bond calculated.

Bloater offered his hand and Bond shook it.

'Well, well, well,' he said. 'Bloater McHarg. How extraordinary.'

At the beginning of World War Two fat boys were rare in Scottish public schools. 'Bloater' McHarg, undeniably heavily plump – hence the nickname – had become something of a pariah, routinely mocked for his perceived obesity. Then Bond had persuaded him to try out for the heavyweight class in his newly founded Judo Society, the first ever at Fettes. Bloater learned fast and seemed to have a talent for the sport and the other boys soon stopped teasing him once they were subject to some of his Judo holds and painful clinches. Bond had left Fettes at seventeen and had lied about his age to join the navy. All connections with his school had been cut and he'd never seen a fellow pupil or a teacher since. Until today, he thought, ruefully, here in Dulles airport, Washington DC.

'It is James, isn't it?' McHarg said. 'You know, I was just thinking about you the other day – not that I think about you a lot – but you saved me, Bond. Though you probably don't remember.'

'I do seem to remember you throwing an eighteen-stone man on his back when we won the South of Scotland Judo League.'

'Leith Judo Club. We won seven–six.' Bloater McHarg beamed. 'My finest hour. You showed me how to fight.' He put his hands on his hips and stared at Bond, shaking his head in happy bemusement.

'I recognised you at once,' McHarg said. 'You've hardly changed. Scar on your face – that's new. Always a handsome devil. What're you doing in DC?'

'Bit of business.'

'We have to get together, have a drink. Allow me to show you an exceptionally good time. I'm a second secretary here at the embassy. I know all the places to go.' McHarg searched his pockets for a card and found one. Bond took it. Bloater's first name was Turnbull. Turnbull McHarg.

'I don't think I ever knew your first name, Turnbull.'

McHarg took a pen from his pocket and scribbled a phone number on the back of the card.

'That's my home number,' he said. 'Call me when you're settled and have an hour free – we'll have a few jars et cetera, et cetera.' He winked. 'Do you ever see anything of the old crowd? Bowen major, Cromarty, Simpson, MacGregor-Smith, Martens, Tweedie, Mostyn, and whatsisname, you know, the earl's son, Lord David White of—'

'No,' Bond interrupted, flatly, keen to stem the flood of forgotten names. 'I haven't seen anybody at all. Not one. Ever.'

'Do call me,' McHarg insisted. 'You can't leave this town without seeing me again. You won't regret it. It's bloody fate.'

It's a bloody nuisance, Bond thought, turning away with a false assurance that he'd call, a grin and a cheery wave. Over my dead body. He left McHarg to whatever errand he was on and continued in search of the car-rental franchises, but hadn't gone more than a few steps when he stopped and cursed himself. You can't hire a car without a driving licence and the only driving licence he had was in the name of James Bond. He considered the options – he had to have a car so perhaps it was worth the risk. Now he was through immigration he reckoned he could play with his two identities as it suited him. In fact it might cover his tracks better – confuse the issue. He went to a desk that said 'DC Car Rental' and asked what cars they had in the high-performance top-of-the-range category. He quickly chose a new model Ford Mustang Mach 1 hardtop. He paid a deposit in cash and was led out to the parking lot.

He liked the Mustang – he'd driven one before – and there was something no-nonsense about this hefty new model – two-tone, red over black – with its big blocky muscled contours and wide alloy wheels. No elegant European styling here, just unequivocal 300-plus horsepower in a brutish V8 Ramair engine. He threw his suitcase in the boot – in the trunk – and slid in behind the wheel, adjusting the seat for the best driving position. Bloater McHarg, who would have thought? My God, who could predict when your past would suddenly blunder into your life? In a way it was surprising that he'd never met any of the other boys he'd known at Fettes. Still, not necessarily something to be wished for. He turned the ignition and enjoyed the virile baritone roar of the engine. He pulled out of the parking lot and headed for downtown DC.

He had booked himself a room in a large hotel called the Fairview near Mount Vernon Square, between Massachusetts Avenue and G Street. He wanted a busy hotel with many rooms, to be just one transient individual amongst hundreds of anonymous guests. As he headed into the city he began to recognise the odd landmark. He didn't know Washington well – it was a place he had passed through over the years, spending the occasional night, mainly in transit for meetings at the CIA headquarters at Langley. He remembered from his reading somewhere that Charles Dickens had called Washington a 'city of magnificent intentions'. A somewhat loaded phrase – seeming at first glance like a compliment – though it could actually be interpreted as a rebuke: why hadn't those magnificent intentions ever been realised? For all its pre-eminent role and status in the nation's political life, Washington, he thought – outside the pomp and grandeur of its public buildings or the tonier neighbourhoods – appeared a run-down, poor-looking, dangerous place. Every time he told people he was going there he received the familiar warnings about where not to go, what not to do. Consequently, his impressions of the city were coloured by this note of caution and edgy guardedness. For most of the time you were in Washington DC you never really felt fully at ease, Bond thought.

His hotel was ideal. The Fairview was a tall featureless modern block with a middle-distance view of the Capitol's dome on its hill. His room was large and air-conditioned, with a colour TV, and the bathroom was clean and functional. He sat down on his bed and flicked through the telephone directory and then Yellow

Pages, finding nothing that led him to AfricaKIN Inc. Then it struck him that Gabriel Adeka had only arrived a few weeks ago. So he called information and was given a number. This second call elicited an address: 1075 Milford Plaza in the Southwest district, south of Independence Avenue. He would check it out in the morning. At least he had found the beginning of his trail.

He unpacked his clothes and toiletries and felt the creeping melancholy of hotel life infect him. The bland room, replicated in thousands of hotels worldwide, made him sense all the drab anomie of the transient, the temporarily homeless – just the number of your room and your name in the register the signal of your ephemeral identity. He thought of Bryce, inevitably, her ripe beauty and their night together and experienced a brief ache of longing for her. Maybe he should never have embarked on this whole business – he should have spent his month's leave in London and come to know her better. It might have been a more therapeutic course of action than revenge . . . He shook himself out of his mood – self-pity was the most rebarbative of human emotions. He had chosen to come here; he had a job to do. He looked at his watch – early evening but midnight for him. Still, he couldn't go to bed.

He went down to the dark loud bar in the lobby – all the other transients drowning their melancholy – and drank two large bourbons and branch water. Then in the half-empty hangar of a dining room he ate as much as he could of a vast tough steak with some French fries. Back in his room he took a sleeping pill: he wanted a full ten hours' unconsciousness before he set about investigating the new configuration of AfricaKIN Inc.

·2·

THE STAKE-OUT

Milford Plaza was a new development and had pretensions. Three six-storey glass and concrete office blocks had been positioned round a large granite-paved public space – the 'plaza' – set out with stone benches and a generous planting of assorted saplings. An oval pool with a fountain and a plinth-mounted piece of modern sculpture – three outsized girders painted in primary colours leaning against each other – contributed to its striven-for airs and graces. AfricaKIN Inc. was on the second floor of the central block.

Bond stood in the filtered neutral light of the building's tall marbled lobby – more plants, a giant suspended mobile twirling gently – and pretended to study the gilt-lettered columns of companies that were renting space. He thought about taking the elevator and actually seeing what the AfricaKIN premises were like but he sensed it might be both premature and possibly dangerous. He needed some time – to watch and evaluate, see who came and went, assess the risk factor. There was no hurry, he told himself; he had time on his side; his name was Bryce Fitzjohn.

He strolled outside. The Plaza was let down somewhat by the

buildings opposite, across the street – a row of assorted pre-war brownstones showing signs of their age faced the pristine glass and granite. There was a temperance hotel – the Ranchester – a thrift shop, an A&P grocery, a Seventh Day Adventist chapel, a Chinese laundry, a jewellers and assorted eating places and a couple of small convenience stores with boarded-up windows.

Bond lit a cigarette and crossed the street wondering if there was somewhere that he could establish a semi-permanent viewpoint. He could have rented a room in the temperance hotel – it was perfectly positioned – but he refused to humiliate himself by staying in such an establishment. However, a little further along and at an oblique angle to the plaza he saw a building, grandly named the Alcazar, with a faded sign saying 'Office Suites To Let. One, Two, Three Rooms. All Conveniences.' Bond looked up at the five-storey facade. If he could rent somewhere high up at the front he'd have a good view of everyone going in and out of number 1075.

An eager young man in a shiny suit who introduced himself as Abe tried to persuade him to take their deluxe suite at the back of the building, which came with two reserved parking spaces in the lot at the rear. Bond insisted on the front. All that was available was a three-room suite on the fourth floor. Abe showed him around as Bond peered out of the windows checking the sight lines. Perfect. Abe wanted three months' rent in advance but Bond, taking out his fat wad of dollars, offered him just one month in advance – with a private, personal bonus of a hundred for Abe himself, for being so extremely helpful. 'It's a deal,' Abe said, trying to keep his smile of joy under control. Bond duly paid his deposit, slipped Abe his inducement, signed the lease and was given a set of keys. 'Welcome to the Alcazar,' Abe said, and shook his hand.

There were dirty, vertical plastic strip-blinds at the windows, no furniture and stained carpet tiles on the floor. The third and smallest of the rooms gave him the best view. All Bond needed was a seat and a pair of binoculars – then he could survey Milford Plaza to his heart's content. It was time to equip himself.

Bond drove west and crossed the Potomac to a suburb outside DC in Virginia. He cruised the shopping malls and the streets until he found what he was looking for. He parked outside a large, brash-looking store painted canary yellow with, along the facade, huge red letters outlined in neon that said 'SAM M. GOODFORTH. GUNS 'N' AMMO'. Beneath that, in a cursive copperplate, a line read 'Your Firearm Dreams Answered'.

Bond pushed open the door and browsed for a while, checking the place out. All the lethal hardware was contained in locked wire-grilled cabinets behind the long sales counter. The rest of the store was filled with army surplus and hunting and fishing equipment and accessories. Bond chose a folding canvas stool and a soft rubber mattress that could be rolled up. He approached the counter with his purchases.

The thin, muscled man who served him was smoking a cigarette and had his hair shaved almost bald in a severe crew cut with a curious tuft at the forelock. Various crests and emblems were tattooed on his pale arms. Despite his martial air his voice was oddly high-pitched and he had a half-lisp.

Bond also bought a pair of binoculars, ex-US Navy, Zeiss lenses.

'Are you the owner?' he asked.

'I'm his brother, Eugene,' he smiled, showing a black tooth. 'Sam's got an appointment with a lady friend.'

'I need a handgun,' Bond said. 'Have you got a Walther PPK?'

'I got thomething better, thir,' Eugene lisped. 'Thmall but thtrong.'

He opened a drawer and brought out a Beretta M1951. Bond liked Berettas, in fact he sometimes regretted giving up his old Beretta for his Walther. He turned it over in his hand, checking it – it was a 'third series' with the smaller sights – cocking it, squeezing the trigger, ejecting the empty clip – it would take eight rounds of 9 mm Parabellum – and slapping it back in.

'Ain't the first time you had a gun in your hand, I can see that,' Eugene said.

Bond liked the weight of the gun. 'I'll take it,' he said, his eye ranging over the rifles, the M5 carbines, machine guns and shotguns racked behind the grilles. Maybe he needed something for longer ranges . . . And then he suddenly thought that powerful telescopic sight might be a real advantage – a sniper-scope – from his room high up in the Alcazar. Something that could zoom in – better than binoculars.

'I might be doing a bit of hunting,' Bond said. 'I want something with a bit of beef – and that can take a strong scope.'

Eugene Goodforth presented him with a choice of powerful hunting rifles – a CZ-550 with a Mannlicher stock, a Mauser Karabiner and a Springfield 1903 in beautiful condition. Bond was more interested in the sights that he was shown and took the latest model Schmidt & Bender scope to the door to see how it worked at long range.

He looked at passers-by down the street. The zoom

magnification was very effective and the little calibrations and illuminated cross-hairs reticle could be changed at the flick of a switch at the side.

He returned to the counter and told Eugene that he needed a rifle that would fit this scope – but one that could be broken up and carried in a bag of some sort.

'Have I got just the baby for you, sir,' Eugene said and went into a room behind the counter emerging with what looked like a black plastic attaché case. He flipped it open and showed Bond the contents.

'Just arrived – a Frankel and Kleist S1962,' Eugene said with reverence in his voice. He took the separate stock, breech and barrel out of their recessed velvet moulds and fitted them together, sliding the scope on top. 'Single shot, bolt action. Point five zero calibre bullet, two-stage trigger set to four pounds.' Bond picked it up and raised it to his shoulder. It was matt black and surprisingly light. Bond fitted his cheek to the cheek rest and drew a bead through the window on a shop sign across the street.

'You turn down the reticle illumination all the way on that scope you can shoot this mother at night, I swear,' Eugene said.

'Perfect,' Bond said. 'You made another sale.'

'What're you after?' Eugene asked with a knowing smile. 'Neighbours?'

Bond laughed. 'Elk,' he said, spontaneously.

'Don't got much elk around these parts,' Eugene said. 'Still, you may get lucky.'

'I'll look hard,' Bond said.

He bought the guns and their relevant ammunition, showed

his Bryce Fitzjohn passport, filled in the documentation – giving as his address his hotel, the Fairview – and marvelled, not for the first time in his life, just how easy it was to arm yourself in the land of the free.

·3·

THE ALCAZAR

The next morning Bond parked his Mustang in an underground garage near the Federal Warehouse and walked the three blocks to the Alcazar, attaché case in one hand, a canvas grip in his other, containing the binoculars, the mattress, three packs of cigarettes and a vacuum flask filled with a weak solution of bourbon and iced water. He could always pop out for a sandwich or a dreaded burger or hot dog if he grew hungry, he reasoned.

Secure in his room, the main door locked, he pulled the little circular chain that turned the blind sideways on to the windows. He set up his folding stool and unrolled his mattress. He sat down and picked up the binoculars. He had an ideal oblique line of sight on to the plaza and anyone entering or leaving number 1075. The binoculars allowed him an initial identification and the sniper-scope provided a genuine close-up with the aid of the zoom-magnification device. However, with the zoom at maximum the hand-shake distortion was sizeable. He needed a tripod, Bond thought – or, even better, the rifle it was designed for.

He assembled the Frankel and fitted the scope. By resting the barrel on the windowsill he achieved perfect stability. Peering through the sight with the distance calibration and the cross-haired reticle in operation made him feel like an assassin. Just as well the gun wasn't loaded, Bond thought: if he saw Kobus Breed crossing the plaza the temptation might prove too hard to resist.

After a couple of hours' watching, Bond began to feel himself stiffening up. He took off his jacket and did some un-strenuous exercises just to keep the blood flowing. He was feeling stronger every day but didn't want to put any undue strain on his healing tissues. He smoked a cigarette, had a swig of his bourbon and water and sat down again.

Through his binoculars he saw a glossy town car pull up in the indented drop-off spot at the edge of the plaza. A black man in a dark suit stepped out and leaned forward to have a quick word with the driver. Adeka, Bond wondered? He picked up his rifle and zoomed in with the scope.

No – even more interesting, and someone else he'd met before: Colonel Denga, lately commander-in-chief of the Dahumian armed forces. There was the handsome face with the matinee-idol moustache. Bond watched him stroll across the plaza to 1075. He was dapper – the suit jacket was cut long and was waisted and the trousers fashionably flared. Just visiting, or was he now something to do with AfricaKIN Inc?

Bond lunched on a ham and cheese sandwich in a diner, had a badly made dry martini in a bar and, curiosity getting the better of him, once again went into the lobby of 1075 and stood by the elevators wondering whether to chance a visit to the office itself. But if Denga was there, he'd be recognised, and – just so he could gain a sense of the lie of the land – he thought it might be more effective to disguise himself somehow, initially. There are disguises and disguises, Bond knew. He could grow a beard and shave his head and no one would think he was James Bond. But the short-term, provisional disguise had its own particular methodology. The key aim was to focus attention on one or two elements of the disguise so that they obscured the other, more familiar ones. Time for some more shopping, Bond thought.

The next morning, Bond strode across Milford Plaza towards number 1075. He was wearing a red and green tartan jacket, heavy black spectacles with clear lenses and a cream pork-pie hat. He rode up in the elevator to the second floor and pushed through the wide, double plate glass doors into the lobby of AfricaKIN Inc.

Everything about the ambience of the long lobby said 'money'. Bond's gaze took in the thick-pile charcoal carpet, the lush plants growing in stainless-steel cubes. At one end there was a seating area composed of curved leather sofas and teak coffee tables. On the linen walls were a couple of large inoffensive abstract paintings. The receptionist – a middle-aged white woman – sat at a mahogany desk with three telephones on it. Behind her on a smoked-glass panel 'AfricaKIN Inc.' was spelt out in large three-dimensional sans-serif aluminium letters. Beyond that Bond could see a wide corridor with offices off it on both sides. It didn't look like a charity, to his eyes, it looked like a successful corporation.

'Welcome to AfricaKIN, sir,' the receptionist said with a smile. 'How may I help you?'

'I'd like to make an appointment to see Gabriel Adeka,' Bond said in a marked Scottish brogue. This is where the provisional disguise should work: if the woman were ever asked to remember him all she could say would be 'Scotsman, spectacles, small hat.' He would guarantee that she'd find it very hard to be any more precise.

'I'm sorry, sir, but that won't be possible. Mr Adeka is extremely busy – on government business.'

'I know him,' Bond said. 'We met in London. I want to make a sizeable donation.' He handed over his card. The receptionist looked at it and handed it back.

'If you care to take a seat, Mr McHarg, I'll see what I can do.' She jotted his name down on a pad. And picked up one of her telephones. Bond wandered off to the seating area and helped himself to some water from the cooler standing there. He saw that there was another corridor, signed with an arrow that said 'Restrooms'. Conceivably there might be a service entrance at the end. Never enter a room without assessing the various ways available to exit it, he reminded himself – Bond had never forgotten his early instructions in procedure. He sat down – he was quite enjoying this – taking care to position himself so that he was screened by a large weeping fig.

He waited. Ten minutes, twenty minutes. Other people joined him until summoned into the office suites for appointments or meetings. Forty minutes passed – the place was busy. Bond sat on, a *National Geographic* magazine open on his knee, his eyes restless – watching, checking, noting. He headed for the restrooms. He was right – there was a door at the end of the corridor that said 'No entry'. He opened it and saw a flight of concrete stairs and a yellow bucket with a mop in it. Bond relieved himself, checked his disguise and returned to his seat.

After he'd been there an hour he began to grow a little worried. Either he could meet Adeka – or he couldn't. He thought of approaching the receptionist again but decided not to – one glimpse of him was all she should have. Then it occurred to him that he was being kept here deliberately, figuring that as long as he was corralled in the lobby anyone could find him. He put the magazine down. Something was now wrong – he was going to abort. He'd been a bit too audacious thinking he'd gain access to Adeka this easily—

Kobus Breed pushed through the glass doors and went straight to the receptionist.

Bond stood up immediately, turned his back and walked unconcernedly down the corridor to the restrooms. He was through the service door in a second and clattered down the stairs. He found himself in a storeroom full of cleaning equipment and rubbish bins. He threw his hat and his glasses into a bin, took off his jacket, turned it inside out and folded it over his arm. He opened another door and emerged at the rear of the elevator banks. Looking straight ahead he made his way through the people waiting for the elevators, strolled easily across the marble lobby with its spinning mobile and walked out into the weak sunshine that was bathing Milford Plaza.

He could still feel the heart-thud of alarm and adrenalin. Breed in Washington DC? Breed summoned to confront this unknown visitor to Gabriel Adeka . . . He had been wearing a dark business suit and a red tie – very smart. Bond remembered that was how he had complimented him in the control tower at

Janjaville. Perhaps that suit he'd been wearing that night was the first indication of his new life as an executive of a global charitable foundation.

Bond began to relax, glancing back as he left the plaza – no one was after him and he had learned a lot from his visit. His request to meet Adeka had brought Kobus Breed from wherever he was residing to investigate. AfricaKIN Inc. had nothing to do with the modest grubby shop in Bayswater. Something much bigger was taking place. Something bigger and very wrong.

·4·

SWITCHBLADE

That night Bond went to see a film called *Bob & Carol & Ted & Alice* but found he couldn't concentrate on it. He left before the end and walked slowly back to the Fairview, smoking a cigarette, his mind working, trying to analyse all the permutations that might make up AfricaKIN Inc. Gabriel Adeka, Colonel Denga and now Breed . . . What kind of strange alliance was this?

He realised he hadn't been paying attention and had taken a wrong turn. He could see the top of the lucent tower that was the Fairview a few blocks away and also the floodlit dome of the Capitol on the hill. He reset his bearings and headed off again, aware that he had wandered into a neighbourhood of near-derelict housing, with many windows boarded up, some of them seemingly damaged by fire. He passed a burnt-out car with no wheels; half the street lights weren't working; stray cats prowled the alleyways. This could happen so easily in DC. One wrong turning and you found yourself in—

'Hey, man, you got a light?'

Bond looked round slowly. Behind him, on the edge of a yellow semicircle thrown by a lamp above a shuttered thrift-store doorway, three young men stood – teenagers, Bond thought. They were wearing jeans and T-shirts and were all smoking, so the need for a light was redundant. Two black kids and a white guy, slightly older. Bond glanced behind him – no one – so just these three to deal with, then. All right, come and get me.

They started to walk purposefully towards him flicking away their cigarettes, numbed and heroic with speed, Bond reckoned. The white kid took something out of his pocket and Bond heard the *whish-chunk* of a switchblade being sprung.

'So you need a light,' Bond said taking out his Ronson and clicking it on. He turned the small wheel that governed the gas valve and the flame flared up three inches.

'Hey, funny guy,' one of them said as they fanned out to surround him.

Bond tossed the flaring lighter at the boy with the switchblade. Reflexively, he ducked and swore and in that moment of inattention Bond grabbed his wrist and dislocated it with a brutal jerk. The boy screamed and the knife dropped with a clatter on the sidewalk. Bond turned on the black kid who was rushing him and kicked him heavily in the groin. He fell to the ground, bellowing and writhing in agony – Bond's loafers were fitted with steel caps at the toe. The other black kid began to back off. Bond stooped and picked up the switchblade and held it out.

'You want this?' he said.

The boy turned and ran away into the night.

Bond found his Ronson and pocketed it – then considered his two assailants. The boy with the dislocated wrist was kneeling, holding his wrist with his good hand and sobbing with the pain, his hand hanging limply and at the wrong angle. The other kid was still on the ground clutching his smashed groin and keening in a high-pitched whine of misery, his knees drawn up to his chest.

Bond stamped down hard on his ribcage and kicked the other kneeling boy in the side with his steel toecaps, knocking him flying, making him scream again. Ribs broken or fractured, he assumed. They would remember him and this night for the next couple of months – every time they coughed or laughed or reached for something.

Bond leaned over them both and swore at them picturesquely, then he added, 'Way past your bedtime, kiddies, run along home.'

He strolled off towards the Fairview, closing the switchblade. It was quite a nice knife, he thought, with a dull ebony handle inlaid with a nacreous pattern of diamonds. He slipped it in his pocket, beginning to feel a little guilty at the unreasonable force of his retaliation. He realised he had vented some of his pent-up rage from Janjaville on these three unfortunates. This was the first 'action' he had seen since he had left the war zone. His blood had come up spontaneously and he had administered swift and efficient retribution. They weren't to know whom they were trying to rob, nor what dark, embittered grudges their potential victim was harbouring: still, he thought, maybe he might have saved them from a life of crime. But he knew he'd taken out his anger on those street punks and punished them for the sins of others. Just their bad luck . . . Tough. He eased his right shoulder as he approached the hotel – no pain – and he massaged the muscle of his wounded thigh. Everything seemed fine after his physical exertions – he was healing fast.

* * *

He spent a fruitless morning the next day in his office in the Alcazar building, scrutinising Milford Plaza but recognising no familiar faces. He started to wonder if there was a rear entrance for more private comings and goings but he had observed that most people arriving by car were dropped off in the indented parking area off the busy street, so he assumed that was the norm.

Then, just before noon, he saw her. Blessing Ogilvy-Grant came out of the main door of 1075 and began to walk across the plaza. Bond zoomed in with the sniper-scope. She looked different – she was wearing a belted beige trouser suit with wide flared trousers but her hair had changed and was now styled in a short bushy Afro, natural and unoiled – very much the young radical, he thought. She stopped at a hot-dog stand to buy a soda and Bond took his opportunity, racing out of his suite of rooms and down the stairs.

When he emerged from the Alcazar on to the plaza he thought he'd lost her but then he caught sight of her heading up the street towards The Mall. She crossed it on 7th Street and he followed her, being very careful, always staying fifty yards or so behind, sometimes crossing the street and doing a parallel follow, looking back to check that she wasn't being covered in any way, before ducking back behind her again.

He felt the contrasting emotions seethe within him. His heart had lurched spontaneously when her face had grown large in the sniper-scope, as he remembered her beauty and the tenderness she'd shown him. Without thinking, he'd approved of this new look she'd created – very American, very cutting-edge. Then he recalled how casually and coldly she had shot him, taking

Kobus's gun and levelling it at his chest without a tremor or any sign of regret. The lover's fond assessment gave way to a bitter, reasoned anger – she had played him exceptionally well, from the moment they had met. She was a highly trained operative, prepared to put her body on the line should it prove necessary, and give herself to her adversary – and also to shoot to kill. He slowed, making sure he kept his distance, assuming that she would routinely verify that she was being followed or not. Bond's expertise had to be at least as good as hers, if not better.

A point worth repeating regularly, Bond told himself, as he watched her turn into a restaurant on E Street called the Baltimore Crab. Bond hovered outside, across the street, watching other lunchers arrive and wondering whom she might be meeting. Perhaps it was just a friend and not sinister business. Even double agents were allowed a personal life from time to time, he told himself.

Bond lit a cigarette and weighed up his options. He had located AfricaKIN. His surveillance was in place and functioning. Nobody knew he was in the US. But there was no point in just watching – some kind of catalyst was needed, and one of his own making; not like Kobus Breed arriving unannounced at the AfricaKIN offices. *Il faut pisser sur les fourmis*, he said to himself with a grin, recalling one of the cruder adages of his old friend René Mathis. Yes, *pisser sur les fourmis* and set the ants scurrying for cover.

Bond crossed the street and pushed open the door of the restaurant. His gaze quickly swept the room. It was bright and airy, decorated in varying shades of blue and embellished with a multitude of nautical motifs on the walls – signal flags, a life belt, a ship's wheel, cork floats and swags of netting. He thought he caught a glimpse of Blessing in the far corner but he looked no further, smilingly approaching the young woman who stood at a lectern at the entrance to the dining room, and asking if he could make a reservation for that evening. The reservation was made, Bond helped himself to a Baltimore Crab business card from the little pile on top of the lectern and left. He was almost one hundred per cent sure that Blessing would have spotted him talking to the woman at the maître d's station. In any event, the next few minutes would prove him right or wrong.

Bond wandered up the street a few yards, hailed a passing cab and climbed in.

'Just wait here for a while,' he told the driver and handed him a $10 note. He hunched down in the rear seat, keeping his eyes on the restaurant door. Sure enough, in about ninety seconds, Blessing hurried out, agitated, looking up and down the street, scanning the faces of passers-by. Bond smiled to himself – the ants were in a real state. Blessing waved down the first cab she saw and got in.

'Follow that cab,' Bond said. 'And there's another twenty in it for you if we're not spotted.'

'Hey, no problem,' the cabbie said. He had a Mexican accent and a droopy, bandit's moustache. 'She your girl?'

'Yes – two-timing bitch.'

'Man, don' get me start on *las chicas*,' the cabbie said and immediately embarked on a long anecdote about his ex-wife in lewd and abusive detail.

Bond let him rant on, keeping his eye on Blessing's cab. He wondered what she would be thinking, what level of shock and astonishment the sight of him would have provoked. To see James Bond saunter into a Washington DC restaurant when she might have assumed he was dead and buried . . . No, Bond thought, the sick jolt of alarm would go quickly and then furious second-guessing would begin. She would intuit almost instantly that this was no coincidence and that he had wanted her to see him. But why? she would ask herself. Then she'd enter the fraught and dangerous labyrinth of pure speculation. This was a man she had shot in the chest in Africa – and yet here he was on her trail in Washington DC. Bond smiled: Blessing's head would be ringing with a hundred alarm bells – she would be well and truly spooked. He sat back – there were many types of satisfaction to be enjoyed in this job.

Blessing's car headed into Georgetown and stopped outside a small, pretty clapboard house on O Street.

'Drive on by,' Bond said to the cabbie, peering out of the rear window to see Blessing run inside, not paying off the driver, keeping her cab waiting, its engine ticking over. They drove on fifty yards and Bond ordered the cabbie to park and wait.

'We go through a lot of zones, mister,' the cabbie said. Bond had forgotten the arcane mysteries of cab-fare calculation in DC.

'Don't worry. I'll pay you well. Get ready to turn around if you have to,' Bond said and fed the man another $20.

'Hey, you can hire me all day, every day, mister,' he turned in the front seat and leered at him. 'I am like to work with you.'

After five minutes Blessing reappeared again, a suitcase in her hand. She locked the front door and hurried into her cab. It pulled away and passed them.

'Don't lose it, whatever you do,' Bond said.

'You got it.'

Blessing's cab headed west out of DC and crossed the Key Bridge over the Potomac. About twenty minutes later it pulled into the forecourt of a large and ugly modern motel called the Blackstone Park Motor Lodge.

'Keep going,' Bond said. They drove on another block or so. 'Stop.'

The cab pulled into the side of the road under a vast billboard advertising Kool cigarettes. Through the rear window Bond could see Blessing paying off her cab and a bellhop picking up her suitcase. So this was where she would be staying. She was smart: she assumed her cover was blown and so she immediately changed address, within minutes. Bond relaxed – he knew where to find her now. She'd check into her room and start making anxious phone calls, warning everyone. The ants' nest would be in swarming disarray.

·5·

SUITE 5K

Bond spent the rest of the afternoon in his Alcazar office watching the comings and goings on Milford Plaza. None of the usual suspects appeared but he wasn't too concerned. As it grew dark he went back to the Fairview, put a pillow and a bottle of bourbon in his suitcase and went out to his car. He drove the Mustang out west across the Potomac to the Blackstone Park Motor Lodge, found a space for his car and went into reception with his suitcase. He had deliberately not checked out of the Fairview – sometimes having rooms in two hotels in a city was better than one.

He was given a large double room in the main block. The Blackstone Park wasn't cheap and nasty, just overused. The sheets on the bed were crisp cotton but the carpet was threadbare and the paintwork was chipped and scarred. The air conditioner worked but hummed a little too loudly. The lavatory was protected by a sheet of cellophane and the tooth-glass had a little cardboard cap on it, but the shaving mirror was cracked and the shower tray's enamel had been scoured through. Anonymous, large, functional – perfect to hide yourself in.

Bond went down to reception and slipped the bellhop on duty $10.

'Keep this between ourselves,' Bond said, 'but I think my wife's checked into this motel under a false name.'

'You mean . . . ?'

'Got it in one,' Bond said, putting on an embittered face. 'Yeah – she doesn't know I know.'

The bellhop's name, according to the plastic badge above his breast pocket, was Delmont. His acne had almost gone but had left his skin dimpled like a golf ball. The wispy moustache he was trying to grow was no asset either, but he bought into the male sodality that Bond offered and they talked briefly of the perfidy of beautiful women like two men of the world.

'She's coloured,' Bond said, 'but pale-skinned, you know. Very sexy with a kind of Afro hairstyle.'

'We got two hundred rooms here, sir,' Delmont said. 'But I'll ask around. A babe like that will have been noticed by my colleagues, know what I mean?'

'I just need her room number,' Bond said. 'I'll give you five bucks for it – leave the rest to me,' Bond smiled. 'I'm Mr Fitzjohn, room 325.'

Bond went back to room 325 and poured himself two fingers of bourbon from his bottle and switched on the television while he waited for Delmont. He watched a game of baseball uncomprehendingly – the Senators versus the Royals – thinking that it made cricket seem exciting. Delmont's knock on the door came ten minutes later.

'She's in suite 5K in the new annexe in back by the parking lot,' Delmont said, folding away Bond's $5 into a small pocket in his jacket. 'She paid for two weeks in advance – so it don't look like she's planning on coming home soon.' Delmont commiserated and said if there was anything else he could do then Mr Fitzjohn shouldn't hesitate. Call the front desk and ask for Delmont.

'A thousand thanks,' Bond said, and he meant it. Life was becoming more intriguing by the hour.

Bond was up at dawn and drove into DC, stopping at a diner for scrambled eggs and bacon and the hot brown liquid that passed for coffee in this country. He took up his position armed with his binoculars and watched the office workers arrive for the daily round.

Just after nine o'clock, Kobus Breed stepped out of a Chevrolet Impala and strode across the plaza to 1075. Ten minutes later Denga's car arrived and there – Bond swivelled the binoculars – there was Blessing herself, walking fast, her head turning constantly, checking to see if she was being followed. Bond smiled. A council of war? The day was young.

An hour went by, then two. Bond dashed to the restrooms at the end of the corridor, cursing the diuretic potency of American coffee, and raced back, hoping he hadn't missed anything or anyone. When he saw Kobus Breed appear twenty minutes later, he relaxed. Kobus was swiftly followed by Blessing.

Bond picked up his rifle and adjusted the zoom on the sniper-scope. There they were – faces close in animated conversation. Bond settled the cross hairs of the sight on Kobus's forehead, watching him dab at his weeping eye with a handkerchief. Then his car arrived and he left. Bond moved the sight to Blessing. Seeing the two of them in ardent discussion had hardened his feelings again, remembering their near-lethal double act in the Janjaville control tower.

He watched Blessing rummage in her bag and take out a pack of cigarettes. She stood there smoking as if in deep thought, pacing to and fro in small circles. Bond moved the cross hairs to her breast. Tempting. Two inches below the right collarbone, exactly where she'd shot him. Just as well he didn't have a bullet in the chamber—

The click by his ear was unmistakeable. The hammer of a revolver being cocked. He could feel the snub muzzle cold on his jawbone.

'No, Mr Bond. Take your hands off the gun then stand up slowly, arms raised.' There was the hint of a Southern drawl in the voice.

Bond did exactly as he was told, standing slowly, turning and raising his arms above his head.

Two young men stood there covering him with their handguns. They both wore navy blue suits and striped ties. One was blond and one was dark, their hair cut short in military style. CIA, Bond guessed at once. What the hell was going on? How did they know his name?

'The gun isn't loaded,' Bond said. 'You can check. I wasn't going to shoot.'

'Good to know,' the blond man said. 'She's one of us.'

·6·

CIA

Bond lowered his arms, his brain in some kind of manic overdrive. 'One of us' . . . ? One question at a time, he told himself.

'I'd like to see your ID,' he asked. 'If I may.'

The blond man took out his wallet and showed Bond his plastic card.

'I'm Agent Brigham Leiter,' he said. 'And this is Agent Luke Massinette.'

Bond smiled. 'So you're the famous Brig,' he said. 'How's Uncle Felix?'

'He's well, sir. In fact I know he wants to talk to you urgently.'

'How did you know my name? How did you know I was here?'

Brigham Leiter holstered his gun, as did his partner.

'The lady you were aiming at is called Aleesha Belem. She told us you were in DC – she saw you in a restaurant, by chance, and gave us your name. We traced the hire of a Ford Mustang to one James Bond at Dulles airport then we lost your trail. Luckily we have this whole plaza staked out. We took your photograph. Aleesha identified it. My uncle confirmed it. James Bond, British agent. We found where you'd parked your Mustang. Followed you to these offices. Followed you back to your hotel.

It wasn't hard to make the connection to a Mr Bryce Fitzjohn.'

Bond couldn't blame himself for sloppy procedure – it was no lapse on his part, just bad luck. How was he to know that Blessing–Aleesha was a CIA agent? He thought further.

'So this Aleesha Belem is working for you. Since when?'

'Over two years now, I believe.'

'She shot me in the chest. In Africa a few weeks ago. Tried to kill me.'

'I don't know anything about that,' Brig Leiter said. 'She's sound – one of our most reliable people.'

'What's she doing in AfricaKIN?'

'I'm not authorised to disclose that information,' Leiter said.

'I think I'd better talk to your uncle,' Bond said. 'Is he back in the CIA or is he still with Pinkerton's?'

'He "consults" for us from time to time. He's still with Pinkerton's, though.'

Bond thought fondly of Felix Leiter – one of his oldest friends and colleagues. They had endured many a tough assignment together over the years. Felix had been badly injured on one of them, back in Florida in the early 1950s, had even lost an arm and part of a leg. Bond glanced at Felix's nephew, Brig. Felix had often talked about him, a 'chip off the old block'. Bond thought he saw something of Felix in the set of Brig's jaw, the thick blond hair, the grey, candid eyes. He wasn't so keen on the other guy, though. Massinette stood back, surly, watchful.

Still, Bond's head was loud with unanswered questions. If Blessing had been in the CIA for two years how had she managed to . . . ? He stopped himself. There would be time enough to settle these issues later.

'I can hook you up with my uncle,' Brig said. 'He's in Miami.'

Bond broke up and packed away the Frankel and followed Brig and Massinette out of the Alcazar and along the street to the temperance hotel, the Ranchester. They rode the elevator to the fifth floor and Bond walked in on a major CIA surveillance team in a room at the front overlooking the whole of Milford Plaza. There were telescopes, cameras with long lenses mounted on tripods, screens displaying covert CCTV links into the lobby of 1075 and the entrance to the AfricaKIN office itself. Everyone who came in and out of that building could be logged and conceivably identified. Bond wondered if 'Turnbull McHarg' had been spotted – somehow he doubted it.

He was put on the phone to Felix Leiter in Miami.

'Felix, it's James.'

'Welcome to DC, my son. What're you up to? You nearly fouled everything up. Why didn't Transworld Consortium tell us you were on a job?'

'Because I'm not.'

'Uh-oh . . .' Pause. 'Don't tell me – you've gone solo.'

'I'd appreciate it if you didn't inform anyone that I'm here.'

There was more silence as Felix took this in.

'James, do you know what you're doing?'

'Of course.'

'Good. Well from now on we take over, right? Go back to London before anyone finds out. Difficult to keep a lid on this.'

Bond looked around the room at all the hardware, the agents, the money being spent on this job and thought of his own puny individual investment in his act of vengeance.

'Felix, will you tell me what's going on here?'

'No.'

'Come on, Felix, it's me – James.'

'Let's just say we're investigating AfricaKIN Inc. We don't believe all their PR schtick.'

'I might just buy that,' Bond said, 'but you already had an agent in Zanzarim weeks ago. How come she was able to intercept me? How come she tried to kill me?'

'It's a long story, James. Go back to London. I'll tell you all about it as soon as possible.'

They exchanged a few more ribald pleasantries and Bond handed the phone to Brig. He watched as Felix obviously gave him a few explicit instructions. Bond had no confidence in what little Felix had told him: something else was at stake here and his own intervention had been a minor bit of grit in a well-oiled CIA machine.

Brig Leiter put the phone down and turned to Bond.

'We can take you back to your hotel, Mr Bond. The Fairview, right?'

'Yes,' Bond said, a little surge of relief and excitement seizing him. They clearly didn't know about the Blackstone Park Motor Lodge. Maybe he was still one step ahead.

He drove the Mustang back to the hotel, followed by Brig and Massinette in their Buick Skylark. Brig came with him into the lobby and saw him pick up his key.

'Mr Bond,' he said, apologetically, 'believe me, this isn't easy for me. Uncle Felix talks about you all the time. It's a real pleasure to meet you – I just wish I hadn't had to pull a gun on you to say hello.'

'Not a problem at all, Brig,' Bond said with a wide smile. 'I'm out of your hair – now I know the truth about Blessing – about Aleesha. I'll head for home, don't you worry. All's well that ends well.'

'Great. Thank you, sir.' They shook hands and Brig returned to his Buick. Massinette was leaning against it, smoking. They climbed in and drove off.

Bond went into the lobby bar to gather his thoughts and ordered a vodka martini, explaining to the barman the best way to achieve the effect of vermouth without diluting the vodka too much. Ice in the shaker, add a slurp of vermouth, pour out the vermouth, add the vodka, shake well, strain into a chilled glass, add a slice of lemon peel, no pith.

Bond took his drink to a dark corner and lit a cigarette, thinking hard. He had assumed that time was his ally, but now time was his enemy. Any more interference with the CIA operation and Felix would call London and they'd ship him off back home with no compunction. Bond reckoned he had forty-eight hours, at the outside.

·7·

THE ENGINEER

Bond left his Mustang in the hotel parking lot and picked up a taxi in the street, telling the driver to take him to the Blackstone Park Motor Lodge. When they arrived there he told the cabbie to circle the block twice. Bond looked out of the rear window as they did so – he wasn't being followed. All the same he made sure he was dropped a few hundred yards up the road and walked back, still checking, doubling back, waiting in doorways. There was no one on his tail.

He stayed in his room until it was dark and, every ten minutes or so, would wander out to the parking lot at the rear to see if the lights were on in Suite 5K. On his eighth visit to the parking lot he saw that the room was finally occupied and the curtains were drawn. He caught the silhouette of a figure crossing in front of a window. Blessing . . . ? Bond went back to his room and slipped his Beretta into his jacket pocket – he was taking no chances.

He knocked on the door of suite 5K and called out 'Engineer.' It was always better than 'Room service.'

He heard Blessing come to the door and say 'Please come back tomorrow.'

Bond put on a Mexican accent. 'The man below he say you got a leak comin' from you bathroom. I gotta check it, Mam.'

'OK, OK.'

He heard the lock turn and he took his gun out of his pocket and held it behind his back. Blessing opened the door and gasped. Bond had his gun in her face and was inside in a second, closing the door behind him. He took the gun from her hand – she was taking no chances either, clearly – and tossed it on the sofa, pocketing his own. Blessing had regained her composure, smiling, shaking her head.

'Yep, "Engineer" is good. I'm going to remember that one.'

She was wearing an eau de Nil satin blouse with balloon sleeves and tight, bell-bottom pale blue jeans. Her feet were bare. She watched, amused, as Bond quickly checked the suite.

'I'm alone, don't worry, James.'

Bond glanced in the bedroom. Suite 5K was deluxe and smarter than his room, designed in the Scandinavian style – all curved pale wood, the bed lower than normal, a thick pile navy rug on a slate-grey carpet, a console stereo, black and white photographs of DC's historic buildings on the walls.

'What do I call you?' Bond asked. 'Blessing or Aleesha?'

'What do I call you? James or Bryce?' She smiled. 'Blessing will do fine. It's actually my middle name, James.'

Bond began to relax. They were on the same side, after all.

'We've got a bit of catching up to do,' Bond said. 'Wouldn't you say?'

'What're you drinking?' she asked, going to the phone.

Bond took the receiver out of her hand.

'Let me do it,' he said. 'Bourbon good for you?'

He ordered a bottle of Jim Beam, two glasses, a bucket of ice and a carafe of branch water and told room service to bill his room – Mr Fitzjohn.

'You're staying here?' Blessing said, astonished. 'Does Brig Leiter know?'

'Not yet. I wanted to have some time alone with you.' He smiled. 'I like your hair like that.'

'Thank you, kind sir.'

The bourbon arrived and Bond mixed them both a strong drink. They clinked glasses and Blessing curled up on the sofa with her legs folded under her. Bond sat in an armchair opposite.

'See if this makes any sense,' Bond said. 'Let's start at the beginning. You were never recruited by MI6 at Cambridge. Instead you were recruited by the CIA when you went to Harvard. Maybe they paid for your graduate studies, just so the cover was good.'

'You're getting warm,' Blessing said.

Bond smiled and continued.

'Then, after your training you were sent to Zanzarim and you got a job with Edward Ogilvy-Grant, UK head of station.' Bond took a slug of his bourbon. 'I would have hired you. Who wouldn't, with your qualifications? You're half-Lowele, you speak the language, your family live in Sinsikrou. Perfect. Somehow I doubt your father was a Scottish engineer.'

'Hotter.'

Bond stood up, lit a cigarette and began pacing around the room.

'For some reason,' he went on, 'the CIA wanted to know what the British were up to in Zanzarim and you became their source. Spying on your ally – we all do it, by the way.' He smiled drily.

'Then you told them I was coming and was to be infiltrated into Dahum. What happened next?'

Blessing reached for her pack of cigarettes, her blouse falling forward for a moment, and Bond saw that she was wearing no brassiere.

'I shouldn't really tell you anything,' she said.

'Then Felix Leiter will tell me when he gets to town. You might as well.'

She sighed and lit her cigarette. 'I miss Tuskers. Lucky Strikes don't do it for me any more.'

'I suppose they ordered you to come with me.'

'Yes. It was a perfect opportunity. They wanted me to get close to Brigadier Adeka – to offer him asylum in the USA. A safe home, money. Everybody could see the war was ending – he had to go somewhere.'

'Why were they so interested in Adeka?'

'I don't know.'

Bond looked sceptical.

'Seriously, I don't – all I had to do was make the offer to him. Make it seem real.'

Bond poured himself another drink. Blessing declined.

'So you set up the fake office and intercepted me.'

'It wasn't difficult. I was Ed Ogilvy-Grant's secretary. I told him you were coming a week later than you actually were. Set up the office, set up Christmas. Gave you the new address. Phoned in and said I was ill.'

'It fooled me,' Bond said, remembering. 'I think the Annigoni portrait of the Queen was the master touch.' He paused. 'Were you told to seduce me?'

'No. That was my own idea.'

'Did you know that Kobus Breed was going to hit us?'

'No. I was genuinely planning to come in with you by boat through the creeks. Kojo, the fisherman, didn't speak English. You would've needed an interpreter, anyway. Then Breed showed up.' Her face darkened. 'It kind of threw me . . .'

'So when you ran off in the firefight you'd decided to go it alone.'

'Yes – in all that chaos it seemed the right thing to do at the moment.'

'So who screamed – you?'

'I didn't hear any scream. Just gunfire, shouting, explosions. I found a thick clump of undergrowth and crawled in. Soldiers walked right by me. When dawn came it was all quiet. I was lost for a couple of days – couldn't find my way out of the forest. Then I found a dirt track and I walked down it until I came across a half-ruined convent with three nuns left behind. They fed me and watered me and eventually I made it to Port Dunbar, about two days before the war ended.'

Bond smiled ruefully, thinking of his own fraught journey on the bush paths.

'Yes, I had some fun in the forest as well.'

'A letter of introduction had been sent to Adeka. In fact, I was expected,' she said.

'But the brigadier was dead by the time you arrived.'

'Yes,' she said. 'I never met him.'

'I did,' Bond said. 'He gave me a medal.'

'Sure,' Blessing smiled. 'But I did meet Colonel Denga – and Breed again. I made the same offer to them – come to the US.

I made it very clear I had the power to bring all this about. My "letter of accreditation" was pretty explicit. When Adeka died I was told that his brother in London, Gabriel, had been contacted and was going to be set up here. They were prepared to spend a lot of money.'

'They?'

'The CIA.' She paused. 'Gabriel Adeka agreed and so the AfricaKIN operation was moved to DC.'

Bond frowned – the whole thing didn't make much sense to him. He sat down again. He was confident that Blessing was telling him what she knew – but what she knew might be very limited.

'Did Breed tell you I was in Port Dunbar?' Bond asked.

'Of course. I told him I wasn't to be mentioned. Anyway, I hardly saw him – everything seemed to be falling apart.' She smiled. 'I'm good – but I don't know how I would have reacted if you and I had met again, there. Best for you to think I was dead.'

Bond considered – there was logic to this. She was on her own mission; he would have been in the way. Too much confusion.

'Why is the CIA so interested in this African charity?' Bond asked, casually. 'Why bring it to America, set them up in those swanky offices?'

Blessing didn't reply immediately. She spread her arms – a gesture of uncertainty. 'To be honest, I don't really know,' she said. 'They only tell me what they think I need. But my feeling is that the person they're really after is Hulbert Linck.'

'What happened to him?'

'He flew out of Janjaville and nobody's seen him since.'

'Didn't he fly out with you on that last Super Constellation?'

'No. There was a DC-3 there as well. I don't know if you saw it.'

'Every detail of that night is burnt in my memory,' Bond said with a cold smile.

'Linck and Kobus Breed left in the DC-3. I flew out on the Constellation with everybody else.'

It still wasn't making much sense to Bond so he changed tack.

'Why did you shoot me?'

Blessing lowered her head, then looked him squarely in the eye. 'Simple. To save you and to save myself. Did you see that hook Breed had with him? He was going to hang you from that, he told me – told me in some detail. Seems it's his special trademark. Also, Breed was very suspicious of me – because I was with you at the beginning. I think he would have killed me that night, in fact.' She smiled, apologetically. 'Killed me and killed you . . . If I hadn't shot you. I shot you exactly where I wanted to, James. We're trained to know what shots will kill and what shots won't. I knew it wouldn't kill you. And Breed was very impressed. He knew I was serious.'

'Does he know you're with the CIA?'

'No. I just represent interested parties with money and influence. He's convinced – even though I wasn't specific.'

But Bond wasn't convinced. Breed may be a psychopath but he wasn't stupid, he thought. He and Denga would be aware that there was a government agency working here, or something similar – too much money, too much power – and recognise it and exploit it. One thing nagged at him: in all their contacts during the final days at Port Dunbar Breed had never told him Blessing had survived the firefight in the forest. He was impressed with Breed's ability to keep that information to himself. It seemed untypical . . .

He lit another cigarette. 'So – the big surveillance at Milford Plaza is to try and nail Linck.'

'Yes.'

'Why? What's so important about Linck for the CIA?'

'I told you – I don't know. Linck must have something we want. Information – some secret. In the end I don't know. Honestly.'

Bond frowned. He had always had his doubts about Linck. 'I never really thought he was just some crazy romantic millionaire who likes lost causes.'

'I think that's what he wants people to think. But there's something more,' Blessing added. 'There's a lot of pressure on me. Too much. It's not normal and it's not fair, to be honest. I'm right in the heart of AfricaKIN. I'm secure. But Brig and the others can't understand why I can't tell them where Hulbert Linck is – or if he's even alive. Sometimes I think that maybe Breed killed him.'

'It's entirely possible,' Bond said.

Blessing stood up. 'Look, I'm going to have a shower. Maybe we can order up some room service, or something.'

'Let's go out and have a proper meal,' Bond said.

Blessing smiled cynically. 'I don't think I should risk being seen dining out with you, James. What if Kobus Breed got to hear about it?'

'Yes – you're right. It's just that I don't fancy the room-service food in this motel.'

She went into the bedroom and soon Bond heard the shower running. He drank another bourbon while he waited, trying to see how the disparate pieces of this puzzle might fit together. And failed. AfricaKIN, Gabriel Adeka, Hulbert Linck, the CIA . . . Kobus Breed had flown out of Janjaville with Linck. More and more Bond felt that Breed was the key to all this.

Blessing came back into the room. She was wearing a boldly printed orange and black cotton dressing gown – short, cut to mid-thigh and belted at the waist. Bond assumed she was naked underneath. Concentrate, he told himself, retrieve as much information as you can.

'Where's Gabriel Adeka?' he asked.

'He runs everything from a big house in Orange County, Virginia, called Rowanoak Hall. It's a kind of clinic – a medical sorting office. A clearing house for the children.'

'What children?'

'The children that the AfricaKIN flights bring in.' She poured herself a tiny bourbon and sipped at it. 'Interestingly, Adeka pays for the big house, not us.' She said. 'We only pay for the office space at the plaza.'

'Have you been there? To this house in Orange County?'

'A couple of times for meetings with Denga. It's almost like a small hospital – state of the art.' She put her glass down. 'I'm hungry.'

'Is Breed there?'

'He stays there. He and Denga seem to work closely together.'

'Old military buddies. Where do these flights arrive?'

'Not in DC. There's a small airport not too far away – Seminole

Field, forty minutes from the house. The kids arrive on the flights and they're taken to the house in ambulances and medically assessed and then they're sent to specialist hospitals in DC, Maryland, Virginia, depending on their problems. It's quite an operation.'

She sat down on the sofa, being careful not to let the hem of her dressing gown ride up. Bond tried to stop himself looking at her slim brown thighs.

'There's a flight tomorrow, in fact,' she said. 'Quite a big deal. We've got someone from the State Department meeting it. It's good cover for us – government participating, approving.'

'Maybe I should check it out.'

'I thought you were going back to London,' she said.

'I am. But there's no tearing hurry. I'm on leave. Convalescing. Somebody shot me in the chest.'

'I feel I owe you an apology,' she said, reaching for her drink and letting the front of her dressing gown gape for an instant before she closed it with a hand.

Bond took a big gulp of his bourbon – remembering her body, that night at Lokomeji in the rest-house.

'I should go,' he said, his voice hoarser than he would have wished.

'Let me say sorry first,' she said and stood up – unbelting her dressing gown, freeing it to fall from her shoulders and crumple on the carpet.

She allowed Bond to study her for a moment then stooped, picked up her dressing gown, slung it over her arm and sauntered into the bedroom, Bond following. She hung the dressing gown on the hook on the back of the door and smiled at him.

'I'm sorry I shot you,' she said and slipped into the bed. 'But I did it to save your life.'

Bond pulled off his tie and began to undo the buttons on his shirt.

·8·

CHELSEA

Bond and Blessing made love, then ordered food and drink – two omelettes and fries and a bottle of champagne – and, after they'd eaten and drunk, they made love again. She was eager and insisting, giving him precise instructions, at one stage rolling him on to his back and sitting astride him, her hands pressing hard on his chest as she rocked to and fro. Bond did as he was told, revelling in her slim brown body, her lissom youthfulness.

Later, when they lay in each other's arms, she told him that she'd been with no one else since that night they'd been captured by Kobus Breed.

'I thought about you a lot,' she said. 'And when I saw you in the restaurant I felt my heart jump, you know . . .' She laughed quietly. 'My first reaction was pleasure – not alarm. What does that tell you?'

'That you've still got a lot to learn,' Bond said.

She punched him gently on his shoulder and kissed him.

'So teach me,' she said.

Bond slipped out of her room in the small hours, having been given all the details about the AfricaKIN flight and the house in Orange County. He had dressed and kissed her goodbye and gave her naked body a final caress as she lay sleepily on the bed amidst the rumpled sheets.

'I suppose we'd better not meet again,' Bond said. 'Until this is all over.'

'I know what,' she said. 'I'll ask to be posted to London.' She sat up and put her arms round his neck. 'That would be fun, wouldn't it, James? You and me in London. Where do you live?'

'You know where I live.'

'No I don't.'

'Chelsea.'

'You and me in Chelsea . . .' She lay back on the pillows, touching herself. 'Think about it, James . . .'

Bond was tempted to tear his clothes off and climb back in the bed.

'There's no harm in thinking,' he said. He kissed her quickly on the lips and left before his resolve collapsed.

As he crossed from the annexe to the main block of the motel Bond paused, some sixth sense making him draw into the shadows of a doorway. He waited, looking about him. The parking lot was almost full, its corralled cars shining dewily in the glow of the arc lights, like some sort of sleeping mechanical herd in its vast paddock. Nobody moving, nobody to be seen. He waited a couple of minutes but there was nothing to worry him. He strode into the rear of the motel, with a wave to the night porter, and rode the elevator up to his room. He requested the motel operator to give him a wake-up call at 5 a.m., slept for a couple of hours then showered and shaved and, as dawn approached, he went down to the lobby and asked the sleepy doorman to hail him a taxi. Thirty minutes later he was breakfasting in the dining room of the Fairview.

After breakfast Bond took a taxi to the BOAC offices on Pennsylvania Avenue and confirmed his return flight to London for the evening of the following day. Now he was glad that he'd booked first class – he could rebook without any problem at the very last minute, and even not showing up was unlikely to be penalised as long as notice was given. He left the offices, hailed a cab and paid the driver $10 to take him round the corner and wait. From the shelter of a doorway he saw agent Massinette stroll into the BOAC offices, no doubt to confirm the flight that Bond was leaving on. The CIA would be reassured and Bond assumed that the surveillance of him would be less thorough. Wait and see. Massinette would acquire the necessary information with a flash of his badge and pass it on to Felix Leiter.

Bond climbed back into his taxi and asked to be returned to the Fairview. There was something about Massinette and his demeanour that troubled Bond – some shortfall in the routine CIA professionalism that Brig Leiter embodied. Bond hadn't liked the sullen, aggressive way that Massinette had stared at him that first time they'd encountered each other. Brig Leiter had zeal, an ethic – that was obvious the minute you met him. Massinette was harder to gauge. Bond told himself to forget it. Maybe Massinette had personal troubles of his own that were souring his view of the world – even agents are human beings, after all.

When he arrived at the Fairview Bond went to the parking lot and sat in his Mustang for five minutes. As soon as he was confident no one was watching him he took a leisurely, round-about route west to Seminole Field airport.

Seminole Field doubled as a commuting hub for small prop planes flying short journeys to Maryland, Virginia and Philadelphia and was also home to three Air National Guard squadrons of F-100 Super Sabres. Consequently the runway was long enough to service the largest transport planes and commercial jets. Bond parked his car and, taking his binoculars with him, joined the small crowd of plane-spotters on an elevated knoll outside the perimeter fence that gave a good view of the main runway, the apron and the small control tower and arrival and departure buildings. The Air National Guard hangars were on the far side of the airport. He checked his watch: according to Blessing the AfricaKIN flight was due in from Khartoum in an hour. Scanning the piste with his binoculars he could see that an area had been cordoned off with portable railings and there was a small row of bleachers to one side where a few journalists and photographers lounged, chatting and smoking.

After about thirty minutes a small motorcade of town cars arrived and assorted dignitaries emerged and were shown into the airport buildings. Bond spotted Colonel Denga and Blessing. There were men in suits and a few women in dresses and hats – AfricaKIN sponsors and officials from the Department of the Interior, Bond supposed. The welcome committee had arrived but clearly Gabriel Adeka wasn't attending. Then three ambulances with 'AfricaKIN' logos drove on to the apron and parked in a row, waiting for the plane.

On time, a Boeing 707 swooped into the airport and touched down, causing a murmur of excitement among the plane-spotters. As it taxied in Bond saw that the words 'Transglobal Charter' were written on the side but there, stencilled on the nose, was the now-familiar AfricaKIN logo. The plane came to a halt, the dignitaries applauded and stairs were taken to the main doors. Gurneys were rolled in readiness from the ambulances and paramedics stood by.

Then the doors opened and the children appeared. First, those who could walk, some with their heads and limbs bandaged, some with little arm-crutches, then some very young and frail ones carried by male nurses, and finally those who were laid on the gurneys for the photo opportunity.

Bond focused his binoculars as the dignitaries briefly flanked the children and the flashbulbs popped. Denga was standing at one end of the group – immaculate in a beige seersucker suit – with a junior senator; an undersecretary of state at the other with Blessing. Hands were shaken, a short speech was made and there was a polite spatter of applause. Bond noticed that all the children who could walk were in a kind of uniform: peaked baseball caps, pale blue boiler suits and neat little rucksacks on their backs, all displaying the AfricaKIN Inc. logo. Charitable work and decent altruism marching hand in hand with very effective PR, Bond thought.

Within minutes the children were installed in the ambulances, which wheeled away to a gate in the perimeter fence, lights flashing. Bond loped to his car and drove round to the side entrance, where he was in time to see the last in the small convoy of ambulances turning on to the highway heading west into Orange County. Two police outriders led the way. Bond slowed, allowing some cars to overtake him – it was going to be an easy follow.

After twenty minutes the ambulances turned off the highway and the road and the countryside around it became noticeably more rural. They were barely an hour out of DC, Bond calculated, but already it felt very remote. They passed fewer and fewer houses. There were meadows with horses grazing, dense copses of wood – elm, walnut, ash – and a pleasing, gentle undulation to the landscape – valleys and streams, groups of small grassy hills. It was the country – but very civilised.

Eventually, after passing through a small village called Jackson Point, the ambulances swept through a gate between twin lodges that marked the driveway to Rowanoak Hall, the new headquarters of AfricaKIN Inc – a far cry from a grubby shop in Bayswater, Bond thought. Here in Rowanoak Hall, Blessing had told him, the children were fed, medicated, assessed and then despatched to the various hospitals in DC and surrounding areas that would best treat the children's wounds, diseases or other ailments. Orphaned children, malnourished, suffering children, children wounded by landmines or ethnic violence, removed from harm's way and brought to safety and succour in the United States of America, no expense spared. African kin indeed, Bond considered: nothing appeared better or more slickly organised or more sanctioned by authority. But what was really going on?

He drove slowly along the country lane that followed the ten-foot-high brick walls of the Rowanoak estate. The house was set in a thickly wooded park, carefully planted in the last century with red mulberry, spruce, cottonwood and hickory trees. There was no extra wiring or alarms fitted to the wall that Bond could see. He pulled into a muddy parking space and shinned up a yellow beech tree that would allow him a better view of the house itself.

Bond focused his binoculars and saw a large and rather ugly red-brick nineteenth-century house constructed in somewhat over-the-top Gothic-revival style. There were battlements, towers, buttresses and clustered crockets, pinnacles and finials and gingerbread trim wherever possible. On the wide gravelled sweep of the driveway in front of the carriage porch of the house the three ambulances were parked and, as Bond watched, they were joined by others sent by the affiliated AfricaKIN hospitals. An hour later, they were all gone, the children despatched. Bond wondered how many other staff remained in the house. From time to time burly men in black windcheaters with walkie-talkies wandered around the lawns and disappeared again. They seemed to be the only evidence of extra security. Bond supposed that they had to be discreet – AfricaKIN was a charity, after all. Was Gabriel Adeka inside? he wondered. And Kobus Breed? He imagined Breed would stay close to Adeka. As far as he could tell neither Blessing nor Denga had accompanied the convoy of ambulances.

Bond climbed stiffly down from his vantage point. Evening was coming on and the sky was darkening as he drove round to the main entrance and found a leafy lane where he could park out of sight but with a view of the gates themselves. As the working day ended, he watched as a small procession of private cars came down the drive from the house, some containing uniformed nurses. There was a man living in one of the lodges who emerged to open the gates and close them, chatting amiably to some of the staff as they departed.

When no more cars appeared Bond assumed that Rowanoak Hall was now empty, down to its core staff – just Adeka, perhaps, and Breed and their aides and bodyguards. He couldn't know for sure without climbing in and doing a headcount himself. But not tonight, he thought. Once he entered those walled acres he had to be prepared for anything and anyone. Perhaps Blessing could tell him more about the personnel left behind once the gates closed for the night. He started his car and headed back to DC. He was hungry – he hadn't eaten since breakfast.

·9·

BLESSING

Bond asked at the Fairview's reception where the best steak restaurant in Washington was to be found and was told that the Grill on H Street was the place to go. So Bond took a taxi there and asked for a table for one. He knew exactly what he wanted and, while his vodka martini was being mixed at the bar, he consulted the maître d' – slipping him the obligatory $20 – telling him the white lie that it was his birthday, and that he was a fussy eater – all to make sure things were arranged precisely as he desired them.

Ten minutes later Bond was led into the dining room to his corner table. The napery was thick white linen, the silverware heavy and traditional and the glasses gleamed, speck-free. The Grill on H Street replicated the clubby values of a Victorian steakhouse reimagined for America, a hundred years on: dark panelled walls, low-wattage sconces, gilt-framed oil paintings of sporting scenes and frontier battles, the odd stuffed animal trophy on the wall, a chequerboard marble floor and venerable, grey-haired men in long white aprons serving at table.

Bond's preordered bottle of Chateau Lynch-Bages 1953 had already been decanted and, as he sat down, a small lacquered tray was brought to his table that contained all the ingredients necessary to make a vinaigrette to his own secret formula: a little carafe of olive oil and one of red-wine vinegar, a jar of Dijon mustard, a halved clove of garlic, a black-pepper grinder, a ramekin of granulated sugar, a bowl, a teaspoon and a small balloon whisk to mix the ingredients together.*

Bond swiftly made his dressing then his filet mignon – *à point* – arrived with a bowl of salad. He had ordered filet mignon because he didn't want a steak that overlapped his plate. It was nicely chargrilled on the outside, pink but not blue on the inside. Bond dressed the salad, seasoned his steak and took his first mouthful of claret. As he ate and drank he allowed himself to enjoy the fantasy that life was good and the world was on its proper course – this being the purpose of eating and drinking well, surely? He ended his meal with half of an avocado into which he poured what remained of his dressing. He drank a calvados, smoked a cigarette and called for the check. His culinary hunger assuaged, a new one replaced it. He was hungry for Blessing, for her slim active body. Hungry for her to give him more precise instructions about what she wanted him to do to her.

Bond sauntered into the lobby of the Blackstone Park, said hello to Delmont, who was working that night, and went up to his

---

* James Bond's Salad Dressing. Mix five parts of red-wine vinegar with one part extra-virgin olive oil. The vinegar overload is essential. Add a halved clove of garlic, half a teaspoon of Dijon mustard, a good grind of black pepper and a teaspoon of white granulated sugar. Mix well, remove the garlic and dress the salad.

room. He waited until ten o'clock and strolled back down to the lobby, exiting through the rear doors into the parking lot. The lights in Blessing's suite were on. He felt a hot pulse of anticipation at seeing her.

He knocked on her door. There was no answer. He knocked again and said 'Blessing – it's James.' Still no answer. He repeated himself more loudly. Nothing. He went back to the night porter at the rear entrance and called her room. The telephone rang and rang – no reply. Odd. The night porter had just come on duty and couldn't enlighten him. Maybe Blessing had come in and had to leave in a hurry, forgetting to switch the lights out . . .

Bond went through to the main lobby and sought out Delmont.

'Hey, Mr Fitzjohn, what can I do for you?'

Bond drew him discreetly aside and lowered his voice.

'Delmont, would you do me a favour? Has my wife come back? You know – the lady in suite 5K in the annexe . . .'

'Give me two seconds.'

Delmont scurried off to reception and swiftly returned.

'She's in her room, Mr F,' he said. 'Arrived about an hour and a half ago. She hasn't left or her key would be there.'

'Of course – thanks, Delmont.' Bond smiled reassuringly but he was worried. He walked casually back to the rear entrance and up the stairs to the second-floor suites. He glanced around but the corridor was empty. He unscrewed the heel from his loafer and worked the blade in between the lock and the door frame. He lunged at it with his shoulder and it gave. Bond pushed the door open.

The lights were on. Blessing's handbag was tossed on the sofa.

Thus far, so unremarkable. Had she taken a sleeping pill and was fast asleep in her bedroom?

'Blessing? It's me . . .' Bond said, then repeated himself, louder. Silence.

Maybe his initial assumption was right – she'd rushed out, called away, urgently. But why leave her handbag . . . ?

Bond felt a premonitory nausea – something was making him reluctant to go into the bedroom. He took a few steps then halted.

A thin dark sticky crescent of blood had seeped under the door to the bedroom.

Bond reached for the handle, turned it and tried to push the door open. It was unusually heavy. Bond gave an unconscious, spontaneous moan because he knew what had happened to Blessing and he knew who had done it.

He stood there in an awful balance of inertia, unable to decide whether to turn away and leave or to confront his darkest suspicions. He felt sick at heart – he knew what he had to do.

He leaned his weight against the door and shoved and pushed it open.

One glance was enough. Blessing was dead – naked, hanging by her jawbone from the hook on the back of the door, blood still dripping from her opened throat.

Bond heaved the door to and sank to his knees.

Kobus Breed.

Bond felt the tears smart in his eyes as he hung his head and thought desperately about Blessing and what she must have endured, a conflagration of outrage making him tremble, igniting his seething anger. Then he stood up, his head clearing. He inhaled deeply – the shock was draining from him to be replaced by a new granite-hard resolve. There was nothing so invigorating as clear and absolute purpose. There was only one objective now. James Bond would kill Kobus Breed.

·10·

ONE-MAN COMMANDO

Bond called Brig Leiter from the Fairview. It was after midnight.

'Red alert, Brig,' Bond said, his voice heavy. 'Bad news – your agent has been erased. I'm very sorry.'

'What? Jesus, no. Aleesha? Where is she? In her house?'

'No, in a motel. It's very nasty. Blackstone Park Motor Lodge, suite 5K.'

Silence. Bond could almost hear Brig's brain working.

'How do you know?'

'I saw her.'

'What was she doing in a motel? And how come you were in her room?'

'She moved. I think she felt safer in a motel.'

'Who killed her?'

'Kobus Breed.'

'My God . . .' there was another pause, then, 'You didn't answer my second question, Mr Bond.'

'I went to her room to ask her something.'

'How did you know she was staying there?'

'I followed her.'

'OK . . . Felix is coming up tonight from Miami.'

'I'm going to miss him,' Bond said. 'I go back to London tonight.' Now Bond paused to let the lie sink in.

'Brig, I don't know what procedures you follow in these circumstances,' Bond said, 'but I think you should get a team round to that motel now and seal the room. I put a "Do not disturb" sign on the door. Lock it down. I wouldn't call the police for twenty-four hours, also. Wait till Felix gets here. He can coordinate with them. You don't want Breed to make a run for it.'

'Yeah, you're right,' Brig said. 'What time's your plane?'

'Nine o'clock this evening.' Let them think for as long as possible that he was going home, he reasoned. They had more important tasks on their hands than worrying about James Bond.

They said goodbye and Bond hung up. He undressed and stood under the pounding shower as if the water would wash away all his bad feelings, his memories of Blessing and her miserable death. Then he tried to sleep but his mind grew busy with the plan that he was forming. He needed to equip himself better if he was going to attack the Rowanoak estate single-handed. He turned his pillow over and rested his cheek on the cooler underside. Why had Breed killed Blessing? There could only be one answer. Breed had followed her to the motel and had seen Blessing with him – Blessing back in contact with James Bond . . . That would have been enough to confer a death sentence on her. Bond recalled that sixth-sense shiver he'd experienced in the parking lot when he left her suite in the annexe – had Kobus Breed been out there watching in the darkness? And Bond knew that the manner of Blessing's death had been a warning directed at him. Breed knew that he could read the signs; Breed was saying to him, I know you're out there – you're next, Bond.

He thought on. Breed hadn't done anything immediately because he wanted to wait until after the flight had arrived and was happy to let Blessing continue with her AfricaKIN duties. So: there must have been something on that flight that came in to Seminole Field that was especially important. Twelve sick children? There had to be something more.

Bond ordered breakfast in his room but only smoked a cigarette and drank a cup of coffee, leaving his eggs untouched. He wasn't hungry. As he left the Fairview he saw Agent Massinette approaching. Bond greeted him amiably enough but Massinette's face remained impassive.

'Brig told me to tell you – we're all locked down at the Blackstone Park. The room's sealed.'

'Good. It should buy you some time.'

'May I ask where you're going, Mr Bond?'

'I'm going to do some shopping – some gifts for friends in London.'

'Yeah? Have a nice day.'

That evening, Bond laid out everything he needed on the bed. Weapons: the Frankel and Kleist, fully loaded and with spare rounds of ammunition; his Beretta with two extra clips; the mugger's switchblade with its diamond inlay; a small aerosol canister of OC – oleoresin capsicum pepper spray (concentrate of chilli pepper with the brand name Savage Heat) – and, finally, a sock filled with $10-worth of nickels and dimes, knotted tight to form a cosh. As for his clothing, Bond had bought a black leather blouson jacket with big patch pockets, a black polo-neck jersey, a black knitted three-hole balaclava and a length of nylon rope. He was going to wear his dark charcoal trousers from his suit tucked into his socks with a pair of black sneakers with thick rubber soles.

He smiled grimly to himself. A one-man commando on a one-man commando raid.

He had a final telephone call to make then he would check out of the hotel and head for the airport. He sat down on his bed and took out Turnbull McHarg's business card.

It was dark when Bond drove his Mustang up to the Fairview's entry-way and the bellhop placed his luggage in the boot. Bond tipped him and glanced around to see if anyone was paying particular attention to his departure. No sign of Massinette but, Bond reasoned, if he were Brig Leiter running this show he'd have a tail on Bond. Routine. Insurance.

Bond drove out to Dulles airport. He couldn't tell if he was being followed. There was a lot of traffic heading out of town. Not far from the airport he pulled into a gas station and filled the tank, watching to see if cars stopped or slowed. He spotted nothing so climbed back into his car and swung out on to the highway back into town, steadily increasing his speed. At the last minute he turned off at an intersection, changed direction and headed back to the airport again. He began to relax. He sped past the turn for Dulles and veered off into the quiet streets of Ashburn and drove around for ten minutes or so, stopping and starting, doubling back suddenly and unpredictably. No one was following him; he could safely choose his own route back out to Rowanoak Hall.

Bond parked the car down a track not far from the house and changed into his dark clothes. He looked at his watch; ten past eleven. By now Brig and Felix Leiter would know full well that he wasn't on the plane for London. Bond had vanished – one rogue male agent gone solo yet again. It was a calculated risk, this solitary assault on the AfricaKIN Inc. headquarters, and he asked himself if Felix might second-guess what he was planning. He doubted it. Only a fool would attempt such a thing. He wondered if they would try to capture Breed – but again he thought they would hold off. Blessing had said that she thought Hulbert Linck was the key target; the CIA wouldn't want to do anything that would scare him away. All in all, Bond reckoned he had this one night to himself. Whatever happened, there would be no second chance for him – his vengeance had to take place in the next few hours before the CIA tracked him down and pulled him in.

He wound the nylon rope around his body and assembled the Frankel and Kleist. Then he filled the pockets of his jacket with his assorted weaponry. He hoped there weren't dogs – he had seen no sign of them – but he had his OC spray just in case. He had once halted a snarling, slavering Dobermann with a blast of pepper spray – it was infallible.

He drove to the furthest point of the Rowanoak estate and parked the Mustang against the brick perimeter wall. He climbed on to the car roof and shinned over the wall, carefully dropping the rifle (safety catch secured) on to the grass on the other side before he lowered himself down. He pulled on his balaclava and moved off through the wooded park towards the distant lights of the house.

As he drew near the Hall he saw a man standing on the back lawn of the house smoking a cigarette. He appeared to have a walkie-talkie in his hand as he paced about, keeping notional guard. The back lawn was illuminated by a powerful arc light high on the fake battlements. The front sweep of gravel was equally brightly lit – no one could approach the house without stepping into this wide glaring disc of light.

Bond moved easily through the trees and bushes of the park so that he could afford himself a good view of the main facade. Here two big lamps threw a pool of light that extended down the drive to the gatehouses. Bond found his ideal position behind a small sycamore and set the Frankel on a low branch to give him a steady firing platform. Bond clicked the switch on the scope to set it to its night-vision mode. Eugene Goodforth had been right – the dimmed red glow of the reticle did not interfere with the vision beyond. Bond's eye settled to the lens of the sniper-scope and he cleared his aim and waited. Five minutes to midnight. He hoped his diversion would be punctual.

In fact it was ten minutes late, but no matter. At ten past midnight Bond saw the headlights of Turnbull McHarg's car pull up at the lodge gates and heard him toot his horn loudly and peremptorily, as Bond had instructed him. When Bond had telephoned him earlier he'd invited Turnbull to a 'surprise' birthday party that wealthy friends were throwing for him at a big mansion house out of town, Rowanoak Hall. He'd given Turnbull precise directions and instructions. Should be fun. Lots of caviar and champagne. And girls. McHarg had been delighted. I'll be there, James. Look forward to seeing you – lots to catch up on. Thanks a million.

Bond knew they'd never let McHarg past the gates but that was all he wanted. A disturbance – something wrong – and his name pointedly mentioned. He could hear McHarg's voice raised, loudly remonstrating with the intransigent lodge-keeper, demanding entry to the party, insisting he'd been specially invited by the birthday boy himself, James Bond.

Bond drew the Frankel snug against his cheek and settled the cross hairs of the reticle on the first arc light. The sound of the big bulb popping almost drowned the gunshot. He shifted aim and took the second light out. In the sudden darkness Bond heard McHarg's profane exclamation of shock and astonishment, then he raced off into the darkness towards the rear of the house.

Secure in a position facing the back of the house, he quickly shot out the rear arc. Only the lights of the house now glowed and he could hear the consternation inside – shouts, doors slamming. Bond slipped the scope off the mountings on the barrel of the Frankel and slid the rifle under a bush – its job was done. He retreated into the darkness of the park, taking the Beretta out of his pocket and cocking it. As he left he saw three men race out of the rear door, guns and powerful torches in hand, running across the lawn, spreading out until they were swallowed up by the wilderness of the park, only the intermittent beams of their torches giving their positions away. Bond tracked them as best he could with the scope. Three guards, Bond thought, and no dogs – thank God. He stood with his back to a tree scanning the pulsing night around him, waiting for a guard to come close – once he had one, he'd have the others. Always wait for them to come to you, he told himself, don't go searching for your prey. He slowed his breathing as much as he could, standing absolutely still, gun poised, waiting.

It was the crackle of a walkie-talkie that alerted him, rather than a torch beam. Then he saw the torch, playing among the trees. He heard the man's voice.

'Dawie – can't see a thing, man. You sure he's in the park? Over.'

There was the inaudible static of a reply.

Dawie, Bond thought: interesting. Some of Kobus's RLI buddies from Dahum.

The man drew closer but he never heard Bond, who, as he passed, brought down the heel of his Beretta on the back of his head. He dropped at once, inert. Bond quickly lashed his hands behind his back and then tied his wrists to his ankles, using the switchblade to cut lengths of nylon rope. He ripped up a clod of earth and stuffed the man's gaping mouth with turf. Then he fired his gun once into the air. He picked up the walkie-talkie, shouted 'Dawie!' fired again and switched it off.

Bond could hear somebody blundering through the bushes then saw a swaying torch beam sweeping through the trees. The man – it must have been Dawie – was shouting harshly into his walkie-talkie trying to summon the third guard to join them.

'Henrick – over here, man,' he shouted. 'We're by the west gate.'

Bond aimed slightly above the torch beam and fired twice.

He heard a scream and saw the torch spin to the ground. Dawie started bellowing.

'I'm down! I'm down! He's over here!'

Bond crept forward as Dawie continued his shouted instructions, guiding Henrick towards him. Then he saw Henrick's jerky torch beam as he ran through the trees.

Bond took his time, making sure he advanced in total silence. Dawie was moaning in pain and Henrick was crouched over his writhing body, looking for the wound. Bond took his nickel-and-dime cosh out of his pocket and slugged Henrick full on the crown of his head. He went down like a cow hit by a humane killer. He was so still Bond wondered if he'd delivered some kind of fatal blow. He held his fingers to his throat. There was a pulse – a thready one.

'I'm dying. Help me,' Dawie said. Bond turned Dawie's fallen torch on him and saw that he'd been hit low and to the side of his abdomen – not fatal, though he was already pallid from blood loss. Bond said nothing, grabbing his collar and dragging him – groaning – to a tree, where he bound his arms behind it. He checked Henrick again – still breathing but out cold. He roped his wrists together and turned him on his side so that he wouldn't drown if he vomited. He fired both their guns into the air a few times then slung them away into the darkness. He wanted whoever was still in the house to think the guards were engaged in a firefight in the furthest reaches of the park. When it all went quiet they would begin to worry – maybe panic: they had no idea how many potential assailants were out there.

He took one last look at Dawie and picked up his walkie-talkie.

'I got him!' Bond yelled into the microphone. Then switched it off.

'If you shout loud enough someone will come for you,' Bond said to Dawie. He knew it wasn't true – he just wanted a few distant incoherent bellowings to be heard back at the house.

'Don't leave me, man,' Dawie said plaintively, then added with surprising poetry, 'I can feel my life flowing out of me, leaving me. I can feel it.'

Bond said nothing and headed off towards the house.

Some of the ground-floor windows were lit up, others had their curtains drawn, Bond observed as he approached. Through a gap in the curtains of the large oriel window of the main drawing room Bond saw Kobus Breed – his jacket off, his tie loosened at his throat – talking urgently on the phone. From time to time he broke off to shout into the walkie-talkie then hurled it away – obviously the lack of response from Dawie's channel was making him furious.

Bond paused outside – he didn't want to go into the house as he had no idea who else might be in there. Better to try and lure Breed outside into the darkness. Then he decided it might be a more efficient plan to climb and maybe break in on a higher floor and he began hauling himself quickly up one of the heavy lead downpipes that drained the roof gutters. In a few seconds he found himself up on the faux battlements with their Gothic buttresses, polygonal chimney pots and profusion of carved stone finials. Bond's mind was working fast – sensing opportunities, weighing up options, minimising risk. He headed for a dark window and accidently bumped into one of the finials decorating a stumpy brick chimney stack. He felt the masonry slide and grate and the round stone ball on the top almost wobbled free. Bond steadied it. It was about the size of a medicine ball and must have weighed close to fifty pounds. He smiled to himself – he had an idea.

He removed Dawie's walkie-talkie from his pocket and switched it on. He turned the channel frequency selection knob very slightly to one side so that it kept connecting and then cutting out. Through gritted teeth and strangulating his voice he repeated certain phrases into the microphone.

'Come in – over – Bond – I have him – come in, come in – not receiving – Bond, repeat Bond, I have him, over.'

He assumed this garbled message would be picked up by Breed and others listening in. Then he searched his pockets for loose change in vain, before he remembered he was carrying a sock full of nickels and dimes. He unpicked the knot and helped himself to a small handful. He crept round the battlements until he had a good angle on to the drawing room's oriel window. He leaned out and flung the small coins down at the glass and heard them rattle and ping as they hit. Then he threw another handful. He raced back to the finial he had nearly dislodged and, with both arms functioning as a cradle, heaved off the crowning stone ball. It was a dense dead weight, incredibly heavy. He shuffled with it to the edge of the battlements that projected out over the wide door that led from the drawing room to the lawn. Come on, Kobus, he said to himself, muscles straining – you must be curious, Bond is out there, Dawie has him.

The door opened slowly and a wand of light from the drawing room fell across the lawn.

Kobus Breed stepped out cautiously, a gun levelled in his hand.

'Dawie?' he shouted into the blackness. 'Where the hell are you, man? You're not coming through on your radio! You keep breaking up!'

Bond looked down on him, his muscles beginning to ache horribly. Breed's head was a small target from this height – but he wanted to crush it like a ripe cantaloupe melon.

Breed stepped out another yard, his gun sweeping to and fro, expecting the danger to lie in the park beyond, not from above.

'Dawie – show yourself! Have you got him?'

Bond dropped the stone ball and took a step back. He heard the impact – the sound of meaty crunching, bone and flesh compacting – and Breed's bellow of acute, hideous agony and surprise.

He peered down. Breed was on the ground, writhing and moaning, his right arm flapping uncontrollably like some broken wing on a bird. The ball had missed his head but seemed to have landed square on his right shoulder, shattering bone, pulverising it.

Bond slid down the drainpipe and, back on the ground, cautiously approached round the side of the building, slipping his Beretta from his pocket. He should just kill him, he thought, but he wanted Breed to know why he was dying, why his pain and imminent execution were recompense for what he'd done to Blessing. There'd be no point in just blowing him away. Bond wanted to taste sweet revenge.

Bond levelled his gun as he drew near. Breed was face down – the stone ball beside his head – and was clearly in massive, intolerable pain and shock. His whole body was now jerking and twitching spasmodically. The stone ball's impact looked like it had shattered the shoulder blade – and the collarbone. The down-force of the dead weight had also blasted the humerus into pieces. Three inches of thick sheared bone stuck through Breed's shirt at the elbow.

Bond turned Breed over with his foot. Breed screamed as his shattered arm dug into the turf of the lawn. But in the good hand that had been underneath his body he had clung on to his automatic pistol. He fired at Bond and missed – his hand was shaking visibly – and fired again, this time the bullet striking Bond's gun and spinning it off and away in a shower of sparks. Bond threw himself down, knees first, on to Breed's chest and felt ribs crack and his sternum bend. He side-kicked Breed's gun from his hand and rummaged in his jacket pocket for the switchblade. No switchblade but the small aerosol can of Savage Heat pepper spray.

Bond sprayed Breed's un-closable open eye with a thick mist of oleoresin capsicum and heard his scream rip up from deep in his lungs. Breed's right arm was useless so Bond stood on his left and let him writhe in the full torment of his pain, his legs kicking convulsively, the potent reduction of chilli peppers working on his seething eyeball. Breed wailed like a baby and Bond happily enveloped his head in another mist-cloud of Savage Heat.

'This is for Blessing, you filth, you scum,' he said, harshly, bending over him, 'and this is from me,' and sprayed his open eye again from a range of one inch.

Bond reached into his other pocket for the switchblade. He

shot the blade out and tugged Breed brutally over on to his front again, burying the knife deep in the back of his neck, severing the spinal cord. Breed's body jerked and then went slack, his screams dying to a burble of popping saliva in his throat.

Bond stepped back, breathing heavily, a little astonished at his own savagery. He massaged his tingling right hand and reminded himself of what Blessing had gone through – no tender mercies from Kobus Breed. He was angry with himself, however: never again, he thought – execute when the moment presents itself. Emotion – desire for just revenge – had undermined his professionalism, and had almost killed him. If you intend to kill – kill. Don't hang around wanting to embellish the act in some way. He could hear Corporal Dave Tozer's harsh voice in his ear: 'DR, you stupid bastard. Disproportionate Response. Any threat – massive overkill. If he spits at you – tear his throat out. If he kicks you in the shin, take his leg off. Take both legs off.'

Bond began to calm. He looked down at Breed's body – a mugger's switchblade sticking out of the back of his neck. He could be carted away later. The fact that no one had appeared from the house when the shots were fired was a good sign. Bond roved around and found his gun. Breed's second round had hit just in front of the trigger, scarring the metal with a raw weal. He cocked the gun, shot the clip out, slammed it back in. It seemed to be working fine.

He took off his balaclava and wiped the smear of sweat from his face. He pushed through the garden door into the drawing room and began to move quickly and watchfully through the public rooms: a library, a smaller sitting room then down a parqueted corridor towards the main hall with its wide solid staircase. Every now and then Bond paused and listened – but he could hear nothing that suggested there was anyone else in the house.

A pair of modern swing doors led off the hall behind the staircase. Bond pushed them open and saw that here the decor changed completely. Another wide corridor stretched before him, painted pistachio green with white rubberised tiles on the floor. It looked like a hospital and from behind closed doors – inset with panels of glass – came the hum of machinery. Bond peered into one room – incubators, centrifuges, sterilisers, freezers. Another room was fitted out like a ward with four beds and a nurse's station. Other doors were labelled 'X-ray' and 'Dispensary'. There was an office with the name 'Dr Masind' on it – a name that seemed vaguely familiar. This was clearly the state-of-the-art receiving clinic for the children from the AfricaKIN flights.

Bond kept listening and kept hearing nothing that alarmed him. He wondered where Gabriel Adeka was – upstairs? Perhaps he should turn back and explore the upper floors. Then he arrived at the end of the long corridor. To the left was a door and to the right a flight of stone stairs that led down to a basement or cellar area. He pushed open the door to find himself in a kind of schoolroom with two rows of desks facing a blackboard. On the floor in front of the blackboard was a pile of what looked like discarded clothing. Bond switched on the light to see that it wasn't clothing but little rucksacks – the rucksacks the kids had been wearing when they disembarked. Bond picked one up – its bottom had been ripped out. He picked up another similarly torn open. All the rucksacks appeared to have been cut apart.

He turned to switch out the light and saw another rucksack

intact on a side table. Beside the rucksack was a Stanley knife. And beside it was a neat stack of what looked like slabs of putty, wrapped in cellophane. Bond picked one up – eight inches long, four wide, one inch thick – about 500 grams, he reckoned. This must have been what Breed was occupied with when Turnbull McHarg had tooted his horn and Bond had shot the arc lights out. Bond picked up the knife and cut away the bottom of the rucksack to reveal in the lining another slab of what he now realised was raw heroin moulded into a flat bar, the size of half a brick. Twelve sick kids, twelve little rucksacks, six kilos of heroin. Who was going to search a malnourished child shivering with fever? Or an eight-year-old amputee? As drug-smuggling went it was heartless, brutal, simple and extremely effective. Each AfricaKIN flight must have its quota of—

Bond heard something – a cough.

He froze, then switched off the light and stepped back into the corridor. He heard the cough again, coming from down the stairs in the basement – lung-racking and feeble. Was there a child down there, Bond wondered? Some sort of isolation ward for the extremely contagious?

He levelled his gun and began to move carefully down the stairs. There was a night light set in the ceiling that gave off a pale pearly glow revealing a wide landing with two doors off it. The cough came again. No child – an adult, Bond thought. There was a key in the lock of the door behind which the coughing continued. He put his ear to the door and heard the sound of laboured breathing. Bond turned the key and then the handle, and shoved it gently open, his gun pointing into the room. The landing light provided enough illumination for Bond to see that there was a man lying on a mattress in the far corner. He groped for a switch, found it and clicked on the light.

The man was shivering, knees drawn up to his chest, lying on a befouled sheet. An African man, naked except for a pair of filthy underpants. He turned towards Bond and muttered something. His head was shaven and he had a small goatee beard. Gabriel Adeka.

Bond stepped forward, recoiling slightly from the feculent smell. Gabriel Adeka in the grip of terrible cold turkey. His face and shaved head were shiny with sweat and his whole body shook with recurring tremors. On a table across the room was an enamel kidney dish, a Bunsen burner attached to a camping gas canister, a length of rubber tubing, some spoons and several syringes still wrapped in their plastic seals. All the paraphernalia required for shooting up heroin.

Bond was thinking hard – so this was why no one saw Gabriel Adeka any more. Breed had turned him into a junkie and kept him locked in this cellar, no doubt on a regime of drug-injection and then deprivation, turning him into this dehumanised, desperate addict.

Gabriel Adeka reached out a shivering hand to Bond, his big eyes imploring, beseeching. Give me more, I beg you, give me my nirvana in a needle.

Except it wasn't Gabriel Adeka, Bond now saw, and grew rigid at the recognition. The last time he'd seen this man he had been lying in a hospital bed in Port Dunbar. Brigadier Solomon Adeka, military genius, the 'African Napoleon', begging for a syringe full of heroin.

'It's a terrible thing, addiction,' a voice said. 'Put your gun down on the table and turn round very slowly.'

Bond did as he was told and laid his gun down beside the syringes and swivelled round carefully.

Standing in the doorway was the tall lanky figure of Hulbert Linck – except his blond hair was cut short and dyed black and he had a full beard. He was wearing a tan canvas windcheater and jeans and was covering Bond with an automatic pistol. He stepped into the room, glancing at Adeka.

'Forgive the precaution, Mr Bond – I hope you understand. This is all Kobus Breed's doing,' he said. 'Breed has kept me and Adeka here prisoners while he and his men use the charity to smuggle drugs into the USA. He's becoming extremely rich extremely fast.' Linck smiled. 'Funny that it should be you, Bond, who's come to our rescue.' He lowered his gun and put it on the table beside Bond's.

'We are very happy to surrender ourselves to you,' Linck said. 'Very happy.'

The first shot hit Linck just in front of his left ear sending a fine skein of blood spraying from his head and the second smashed into his chest, slamming him heavily against the wall. He slid down it, leaving a thin smeary trail of blood and toppled over. Adeka screamed and gibbered, huddling in the corner.

Agent Massinette irrupted into the room, gun levelled at Adeka. He was followed immediately by Brig Leiter. Bond heard the clatter of other footsteps coming down the corridor overhead.

'You OK, Mr Bond?' Brig Leiter said.

Bond had his eyes on Massinette, who was crouching over Linck's body searching his pockets.

'Why the fuck did you shoot him?' Bond said, his voice heavy with fury.

Massinette turned and stood up.

'He had a gun and was going to kill you.'

'He was putting his gun down. He was surrendering to me.'

'It didn't look like that from the bottom of the stairs,' Brig said. 'We couldn't take any chances.'

Massinette stooped and took something from Linck's pocket. He had another gun in his hand, a little Smith and Wesson .22 revolver, it looked like.

'This was in his pocket, Mr Bond,' Massinette said. 'He was fooling you. He had other plans.'

Bond looked at the two agents.

'I apologise,' he said, though he knew full well that Massinette had just planted the second gun on Linck's body. But why? He stopped himself from trying to answer that question as Felix Leiter came into the room.

'You took your time,' Bond said. 'Still, very pleased to see your ugly face.'

They shook hands warmly. Right hand to left hand.

'The company you keep, James,' Felix said, tut-tutting with a smile. 'Where's Kobus Breed?'

'Out on the back lawn – dead. I'll show you. You'd better get some medical help for Adeka here. He's in a bad way.'

'I'll get on to it,' Brig said, taking a walkie-talkie out of his pocket and calling for an ambulance and medics.

Bond and Felix climbed the stairs and moved through the clinic towards the hallway.

Felix clapped Bond on the back.

'Your friend Mr McHarg called the police with some story about a mansion, gunshots and someone called James Bond. When we'd discovered you weren't on the plane to London we'd put out an APB on you. The police called us and asked if this Bond fellow was part of our operation. Very clever, James.'

'Sometimes you earn your own luck,' Bond said, deciding not to mention his suspicions of Massinette just at this moment. For all he knew Brig Leiter may have been a part in the assassination of Hulbert Linck and he wanted to ensure his facts were right before any accusations were made.

Bond paused in the hallway and looked up the stairs. Linck must have been waiting up there somewhere, he supposed. But why would the CIA want Linck dead . . . ?

'Got a cigarette?' Bond asked.

Felix reached into his pocket with his good hand and shook out a packet of Rothmans. Then with the elaborate titanium device that had replaced his other hand – a small curved hook and two other hinged digits – he took out a book of matches. Bond watched in some amazement as the claw selected, ripped off and lit a match before applying it to the end of Bond's cigarette.

Bond inhaled deeply, relishing the tobacco rush.

'That's quite a gadget you've got there,' he said. 'New model?'

'Yeah,' Felix said with a grin. 'I can pick gnat shit out of pepper with this baby.'

Bond laughed. 'Thank God you're here, Felix. Have I got a tale to tell you. Come on, I'll show you Breed first.'

They went to the main drawing room and Bond pushed through the garden doors and stepped out on to the lawn.

Kobus Breed had disappeared.

·11·

A SPY ON VACATION

'We found two guards,' Leiter said. 'One of them had almost bled to death and the other was trussed up like a Thanksgiving turkey.'

It was dawn and they were standing on the gravelled sweep in front of the house. An ambulance had taken Adeka to hospital while police and forensic teams were searching the building. Forty kilos of heroin had been recovered.

'The third guard was called Henrick,' Bond said, leaning against a police car. 'I slugged him – but he seemed so unconscious I didn't bother to bind his ankles. He must have come round, untied himself somehow, gone back to the house and found Breed's body. Must have carted it away for some reason.'

'You sure you killed Breed?' Felix asked.

'I *was* sure,' Bond said. 'Now I don't know. He was shockingly injured.'

Bond felt sick and angry with himself. Had Henrick simply wanted to deny the authorities a corpse? Or had there been some vital sign of life in Breed's ruined body? Was Breed lying at the bottom of some river nearby weighted with stones? Or was he in some secret surgical theatre being put back together?

Bond was troubled – perhaps the *coup de grâce* of the switchblade had just missed.

'Don't worry about Breed,' Felix said. 'We'll pick him up. If you did the damage you say you did he'll have to find a doctor or go to a hospital. Or maybe he'll just die.'

'Possibly,' Bond said, wondering if there was any way Breed could be realistically patched up. His right shoulder and arm had been shattered, pulverised. He wondered what kind of new deformities a living Kobus Breed would display.

'Don't look so serious, James,' Felix said. 'You broke up a giant drug-smuggling operation. We got the bad guys – most of them – and saved Gabriel Adeka. Not bad for a British spy on vacation.'

Bond decided to tell Felix the reality of the situation.

'He's not Gabriel Adeka,' Bond said, flatly.

'You need to go back to your hotel, take a shower, have some breakfast, sleep for a day – and you'll be your old self again.'

'I'm sorry, Felix,' Bond said. 'That man's not Gabriel Adeka – he's Solomon Adeka. Brigadier Solomon Adeka, former C.-in-C. of the Dahum armed forces. He's disguised as Gabriel Adeka – people are meant to think he's Gabriel Adeka. But he isn't.'

'How do you know?' Felix wasn't smiling any more.

'Because I've met him. And I've met his brother. I recognised him. I know them both.'

'Can you prove it?'

'Yes. But . . .'

'But what?'

'It's complicated.'

'Let nothing stand in the way of proof, James.'

'All right,' Bond said, calling Felix's bluff. 'Can you whistle us up an aeroplane?'

·12·

ZANZARIM REVISITED

Bond felt very strange being back in Port Dunbar. It was as if the events between his last visit and this one had taken place in a malign parallel universe. Here he was standing in the cemetery that ringed the small cathedral almost exactly in the same location – at the back, the modest spire of the cathedral to his left – as when he had witnessed Brigadier Solomon Adeka's funeral. Except that this time he was alongside Felix Leiter and the guard of honour had been replaced by a magistrate and his clerk, some officials from the interim government of Zanzarim and a small, tracked, orange excavator that was manoeuvring into position in front of Solomon Adeka's grave.

Twenty-four hours after the events at Rowanoak Hall, Felix and Bond had been flown out of Andrews Field on a USAF Boeing 707 transport. They had been met at Sinsikrou airport by the American ambassador to Zanzarim and then, in a small convoy of embassy cars, they had been driven down the transnational highway to Port Dunbar, where government officials received them at the cathedral and informed them that all relevant permissions and waivers from the ecclesiastical authorities for the disinterment of Solomon Adeka's body had been granted. Bond had been impressed by the level of power and influence such despatch had displayed. It seemed that Felix Leiter just had to snap his fingers and all his demands were met. Why such efficient haste? Bond wondered. Why were they being treated like visiting dignitaries? Once again he felt there were other agendas beside his own that were for the moment invisible to him. He was also aware – because he knew Felix so well – that he was not telling him everything. No matter: he could bide his time because Felix would indeed tell him if he insisted – they were too good and too old a pair of friends to hold anything back if total honesty was demanded. But Bond decided it might be more interesting to watch and wait.

Driving through the city towards the cathedral, Bond could see from the windows of their limousine that Port Dunbar had reclaimed its usual bustle and energy. The journey south had also demonstrated that almost every sign of the civil war was being swiftly erased. There were some temporary Bailey bridges across rivers; here and there a few burnt-out vehicles waited to be carried away for scrap. And there were many more Zanza Force soldiers on the streets – manning checkpoints, directing traffic – than was normal for a peaceful country. All the same, Bond thought, you would hardly believe a bitter civil war had raged here for two years, remembering the time he'd spent in the beleaguered Republic of Dahum as it entered its final days and hours. Once again he thought it was as if he'd existed in a parallel universe or a dream of some kind. A bad dream, Bond corrected himself, because it featured Kobus Breed.

There was a call from the graveside and Bond and Felix made their way towards the small crowd that had gathered now that the key moment was at hand.

The tracks of the digger clattered noisily as it lined itself up and its lobster claw delicately began to scrape away the packed earth in front of the gravestone.

'I remember this funeral well,' Bond said. 'It was all very elaborate and formal. Very cleverly planned – orations, rifle salutes, grieving populace . . . How is Adeka anyway, have you heard?'

'They say he's doing very well,' Felix said. 'Getting the best possible help. Should make a full recovery.'

'Must be strange coming back from the dead.'

'Ha-ha,' Felix said, drily. He was still highly sceptical, but he knew this was the one and only way of proving or disproving Bond's claim.

The lid of the coffin was revealed and six gravediggers stepped forward. After some diligent spadework the whole of the coffin was uncovered and heavy strapping was tied to its brass handles and attached to the digger's boom. Slowly, easily, the coffin was raised, lifted clear of the earth and lowered to the ground. Two of the gravediggers prised open the lid with jemmies.

The gasp of astonishment from those peering in was almost comic. Three sacks of cement were removed and laid beside each other on the parched turf.

Felix looked serious and prodded a sack with his foot as if it might suddenly become corporeal. He looked at Bond.

'Looks like three sacks of cement to me,' Bond said.

'Well, I'll be hog-tied,' Felix said, not amused. 'You were right.'

Bond shrugged modestly.

'So,' Felix said, 'if the man we've got is Solomon Adeka, where's his brother Gabriel?'

Bond lit a cigarette. 'I suspect that if I took you to a small shop in Bayswater and you dug up the concrete floor you'd find his mortal remains.' He paused, thinking. 'It was all very elaborately planned.'

Felix looked shrewdly at Bond.

'Do you know what's going on, James?'

'About eighty per cent, I reckon,' Bond said with a smile. 'I have a feeling you might be able to supply the missing twenty.'

Felix prodded a bag of cement again with his shoe, thinking. Then he looked up.

'Let's go and get a serious drink someplace,' he said.

The Grand Central Hotel in Port Dunbar had possessed a variety of names in its short history: the Schloss Gustavberg, the Relais de la Côte d'Or and the Royal Sutherland. Now it was the bland Grand Central, having been requisitioned by the Dahum junta for use as its centre of government bureaucracy during the civil war. It was as if all that history was meant to be effaced by the re-christening. The Grand Central heralded a new and more prosperous future.

There was a bar on the ground floor with a wide veranda that looked over the newly renamed main street – Victory Boulevard. The veranda was crowded so Bond and Felix found a seat in a dark corner underneath a whirring ceiling fan. Bond surveyed the clientele – half a dozen black faces, all the rest white – and all men, men in suits, perspiring over their cold beers.

Bond signalled a waiter over.

'Do you have gin?' he asked.

'Yes, sar. We have everything now. Gordon's or Gilbey's.'

'Good. Bring me a bottle of Gordon's, two glasses, a bucket of ice and some limes. Do you have limes?'

'Plenty, plenty, sar.'

The ingredients were brought to their table. Bond filled the glasses to the brim with ice then poured a liberal few slugs of gin on to the ice and squeezed the juice of half a lime into each glass.

'It's called an African dry martini,' Bond said. 'Cheers, Felix.'

They clinked glasses and drank. The gin was ideally chilled, Bond thought, and the freshness of the lime juice took the edge off the alcohol. They both lit cigarettes, Felix holding his delicately between two of the pincers of his tungsten claw.

'So, Felix,' Bond said, looking at him squarely. 'We know each other too well. Total honesty from us both. Deal?'

'Nothing but,' Felix said.

'Shall I start the inquisition?'

'Fire away, Torquemada.'

Bond paused.

'Why did Massinette kill Linck?' Bond saw Felix's eyes flicker – he wasn't expecting the unravelling of the story to begin there, obviously. He drew on his cigarette, nodded, pursed his lips, buying a few more seconds.

'Because he was going to kill you.'

'Not so. Linck had just "surrendered" to me. He'd put his gun on the table.'

'He had another gun. It was a ruse.'

'Massinette planted that gun,' Bond said. 'I saw him do it.' He paused again. 'Massinette was there to kill Linck, come what may. Linck was going to be killed. Why?'

Felix sighed. 'Total honesty – I don't know. And believe me, Brig doesn't know. Massinette was assigned to the Milford Plaza operation. He's not regular CIA personnel.'

'So what is he? Some kind of CIA contract killer?'

'Like a Double O? Maybe. It doesn't smell good, I have to admit. But Massinette sticks by his story. He killed Linck to stop him killing you.'

'How convenient.'

Felix topped up their glasses from the gin bottle and looked around the room.

'OK. Here's the thing, James. Let's start at the beginning. This is what I know as far as I know.'

Felix lit another cigarette and proceeded to outline the facts. Towards the end of the war in Dahum, when the heartland was shrinking and the military and humanitarian situation was becoming ever more desperate, Brigadier Solomon Adeka was secretly approached by one Hulbert Linck, a philanthropic multimillionaire with an altruistic love of freedom and Africa. Linck offered to supply arms, aircraft, white mercenaries, ammunition, food, essential medical supplies – anything to keep Dahum alive.

'But there was a price to pay,' Bond said. 'Altruism is expensive.'

'Exactly. There always is. There's no money in the free-lunch business,' Felix said and gestured at the crowded bar and the veranda beyond. 'You see all these white men?'

'Yes,' Bond said.

'Who do you think they are?' Felix didn't wait for an answer. 'They're oil company executives.'

'Flies round the Zanzarim honey pot,' Bond said.

'Indeed. The Adeka family have been important chiefs in the

Fakassa tribe for hundreds of years. The Zanza River Delta is their tribal homeland. Solomon Adeka is the sovereign chief.'

'No he's not,' Bond said. 'He couldn't be. His older brother is – Gabriel Adeka. I'll explain when you finish.'

'Anyway, the price Hulbert Linck demanded for his military aid was a twenty-five-year lease on the oil rights in the Fakassa tribal homelands. Profits to be split fifty-fifty. Solomon Adeka granted him the lease – anything to save Dahum.'

'So Linck owned the land where the oil was.'

'In fact it's owned by a company in Luxembourg called Zanza Petroleum SA. It's Linck's company. He had all the leases. Signed and sealed.'

Bond was thinking – pieces were fitting together, fast. Signed and sealed – but by the wrong Adeka brother.

'And Linck certainly tried hard,' Bond said. 'I give that to him. For him a free independent Dahum was the best option. I saw what he did, what he spent.'

'But it was never going to work,' Felix said. 'Dahum was never going to win this civil war, was never going to be an independent state. Too many powerful countries had other plans.'

'And Linck was no fool. He could see the writing on the wall, eventually. His leases weren't going to be worth a penny when Zanzarim was reunited. And that's when the conspiracy started,' Bond said. 'Plan B began when they saw that the war was going to be lost.' He sipped at his drink. 'And I suspect another factor was when Linck discovered that the leases weren't Solomon Adeka's to sell. With the war over and the older brother, Gabriel, on the scene Zanza Petroleum would be no more.'

'Go on,' Felix said, leaning forward. 'This is where it gets confusing for me. Remember I thought Gabriel Adeka was alive and well and living in Washington DC.'

'The only way for Linck to keep the integrity of his oil leases going was to have them "authorised" by the older brother – the paramount chief of the Fakassa. How was that to be achieved? Solomon Adeka had to "die" and become Gabriel . . .' Bond felt more clarity arriving as he articulated the plan to Felix. 'I think Linck contacted Gabriel Adeka in London right at the end of the war. Spun him some sort of story about aid to Dahum. That's why the two Constellations I saw suddenly had AfricaKIN painted on them. Even that last night as everyone was fleeing. Linck knew about Gabriel and that he was the older brother – that proves it.' Bond thought further. Gabriel Adeka must have been found and located, agreed to 'partner' Linck in the airlift to Dahum. Perhaps it was just a ruse to gain his confidence. He might even have been dead already when that last Constellation touched down at Janjaville.

'From Linck and Solomon Adeka's point of view the key thing was to have Gabriel Adeka dead,' Bond said, adding – 'not only dead but "disappeared". There would be no body. As far as anyone in London was concerned Gabriel had gone to America to set up the new charity – AfricaKIN Inc.' Bond remembered his encounter with Peter Kunle at the Bayswater offices. How Kunle had been surprised at Gabriel's untypical complacency about his borrowed typewriter, not living up to his usual impeccable behaviour patterns.

'You're saying Adeka and Linck planned all this,' Felix said, frowning. 'To kill Gabriel.'

'Yes, I'm afraid so. The rewards were immense. Fratricide has a long history – starting with Cain and Abel.' Bond added more ice to his glass. 'Solomon Adeka feigned his terminal illness and his death. By the way – you might want to interrogate an Indian doctor called Dr Masind. He was in Rowanoak as well. He must have done the drugging, written the death certificate. It was very effective. Solomon "dies", the war ends and enter the CIA. Gabriel Adeka, meanwhile, has been invited to set up AfricaKIN in Washington DC.' Bond smiled. 'The timing was perfect. Gabriel Adeka apparently leaves London – suddenly he's not there – and another "Gabriel Adeka" arrives in Washington. Meanwhile Solomon Adeka has been buried with full military honours in Port Dunbar.'

Felix shook his head cynically. 'How were we to know? You meet a man who says he's Gabriel Adeka. How could we know that it was the younger brother, Solomon? He had a shaven head and a small goatee, just like Gabriel. Solomon was dead and buried – who's going to be suspicious?' Felix nodded, almost as if he had to convince himself of the elaborate nature of the subterfuge.

'I bet you didn't see much of him,' Bond said.

'No, that's true. There were some initial meetings – "Gabriel" was unwell, we were told – this Colonel Denga was the frontman. Very efficient. Very precise.'

'Part of the team.' Bond lit another cigarette. 'I'm pretty sure this was how it must have happened. Gabriel Adeka was lured into a kind of collaboration with Linck and his aid plans for Dahum. At some meeting an unsuspecting Gabriel would have been killed – probably by one of Kobus Breed's buddies and the body disposed of – buried under fresh concrete in the Bayswater office. Breed is Linck's enforcer – he would have arranged everything. Maybe he's his partner, for all I know. I bet you it was Breed who saw other opportunities for AfricaKIN and its "mercy flights". Maybe Linck was in on it.' He shrugged. 'Clearly he's a man who likes to make a profit, one way or another.' Bond spread his hands. 'But we'll never know now, thanks to Agent Massinette.'

Felix wasn't going to follow this line of speculation, Bond saw. He shook his glass, making the ice cubes spin.

'So, just to be on the safe side, to keep their control, they turned Solomon into a junkie,' Felix added, nodding to himself again.

'Absolutely perfect control,' Bond said, adding more gin to their glasses. They were halfway through the bottle. 'Linck and Breed were running things now. They didn't want their Adeka brother changing his mind in any way.'

'So you reckon Linck wasn't a prisoner at all,' Felix said.

'No. Why would a prisoner dye his hair and grow a beard?' Bond posed the question. 'That little ploy was Linck's escape route, or so he hoped. Kobus Breed was the mastermind. So Linck would have had us believe.'

'Why didn't he just run for it? Why did he surrender to you?'

'You answered that. While he was alive he still – just about – owned Zanza Petroleum. Linck must have known that the whole AfricaKIN cover would be blown. Better to present himself as a victim along with poor Gabriel Adeka. You said the leases were all legal. He might have been able to pick up where he left off. He could have claimed some sort of negotiating position, at least.'

'Except he hadn't reckoned on you – the fact that you knew both brothers.'

'Linck didn't know that. And Massinette blew him away the moment he saw him.' Bond clicked his fingers. 'Just like that. I wonder why . . .'

'I think I may be able to answer that question, now.' Felix nodded. Bond could see clarity was visiting him, also.

'OK,' Felix continued, 'one more thing. I can now understand how the real Gabriel Adeka could be made to disappear in London. And suddenly reappear in Rowanoak Hall. Solomon was "dead" – you'd been to his funeral. How did he get to the US?'

'It was something Blessing told me – Aleesha Belem. She reminded me that there had been another plane that last night at Janjaville – a DC-3. She said Breed and Linck flew out separately on the DC-3 while everyone else was on the Super Constellation. I didn't see that, of course – I was minding my own business bleeding to death.' Bond smiled, wryly. 'I suspect there were a few crates loaded on the DC-3 at the last moment. One of them would have contained Solomon Adeka, drugged and comatose but very much alive and ready to assume his new identity. Gabriel was dead – long live Gabriel. You weren't going to ask any difficult questions – even if you had any – because you were so very pleased to welcome him and AfricaKIN to the US. I wonder why? Sorry to repeat myself . . .'

'Follow me,' Felix said and strolled on to the veranda. Bond joined him. Just below the edge of the veranda was a long row of cars and trucks and utility vehicles. All new and each one with the logo of an oil company on its side. Shell, BP, Texaco, Elf, Agip, Esso, Mobil, Gulf.

'Take a look,' Felix said. 'Every oil company in the world wants to stick its nose in the Zanzarim trough.'

Bond looked at the shiny new vehicles, looked back at the perspiring white men in the bar of the Grand Central Hotel.

'You've got to understand, James,' Felix said, 'the civil war here fouled everything up. Oil had been discovered, sure. But you can't develop oilfields if a war is raging on top of them. It was a disaster for the oil companies. And when the war didn't end in a few weeks and began to drag on and on – one year, two years – and it looked like there was going to be this interminable stalemate—'

Bond interrupted. 'And certain Western governments agreed that if there was some way of stopping the war it would be in everybody's interests.' Bond frowned: not quite everybody's – but he saw how a congruence of different ambitions had merged unknowingly, unwittingly. Britain, the USA, the international oil companies, Hulbert Linck's vicious opportunism, the greed of a younger brother . . .

'Here we are in the heart of the Zanza River Delta,' Felix said. 'We're standing on a gigantic ocean of oil, untapped, barely explored. We don't know how vast these reserves may be. It could be bigger than the Ghawar field in Saudi. These fellows' – he gestured at the bar – 'will figure it out any day now. But it's not just any old oil. It's "light crude". The best oil in the world, so much easier to refine. The world wants it and the world is going to get it.'

Bond smiled cynically. 'And someone like Hulbert Linck couldn't be allowed to stand in the way. Enter Agent Massinette.'

'I don't like to admit it,' Felix said. 'But I can see why it was in everyone's interests if Hulbert Linck was dead – killed by an agent in a shoot-out, for example, during a raid.'

They wandered back to their seats. Felix had a sour expression on his face – a man who had just come face to face with an unpleasant truth about the business he was in, Bond thought.

They sat down and Bond added a fresh splash of gin to their glasses. Felix dropped in more ice cubes.

Bond looked at him. 'You say "everyone's interests", Felix, but what you mean is the West.'

'Of course. Figure it out. We don't want to get our oil from the Gulf, if we can help it,' Felix said. 'It's the proverbial powder keg. Islam, Palestine, Israel, Shia and Sunni – it's a goat-fuck. Zanzarim alone could provide up to forty per cent of all US and UK oil needs, I've heard it said. Forty per cent – and not a camel in sight. It changes everything.' He lit a cigarette and spread his arms. 'This is the new Gulf, James. Right here in West Africa. It suits us fine.' He stood up. 'I've got to make a quick phone call. I saw a payphone in reception. Don't finish that gin, I'll be right back.'

He wandered off and Bond sat back in his chair thinking. Sometimes, he reasoned, the stakes – the rewards – can become so high that illegitimacy, malfeasance, even murder seem entirely reasonable, not to say logical, courses of action. All this oil was waiting under the ground in the Zanza River Delta – and one man, Hulbert Linck, knew too much, could cause potential problems, could stand in the way of the new order being established. Wouldn't it just be so much easier if he wasn't there any more? That he didn't have to be factored into any plans? Someone very high up in government circles, someone very important, would make a decision. Don't we have 'people' who can sort these kind of things out for us? Yes, sir. I believe Luke Massinette is the ideal man for the job. And he's available. Fine – so make sure he's an integral part of the search for Hulbert Linck and tell him exactly what to do once we've found him. Don't mess up.

Bond lit a cigarette. 'Dirty tricks' were as old as history. As old as diplomacy. As old as spying. All the same, he had to admit, sometimes the sheer candid ruthlessness of absolute power did shake you up somewhat. He understood why Felix had worn that expression on his face for a second or two.

Felix returned. 'You can telephone the USA from Port Dunbar. That's what I call progress.'

'Realpolitik is not just a German concept,' Bond said. 'Everything can be made to happen.' He smiled. Felix nodded. They both knew the global subtext now, the underlying story.

'What're you going to do with Adeka?' Bond asked, changing the subject.

'I think he likes it in Washington DC. He'll become a wealthy man once the leases are renegotiated with the government of Zanzarim. We can keep an eye on him – and Colonel Denga and this Dr Masind, if necessary. The drug-smuggling issues give us a little leverage. I'm sure they'll behave.'

'Will Adeka be Gabriel or Solomon?' Bond asked.

'I don't think we really give a damn, to be honest. Now everything's sorted out to our satisfaction.' Felix looked serious and placed his glass down on the table.

'I think we just figured it all out, didn't we?' Felix said.

'Yes,' Bond said. 'How would you express it? We picked the gnat's shit out of the pepper.'

Bond sat back and drained his glass. They looked at each other: two men who knew all too well how the world worked. Bond thought to himself about what had happened – he called it the Thomas à Becket solution. Henry II had understood this in 1170 as clearly as those who had wanted Hulbert Linck eliminated 800 years later. 'Will no one rid me of this turbulent priest?' – so Henry II had asked his leading question. And Thomas à Becket had been duly assassinated. Will no one rid me of Hulbert Linck . . . ? Step forward Agent Massinette. Sometimes the easiest way to solve a problem is to make it go away.

Bond shrugged and smiled. 'At root, most problems are very straightforward. And the solution is usually very straightforward as well. Though sometimes brutal.'

'Except that often it doesn't *seem* straightforward.'

'Ah, but we like that,' Bond said. 'The more smoke and mirrors the better.'

Felix looked at him, closely.

'In the midst of all this smoke, there's just one thing that strikes me, James.'

'What's that?'

'There are very few people in the world who know about Gabriel and Solomon Adeka. Denga must know. Linck did, but he's dead. This Indian doctor, Masind, does. And Kobus Breed – he's probably dead, or out of action anyway. It just strikes me that you – you – are maybe the only person around who's actually ever been face to face with both the brothers.'

'What're you saying, Felix?'

'That you're a man with a very, very privileged piece of information indeed. I would keep it to yourself, James. I certainly won't mention anything of what you told me to any of my people. You know as well as I do that knowledge is power – but owning this kind of knowledge can be as dangerous as owning an unexploded bomb . . . Just be careful, OK?'

'I'll try,' Bond said, and smiled.

PART FIVE

CODA IN RICHMOND

·1·

UN PAYSAN ÉCOSSAIS

M's office was bluey-grey with hanging strata of pipe smoke and Bond's eyes began stinging within two minutes of their meeting commencing. He must have been smoking all day, Bond thought, and usually that was a sign of trouble.

But M seemed genial – or at least the impenetrable mask he wore was genial. He had sat there without a word, attending to Bond's narrative of events, puffing away on his pipe, with a nod and a smile from time to time, almost like an uncle patiently listening to his nephew recount the details of his school's sports day.

'And there you have it, sir,' Bond said. 'The scramble for Zanzarim's oil is in full enthusiastic swing. I saw it with my own eyes – every oil company in the world wanting a piece of the action.'

'And we're at the head of the queue,' M said, putting his pipe down and smoothing back his thinning hair with the palm of one hand. 'Excellent,' he said thoughtfully to himself, pursing his lips and tugging at an ear lobe. Bond knew the signs, it was not a moment to interject. M would speak in his own good time.

'I should probably discipline you in some way, 007,' M said finally. 'For going solo in such a dramatic and headstrong manner – for vanishing like that. But I've decided that would be perverse.'

'May I ask why, sir?'

'Because – paradoxically, even astonishingly – you achieved everything that was asked of you. The war is over and Zanzarim is reunited. A little corner of Africa is at peace and has a bright, prosperous future. Thanks to your efforts.'

'And we can acquire all the oil we need.'

M's eyes sharpened.

'Cynicism doesn't suit you, 007,' he said. 'Oil has nothing to do with us. We – you and I – are just naval ratings on the ship of state. We were given a task and we carried it out. Or rather you did all the hard work – I only put you forward as the right man for the job.' He allowed himself a half-smile. 'And it turned out I was correct. I know it hasn't been an easy time for you but we'll find a way of recognising that, James, don't you worry.'

Bond noticed the deliberate use of his Christian name. The mood was mellowing again, but he wanted to make his point.

'All's well that ends well,' Bond said. 'For both of us.'

'Us?'

'The British and the Americans. We seem to be sitting pretty.'

'And what could be wrong with that?' M stood up, signalling that the meeting was at an end. Bond rose to his feet also, as M came round from behind his desk. 'Don't go there,' he said, his voice leavened with delicate warning. 'It's not our affair. We're servants of Her Majesty's Government, whatever its political hue. We are part of the Secret Intelligence Service. Civil servants in the pure sense of the term.'

'Of course,' Bond said. 'As you know, sir, *je suis un paysan écossais* – all this multinational, macroeconomic forward-planning is lost on me.'

'He said, disingenuously.'

They both smiled and moved to the door, where M briefly rested his hand on Bond's shoulder.

'You did exceptionally well, 007. Did us proud.'

It was a significant compliment, Bond knew. And suddenly he saw how much had been at stake; how his obscure mission in a small African country had possessed a geopolitical resonance and fallout that he could never have imagined. That he would never have wanted to imagine when he had set out on it, he told himself.

M patted his shoulder again, avuncularly.

'Come in and see me on Monday morning. I think I might have an interesting little job for you.'

No rest for the wicked, Bond thought.

'See you Monday morning, sir.'

'Any plans for the weekend?'

'I have to return some lost property.'

·2·

OUT OF THE DARK

Bond knocked on Vampiria's door. He had had his hair cut and a massage and was wearing his dark navy-blue worsted suit, a heavy cream silk shirt and a pale blue knitted silk tie. He sensed he was back to normal – feeling as well as he had in months.

Bryce Fitzjohn opened the door to her caravan. She was wearing a ginger gaberdine double-breasted trouser suit with a white cashmere polo neck and her hair was pinned up in a loose bun.

'Too early?' Bond asked.

'No – perfect timing. Vampiria is no more, consumed by hell-fire.' She looked him up and down approvingly. 'You seem very fit and well, Mr Bond. Step inside. I don't want to kiss you with half the crew looking on.'

He went inside and they kissed, gently, passionately. Bond felt a kind of release inside him, a rare surge of well-being. Perhaps he could let everything go for twenty-four hours and be himself with this wonderful woman.

'How was your trip to Americay?'

'It was . . . interesting.'

'No new scars?'

'A scar-free sojourn, I'm glad to report.' He smiled, reassuring her, but he made the qualification to himself – at least none visible.

Bond drove her back to Richmond in his Interceptor II.

'Is this a new car?' Bryce asked.

'On approval. I'm not sure I can afford it.'

'Are you all right, James?'

'I am now,' he said with real sincerity. 'I was feeling a bit out of sorts – and then I saw you again.'

'We do our best,' she said, reaching over to touch his cheek with her knuckles. There was an understanding between them, Bond thought. So much of what they communicated was unspoken. She already knew him, it seemed – his necessary reticences, places he couldn't go – and he received in return her covert messages of desire and affection, of real warmth. The hidden currents of their conversation were deep and strong.

Back at her house she told him they were having a repeat meal: champagne, a steak and a tomato salad and a great bottle of red wine. When she went into the kitchen to decant the wine – she'd chosen a Chateau Cantemerle 1955 – Bond slipped into her study and replaced her passport in the top drawer. Dennis Fieldfare had swiftly reconstituted it in its original form – it looked completely identical to the one he'd purloined, though maybe one day Bryce would wonder how she'd acquired those US immigration stamps while she'd been busy filming *Vampiria* in the Thames Valley, but Bond reckoned he'd managed the duplicity without being discovered. She would have no idea how helpful she had been.

They ate, they drank and later they made love like old and practised familiars.

'I'm so glad you're back,' she said, lying in his arms, smoothing the forelock from his brow with a finger. 'I've missed you, absurd though it may sound. And remember you promised me a holiday.'

'I'm going to take you to Jamaica,' he said. 'Ever been there?'

'No, I haven't. How rather wonderful.'

'Stand by for the trip of a lifetime.'

'How can I possibly thank you, Mr Bond?' she said, shifting forward and kissing him, letting her tongue linger in his mouth. 'Maybe I can think of something a little out of the ordinary . . .' She flicked the sheet away from his naked body.

Bond woke. He had heard a noise. He heard it again – a sharp patter of fine gravel thrown against the windowpane almost like a rain-shower. He looked at his watch – 4.55 a.m. Bryce was soundly asleep. Bond slipped out of bed and parted the curtains an inch and peered out. The opaque grey expanse of the lawn, lit by the moonlight, was revealed below and beyond it, through a fringe of trees, flowed the silvered river at high tide. Then he thought he saw some shadow move in the darkness and felt himself tense, suddenly. He gathered up his clothes and shoes and quietly left the bedroom, dressing quickly on the landing. He pulled on his socks and shoes and then his jacket, shoving his tie into a pocket. There was somebody out there in the garden, he was sure, and he was going to find out who it was.

He went downstairs, not switching on any lights. It was an old burglar's trick, he was aware – throw some gravel at the bedroom windows and if no lights go on you're pretty much safe to plunder the ground floor. He picked up the poker from beside the fire in the drawing room and crept through to the kitchen and its door on to the garden. Keeping out of sight, he peered through the kitchen windows at the ghostly expanse of the garden within its high walls. Once again he thought he saw something shift in the big herbaceous border by the fig tree. Were his eyes playing tricks with him? But the thrown gravel was no illusion. Perhaps he should just switch the lights on and the interloper would get the message and try to rob another big house in Richmond instead. But Bond had a strange sense about this wake-up call. Thrown gravel. Thrown coins . . . Perhaps somebody wanted to lure him out into the darkness. Well – he was ready for that.

He opened the door and stepped outside. It was cold and his breath condensed, the first intimations of the winter that was approaching. He gripped the poker hard in his fist and walked down a brick path towards the wall and the gate on to the river promenade. He stopped – listening hard. Nothing. A breeze swirled by and leaves rustled. Bond headed for the herbaceous border where he thought he'd seen the movement in the shadows.

He stood at the lawn's edge looking at the plants in the border for any sign of broken stems or leaves. He reached into his pocket for his lighter and clicked it on, crouching and holding the flame close to the ground. Some leaves had fallen, one plant was oddly bent over. He moved the flame so it cast an oblique light – and he saw the footprints. The soil was moist and the freshly moulded imprints were an inch deep, four of them. Someone had been in this garden, hiding. What was odd was that one footprint, the right, seemed unnaturally turned into the other, and the right heel seemed implanted deeper than the left – and there were a series of round holes beside them also, as if a stick or a cane had been used to rest on. This is madness, Bond thought – but another more rational part of his brain was saying this could be someone deformed, someone who cannot walk unaided. A cripple of some kind . . .

Then he heard a noise in the street beyond and ran to the garden gate, turning the key that was in the lock and flinging the door open. He stepped out on to the street. The tide was now fully ebbing in the river, flowing strongly back towards the sea. Bond looked left and right. The river-road here in Richmond was well illuminated by street lights but there was no sign of anyone. He thought he heard a car engine kick into life a street away, and pull off into the night.

He felt a great sinking of heart as he realised what he had to do. There was no other option.

Bond went back into the house and poured himself an inch of brandy in a tumbler, took a gulp and then went into Bryce's study, sat down at her desk and wrote her a brief note on a sheet of her writing paper.

Darling Bryce,
I have to go away suddenly, 'on business'. You are too good for me and I could never make you happy. These few wonderful hours I've shared with you have given my life real meaning. I thank you from the depths of my heart and soul. Goodbye.
With my love, J.

He finished his drink and weighted down the sheet of paper on her desk with his empty glass. She'd find it in the morning when she came down to look for him, calling his name. It was Sunday – they had made plans for Sunday.

Bond closed the door softly behind him and slipped into the front seat of the Interceptor. He sat there for a while, running through his various decisions, his mind constantly returning to the horrific images of Blessing, dead at the hand of Kobus Breed. Perhaps what had happened in the garden had been nothing more than a Richmond burglar trying his luck, but Bond knew he couldn't live with the possibility of Bryce becoming a victim – like Blessing – because of her association with him. He couldn't put her in harm's way – particularly if the harm was to be administered by a man like Breed.

He started the engine – its throaty purr was so quiet he doubted Bryce would wake – and drove slowly out of her driveway, the gravel crunching under his wide tyres.

There was a distinct lemony-pewter lightening in the east, heralding the beginning of the new day – a clear sky with no clouds. Bond turned the Interceptor on to the London road and put his foot on the accelerator, concentrating on the pleasures of driving a powerful car like this, trying not to think of Bryce and whatever dangers had been lurking out there in the darkness of her garden.

He drove steadily homewards, his face impassive, his mind made up, an unfamiliar heaviness in his heart.

He pulled into the square off the King's Road and sat for a

moment in his car, thinking, already half-regretting his act of spontaneous chivalry – of leaving Bryce unannounced, so suddenly, clandestinely in the night. She'd be shocked and hurt after the time they'd enjoyed together, and the love they'd made – she'd never think such an abandonment was done to keep her safe from the merciless savagery of Kobus Breed. All she knew about James Bond was his name – she didn't have his address or telephone number. She'd never find him, however hard she cared to look. And where would *he* ever find someone like her again? he wondered, with some bitterness. That was the price he paid for the job he did, he supposed. Falling in love with a beautiful woman wasn't recommended.

Bond sighed. It was a calm and beautiful Sunday morning. Tomorrow was Monday and he remembered that M had said he had an 'interesting' little job for him. Life goes on, he thought – it was some consolation . . . He stepped out of his car into a perfumed, sunlit day and as he strolled towards his front door somewhere a spasm of church bells sounded and a gang of pigeons, feeding in the central garden of the square, clapped up into the dazzling blue of an early morning sky in Chelsea – and vanished.

IAN FLEMING

Ian Lancaster Fleming was born in London on 28 May 1908 and was educated at Eton College before spending a formative period studying languages in Europe. His first job was with Reuters news agency, followed by a brief spell as a stockbroker. On the outbreak of the Second World War he was appointed assistant to the Director of Naval Intelligence, Admiral Godfrey, where he played a key part in British and Allied espionage operations.

After the war he joined Kemsley Newspapers as Foreign Manager of the *Sunday Times*, running a network of correspondents who were intimately involved in the Cold War. His first novel, *Casino Royale*, was published in 1953 and introduced James Bond, Special Agent 007, to the world. The first print run sold out within a month. Following this initial success, he published a Bond title every year until his death. Raymond Chandler hailed him as 'the most forceful and driving writer of thrillers in England'. The fifth title, *From Russia with Love*, was particularly well received and sales soared when President Kennedy named it as one of his favourite books. The Bond novels have sold more than sixty million copies and inspired a hugely successful film franchise which began in 1962 with the release of *Dr No*, starring Sean Connery as 007.

The Bond books were written in Jamaica, a country Fleming fell in love with during the war and where he built a house, 'Goldeneye'. He married Anne Rothermere in 1952. His story about a magical car, written in 1961 for their only child, Caspar, went on to become the well-loved novel and film *Chitty Chitty Bang Bang*.

Fleming died of heart failure on 12 August 1964.

By Ian Fleming

James Bond novels
Casino Royale
Live and Let Die
Moonraker
Diamonds are Forever
From Russia with Love
Dr No
Goldfinger
For Your Eyes Only
Thunderball
The Spy Who Loved Me
On Her Majesty's Secret Service
You Only Live Twice
The Man with the Golden Gun
Octopussy and The Living Daylights

Non-fiction
The Diamond Smugglers
Thrilling Cities

For children
Chitty Chitty Bang Bang: The Magical Car

www.ianfleming.com

IAN FLEMING
Casino Royale

Surround yourself with human beings, my dear James.
They are easier to fight for than principles.

In *Casino Royale*, the first of Fleming's 007
adventures, a game of cards is James Bond's
only chance to bring down the desperate SMERSH
agent Le Chiffre. But Bond soon discovers that
there is far more at stake than money.

'Ian Fleming has discovered the secret of narrative
art...the reader *has* to go on reading'
John Betjeman

First published in 1953

IAN FLEMING
Live and Let Die

You start to die the moment you are born.

Live and Let Die, Ian Fleming's second 007 novel,
takes Bond from Harlem to Jamaica in a frenzied
hunt for the brilliant deadly gangster Mr Big
and his macabre network of associates.

'Speed...tremendous zest...communicated excitement.
Brrh! How wincingly well Mr Fleming writes'
Julian Symons, *Sunday Times*

First published in 1954

IAN FLEMING
Moonraker

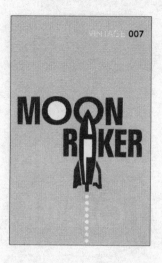

*For several minutes he stood speechless,
his eyes dazzled by the terrible beauty
of the greatest weapon on earth.*

He's a self-made millionaire, head of the Moonraker
rocket programme and loved by the press. So why is
Sir Hugo Drax cheating at cards? Bond has just five
days to uncover the sinister truth behind a national
hero, in Ian Fleming's third 007 adventure.

'Irresistably readable'
Observer

First published in 1955

IAN FLEMING
Diamonds are Forever

The twentieth century looked out at him from the piece of newsprint and bared its teeth in a sneer.

From the diamond mines of Sierra Leone to the jewellers of Hatton Garden, from race track to casino, Bond must infiltrate and destroy the criminal network of the Spangled Mob in Fleming's fourth 007 adventure.

'The remarkable thing about this book is that it is written by an Englishman. The scene is almost entirely American and it rings true to an American. I am unaware of any other writer who has accomplished this'
Raymond Chandler

First published in 1956

IAN FLEMING
From Russia with Love

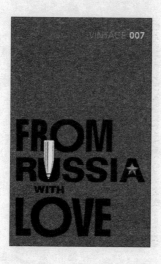

We are here to find a target who will fulfil our requirements. Someone who is admired and whose ignominious destruction would cause dismay.

A beautiful Soviet spy. A brand-new Spektor cipher machine. SMERSH has set an irresistible trap that threatens the entire Secret Service. In Fleming's fifth 007 novel Bond finds himself enmeshed in a deadly game of cross and double-cross.

'Mr Fleming's tautest, most exciting
and most brilliant tale'
Times Literary Supplement

First published in 1957

IAN FLEMING
Dr No

*The first shot had been fired. There would be
others. And whose finger was on the trigger?
Who had got him so accurately in their sights?*

Crab Key island is desolate and remote. So why is
Dr No defending it so ruthlessly? Only Bond can
uncover the truth, in Fleming's sixth 007 adventure.

'The purest Fleming...the most artfully bold,
dizzyingly poised thriller of the decade'
New York Herald Tribune

First published in 1958

IAN FLEMING
Goldfinger

You're stale, tired of having to be tough. You want a change. You've seen too much death.

In Fleming's seventh 007 novel, a private assignment sets Bond on the trail of an enigmatic criminal mastermind – Auric Goldfinger. But greed and power have created a deadly opponent who will stop at nothing to get what he wants.

'Nobody else does this sort of thing as well as Mr Fleming...it offers more passages of sustained excitement than we are likely to get from any other thriller this year'
Sunday Times

First published in 1959

IAN FLEMING
For Your Eyes Only

Includes *From A View to A Kill* * *For Your Eyes Only* *
Quantum of Solace * *Risico* * *The Hildebrand Rarity*

*Private armies, private wars. How much energy they
siphoned off from the common cause, how much fire
they directed away from the common enemy!*

Five stories. Five missions. Five glimpses into the mind
of a spy. From Jamaican estates to brooding French
forests, Bond is tested to his limits by the world's
most dangerous men and the dark secrets they keep.

'Mr Fleming's licensed assassin is in good
form... Few men can have been able to mix
business with pleasure so successfully as Bond'
Times Literary Supplement

First published in 1960

IAN FLEMING
Thunderball

He was one of those men – one meets perhaps only two or three in a lifetime – who seem almost to suck the eyes out of your head. He was their Supreme Commander – almost their god.

SPECTRE is a merciless new enemy – a group of the world's toughest criminals, headed by the brilliant Ernst Stavro Blofeld. When two NATO atom bombs go missing, Bond must unravel SPECTRE's intricate plans and prevent a global catastrophe, in Fleming's ninth 007 adventure.

'A sensational imagination, informed by style, zest and above all knowledge'
Sunday Times

First published in 1961

IAN FLEMING
The Spy Who Loved Me

You take a wrong step, play the wrong card in Fate's game, and you're lost in a world you had never imagined, against which you have no weapons. No compass.

Vivienne Michel is running away – from pain, from rejection, from humiliation. When she stumbles into a criminal plot, her life seems over...until a chance encounter with James Bond turns her world upside down. Ian Fleming's tenth 007 novel is a unique view of Bond, through the eyes of a woman who loves him.

'Ian Fleming keeps you riveted. His narrative pulls with the smooth power of Bond's Thunderbird'
Sunday Telegraph

First published in 1962

IAN FLEMING
On Her Majesty's Secret Service

*He was a man with years of dirty,
dangerous memories – a spy.*

James Bond has had enough. Enough of Service life,
of fruitless manhunts, of taking orders. But Blofeld
is back – older, leaner and more dangerous than
ever, with a deadly secret at the heart of his luxury
ski resort. Bond must rediscover his passion for what
he does best, in Fleming's eleventh 007 novel.

'No book comes closer to the heart of 007'
Val McDermid

First published in 1963

IAN FLEMING
You Only Live Twice

You only live twice:
Once when you are born
And once when you look death in the face.

Doctor Guntram Shatterhand's Garden of Death
is a magnet for suicides from all over Japan. James
Bond – grief-stricken and erratic – must kill him to
save his career in the Service. But as Shatterhand's
true identity is revealed, Bond is forced to confront
his past, in Ian Fleming's twelfth 007 adventure.

'A sensational imagination'
Sunday Times

First published in 1964

IAN FLEMING
The Man with the Golden Gun

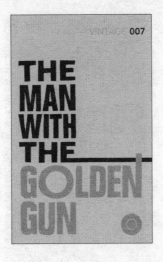

*Mister, there's something quite extra
about the smell of death. Care to try it?*

After a year missing in action, Bond is back...
brainwashed by the KGB and on a mission to
assassinate M. To prove his worth to the Service,
he must hunt down and eliminate his fiercest
opponent yet: 'Pistols' Scaramanga – The Man
With The Golden Gun. Ian Fleming's final 007
novel is a fitting tribute to a unique British hero.

'As fast-moving as ever...an immensely readable tale'
Scotsman

First published in 1965

IAN FLEMING
Octopussy and The Living Daylights

Includes *Octopussy* * *The Property of a Lady* *
The Living Daylights * *007 in New York*

This was going to be bad news, dirty work.
This was to be murder.

Four classic moments in the life of a spy. From
avenging the wartime murder of a friend to sniper
duty on the East–West Berlin border, James Bond's
body, mind and spirit are tested to their limits.

'Mr Fleming is the best thriller writer since Buchan'
Evening Standard

First published in 1966

www.vintage-books.co.uk